# STAY AWAY, JOE

# STAY

# AWAY,

# JOE

a novel by **DAN CUSHMAN**

**THE VIKING PRESS · New York · 1953**

Library of Congress catalog card number: 52-12887

Printed in U.S.A. by H. Wolff, N.Y.

*For Betsy—*

*my captive audience*

STAY  AWAY,  JOE

# Chapter I

When it became apparent that his youngest son was about to be kicked to death inside the corral, Louis Champlain stopped carving the little wooden bear and sat up straight with concern.

"Joe!" he called. "Do you hear me, Joe? You leave those gray bronc alone. Sometam you get killed by those bronc."

With a hammering and splintering of poles the bronc had climbed the corral; his ears and one wild eye were briefly visible over the top rail, and Joe, a small boy of nine or ten, was somewhere on the ground, scurrying to escape.

"Did you use spurs on those bronc?" his father called in his excitable Coyote-French. "Goddam you, Joe, you take off those spur."

Little Joe popped into view quick as a steel spring. Pete, his older brother, was now at the horse's head, pulling at the reins. The bronc half fell, and when he got up Joe was once again in the saddle. He took time to pull his black hat down with both hands; he grabbed the reins; the bronc backed free of the corral, lunged, broke rhythm, and sunfished. Little Joe was dumped to the ground. He lay, face down, while the bronc bucked over him and around the corral with empty stirrups whopping; but a second later Little Joe was in pursuit, limpity-hobble, in spurs and boots too large for him.

Louis shouted, "Joe! Pete! You hear me? You be careful with those bronc."

They paid not the slightest attention to him, so Louis sat down again and resumed carving the bear. The wood was soft, and the bear's hindquarters took shape with swift plasticity in his fingers. A woman, broad and stolid, had stopped clattering pans inside the kitchen and was in the doorway. Louis knew she was there and said without turning, "Ol' woman, you watch those boy of yours. By gare, sometam those gray bronc kill those boy."

"I'd sell that no-good bronc. Gus Podonik said he'd pay you ten dollars for that bronc."

"Ten dollaire!" cried Louis in derision, making a spiral gesture with the blade. He was a medium-tall, dehydrated man, and at that moment he seemed to be all nose and eyeballs. "Sometam I take him to the race and win four-five hundred dollaire."

She stood, sweating from the cookstove, while her husband shredded the long fibers of wood, making hair for the bear's hindquarters and his foolish little tail. A radio had been playing behind her; now she stalked out of sight and turned it on full blast, in defiance, filling the house and the yard with the raucous robot noise of a give-away show.

At the corral, Pete had mounted a gentle bay and brought the bronc under control. Joe got in the saddle and waited for trouble, but the bronc stood perfectly still. Joe cried "Yippee!" and jumped around, but the bronc was good for only a few cat hops. Joe fanned him with his hat, he tried the spurs, but the bronc was almost docile. When Pete let down the gate he trotted willingly outside.

"Hey, Pa," Joe called. "Look, I'm riding the gray bronc."

"By gare, yes." Louis got up and shouted through the door, trying to be heard over the radio, "Mama! Ol' woman, come see how that boy of mine has ridden the bronc. By gare, you wait, one of these tam those boy will be a bronc rider at Madison Square Garden like *Big Joe.*"

The radio blared on. Mama did not come to the door; mention of riding at Madison Square Garden only made her bang the pans more loudly. Louis Champlain did not notice. He was aware only of the bronc and Little Joe. He rolled a cigarette of Bull Durham and wheat-straw paper, lit it, and dragged on it, letting the smoke out through his nostrils—all without taking his eyes off Little Joe. Bump-bump-bump, Little Joe rode proudly across the yard in his long-stirrup Indian style. The bronc had a rear-shifty way of going that was no recommendation in most eyes, but Louis had an extra sense for horses, and

he had long known that this gray could run like a jack-
rabbit if anyone ever got his meanness under control.

He looked around for Mama, but she had not come out.
So instead he spoke to a very old Indian who was seated
beside the house, crosslegged in the dust, sunning himself, his sombrero over his eyes.

"Gran'pere," Louis said, raising his voice to get above
the hoarse bursts of laughter that beat remorselessly from
the radio, "did you know that Little Joe had ridden the
gray bronc?"

Grandpere stirred himself with a series of movements,
one at a time and slow. He was so old that years could
leave no further mark on him. His flesh was pulpy and
pouchy, his skin was like a withered potato, his hair had
turned to a gray spiderweb, so thin that it made braids no
thicker through than a man's little finger. Here and there
from the wrinkles of his throat and cheeks an inch-long
whisker grew stiffly. At one time he had been a large
man, tall, broad, and muscular; but now his body was
wasted, and his back stuck up like the breast of a chicken
beneath the faded Monkey-Ward blanket that covered
it, and his arms where they were visible were skeletons
hung with skin.

"Uh!" he said. "Good!"

"You like to roll cigarette, Gran'pere?"

Grandpere reached for the tobacco and paper that
Louis handed him; then he sat perfectly still with the
makings in his hands, staring out across the foothills
studded with sage and jackpine, at the ragged brush of
the creek, at the graveled road which wound along the

sidehills from the Agency to Montana State Highway 29
and the town of Big Springs eighteen miles away.

"Bronc bad. *Muche!*" Grandpere made the hand signs
which, coupled with the Cree word, indicated very bad,
snaky bad, weasel-smart and snaky bad. "Joe will be wild
horse rider some day. That young Joe will be a mighty
bulldogger at Madison Square Garden, a chief, like *Big
Joe.*"

"Don't you let ol' woman hear you say that, Gran'-
pere."

"Ha-ya, I have seen the days when they knew how to
treat old squaw. In the old days that squaw of yours with
her Philco devilbox and her rattlesnake tongue would be
stripped naked and painted red, and horse-dragged by
lariat ropes through the crick. Ay-ya, it was better in the
old days."

He fell silent. The radio roared on inexorably. "You
can say that again," quipped the radio M.C. His stooge
*did* say it again, and the audience rocketed waves of
laughter. When it became so funny they could no longer
express themselves in laughter they burst into loud ap-
plause.

A car was coming along the county road, an unfamiliar
car, and Louis kept a half-interested watch as he worked
with his knife point, shagging the coat of the little
wooden bear. As it came closer he could tell it was a Cadillac sedan, one of the big ones, somber and hearselike.
When it slowed at the open gate and turned in, Louis
said, "Goddam!" and stopped his knife to watch.

Swinging and sagging on its springs, one wheel at a

time, the Cadillac descended to the creek, forded it, came up with its tires streaming water, and crossed the yard as far as the litter of cast-off wagons and machinery would allow. Then it stopped. Two men sat in the front seat, looking at Louis.

Smiling and bowing, recognizing the driver, Louis said, "M'shu Wilcox!" and "Good day, M'shu!" to the other. He crossed the yard with the slightly toed-in manner of one who has spent all his life in moccasins, saying, "This is a great day in my life! My old friend come to honor my house!"

Pete and Little Joe, on horseback, burst from the creek and rode dangerously across the junk litter of the yard, almost trampling their father underfoot as they bore down on the Cadillac.

"Hello, Mr. Wilcox!" Pete shouted.

"Mr. Wilcox, look, I'm riding the gray bronc!" screamed Little Joe.

"This is a Cadillac, ain't it, Mr. Wilcox? Is it a new Automatic? What horsepower does she have? My brother Joe's going to drive a Cadillac home when he comes off the rodeo circuit."

"You want me to make him buck, Mr. Wilcox?"

Wilcox, a thin, graying, correct man of fifty, could not help being pleased at the excitement his arrival had occasioned. He got out from behind the wheel, putting on his suit coat, smiling, his rimless glasses shining briefly in the sun.

"Well, Joe, that is a fine horse," he said. And to Pete, "No, young man, I'm sorry, but this magnificent vehicle is not mine. I was merely driving it for Congressman Morrissey."

Louis said, "You say Congréss? Congréss at my house? Ol' woman, Congréss he has come from Washington to visit with Louis Champlain!"

Wilcox said, "Congressman Morrissey wants to look your place over."

"Eh!" said Louis in a startled manner. "Well, she is here."

Morrissey, a short, thick-bodied man, got out and looked all around. His eyes, after taking in the house, the corrals and sheds, and all the broken wagons and cars, came to rest on the unfinished bear in Louis' hands. "Well, well," he said, "I see you're interested in sculpture."

"Eh? Oh, this ol' bear! I carve him all-tam." Louis rubbed off some fragments of wood between his fingers. "This is ol' brown bear. Plenty long tam since ol' brown bear come around this mountain. Like Gran'pere say, he leave country with buffalo. Gran'pere remember him all right."

Wilcox said, "The old man is over one hundred years old."

Morrissey took an interest in Grandpere, who was still sitting in the dust beside the house, the cigarette long dead in his fingers. "Is he really?"

"Sure," said Louis. "I guess a hundred and five."

Something of a hypochondriac and a secret student of the actuary tables, Morrissey asked, "By the way, what are his dietary habits?"

"Eh?"

"What has he lived on? What's he eaten most of his life?"

"Meat. Sometam, when I was little boy, Gran'pere was then maybe sixty years old, he come live with us, *my* papa, bring whole damn beef. Last all winter, all spring. Next June you'd tie a string around your nose to smell those beef, but Gran'pere eat him all up, every bit. One tam I saw this picture show, Popeye. So I come home and tell Gran'pere. 'Why you don't eat spinach every day, make you young again, chase squaw?' He say, 'You give me raw meat from old-tam buffalo, I chase squaw all right.' Maybe he'd do it, too—I don't know."

"Pretty fair pasture he has here," said Wilcox, motioning toward the ridge.

"How many cattle do you run?" Morrissey asked Louis.

"Cattle? I do not have one cow."

"How much land do you have?"

"Big Joe's got six hundred and forty," cried Pete, "but it's mortgaged for five hundred bucks."

"They can't collect the mortgage because he's Indian," said Joe.

"He got the Purple Heart."

Morrissey kept looking around the clearing at the sheds and the log house. Nothing in the scene cheered him. He walked away while the kids were arguing and stopped in front of a derelict touring car. It was a Star. "My God," he said. He had forgotten there ever was such a make.

He walked back and asked Louis, "Exactly what was your income here last year?"

"In-come?"

"Yes, how much money did you make?"

"I don't know. I never figure it out."

"Didn't you report to the Internal Revenue?"

"No."

"Haven't you ever heard of income tax?"

"Oh, sure, all-tam. But government tells me I am Canadian Indian. Ol' Canadá, she don't know me."

"I know all that, but about what do you make? I'll have to have that in my application."

Wilcox said, "Try and think of the cash you got in last year."

Louis stood rubbing the bear, his eyes thoughtful on the far horizon. "Last winter I trap the musk-a-rat. Pretty soon the game warden come around and said, 'Louis Champlain, let me see your license.' Goddam, I would go to jail but for my daughter Mary, work in the bank, pay my fine. Congréss, you are a great man. You drink tea with ol' Presidenté, no? Maybe you get me back my money?"

"Oh, of course, of course. How many acres did you say you had?"

"Eighty. I have him mortgaged, though, long tam. But Big Joe, he's got section land. You see, Joe's mother, she was Assiniboin, an American Indian."

Wilcox said, "That was his first wife. They had one child. He's away now; he's a Purple Heart Marine vet,

World War Two and Korea both. Then there's Mary—
she's his daughter by his present wife. I was telling you
about her."

Morrissey nodded. He understood all about Mary. She
had been the star pupil when Wilcox was superintendent
of schools at Big Springs, and now she was employed at
the Big Springs State Bank by Hy Slager, who had
been a delegate to the Republican National Convention
every four years since Teddy Roosevelt. Mary was the
real reason why the heat was on to get this experimental
aid for the landless Indians—or at least she was the reason why the Champlains had been chosen.

He said, getting Wilcox over by the Star, "You're
sure this is the best bet? I mean—well, he seems a little
bit shiftless." He hurried to add, when Wilcox looked
offended, "Oh, I'm not doubting your judgment."

"Of course, if the place was already prosperous—"

"That's right, if it was prosperous he wouldn't need
help."

Louis was saying, "Goddam, times are bad! Every
year, reservation she's bigger, but no land for me. Am I
not Cree Indian halfway? Damn ol' government give
Charley Three Bird two hundred acre. Don't I get maybe
one hundred acre? Goddam."

"We're going to fix that up," said Wilcox benevo-
lently. "Right, Congressman?"

"Sure, sure." Morrissey had decided to make the best
of it. After all, 438 men and women of the Big Springs
community had signed a petition requesting emergency
aid for the landless Indians, and 438 was not a number

to be taken lightly by a congressman running for re-election that very fall. He was quite certain he could secure a small rehabilitation grant, especially in view of the fact that the eldest boy was a Purple Heart veteran of Korea. "Yes, yes!" he cried, slapping Louis on the shoulder. "We're out here to put you in the cattle business."

"Eh?"

"I mean we can make it possible for you to secure some cattle—a few, twenty head perhaps, surplus derived from the experimental herd at Fort Price Reservation. Pure-bred Herefords."

Louis whispered, "For *me?* For me this?"

"Mind you, there's nothing certain about it, but it's my belief. And of course, we had to speak to you first."

"By gare, anything ol' Congréss say, she is done. Down at Big Springs, I hear talk about Congréss. 'He is a great man,' they say. 'He has got plenty thing from Washington, he is drink tea with ol' Presidenté.' Oho! If Congréss say he will get those cow for his poor friend, Louis Champlain, then I am like seeing those cow right now."

"Now, Louis!" cautioned Wilcox.

"Oui?"

"Louis, I want you to understand one thing. Our reputation is riding on this. If it's successful, then we're successful. If it's a failure—well, you can see what people will say about Congressman Morrissey and myself."

"Eh, by gare!"

"This is an experiment. We're trying this out with

you. If you build this herd up, clear your indebtedness, add to your holdings, then the government may adopt such a policy of rehabilitation for other landless Indians. It depends on *you!*"

Louis Champlain stood very straight, his head tilted slightly back, his hands raised to shoulder height and pointed toward the sky. He spoke, and his voice trembled with the solemnity of a vow. "You, Congréss! You M'shu Wilcox, my friend! Hear me, Louis Champlain, he's speak: I will do this thing. I will take care of those cow. I will raise many fine, strong calf. 'B'shu M'shu Champlain,' people will say. 'This is fine suit of clothes you are wearing. Did you get this suit at Lou Lucke's in Havre, eh?' They will say, 'And what a fine silk dress your old squaw is wearing!' This they will say. And when they do, 'Voilà!' I will say. 'Congréss, he has done this thing. M'shu Wilcox, he too has done this thing.' Then they will come to my ranch, and I will point to my fine, fat cows and say, 'This I, Louis Champlain, have raised. All this to prove that landless Indian is good man. All this to prove that my dear friends, Congréss and Wilcox, they are damn good, too.' "

In the Cadillac, rolling back across the clearing, Wilcox said, "Well, don't you think he'll make a go of it?"

"Mr. Wilcox," said Morrissey, "I want every man and woman whose name appears on that petition to be notified that I alone am responsible for this. But aside from them, I'd rest just as easily if no living soul in this great state of Montana knew about it."

# Chapter II

When the nineteen heifers and the young bull arrived, Louis Champlain sat on the front step all night, listening to the sounds they made. Every hour or so Annie called him through the open window, asking why he did not come to bed, but each time he said, "Be quiet, ol' woman, while your husband listen to his fine, fat cows."

At dawn, carrying a brush and curry comb, Louis went out to comb from their coats the slobber and manure they had accumulated riding in the stock trailer from Fort Price. They were already up, grazing the buffalo grass in the little triangular field across the creek. He walked around, talking to them, trying to get close, but the heifers kept running out of reach, and the young bull crashed back and forth through the brush, snorting and pawing dirt. Finally Louis sat down in the fence corner, without using the brush and curry comb, and rolled and smoked cigarettes and looked at his cattle.

Finally, hearing the sharp ke*whack* of Annie's ax on firewood, he started for the house. Pete and Little Joe were already in the corral, getting their broncs saddled.

"Eh?" said Louis, looking through the poles. "You boys eat breakfast?"

"We'll eat after while," Pete said. "We're going to practice bulldogging the heifers."

"I'm going to ride the bull," cried Little Joe. "I'm going to fix me a circingle."

"By gare, you run those cow, I'll tear your hide off with quirt." When they paid no attention to him, Louis clambered over the corral fence, ran to the shed, and came out swinging a latigo strap. He swung it over his head and pounded the ground with it so hard it frightened the gray bronc into breaking loose from Little Joe and bucking around the corral. "You hear me, you boys? You bulldog those cow, or ride those bull, your papa, he'll tear your hide off." He stopped, drawn very erect, shoulders against his neck, and let his breath out. He cursed solemnly, after the manner of a devout believer. "Take those saddle off. Yes, by gare, today you hitch team to wagon. Today is work, drive over to Big Joe's field and fix fence, set posts, string new wire."

"We got no wire," Little Joe wailed. "We ain't got any posts either."

"Then you chop good strong jackpine posts on hill. You get him wire off county fence. You want my cows to get over in Pomeroy's range? That thief Billy Pomeroy maybe steal my cows." Billy Pomeroy, manager of the big Lazy Y Quarter Circle ranch to the south, had once caused three of Louis' horses to be impounded after they had fed most of a winter on his haystacks. "By gare, you

fix him fence up good and strong to keep Pomeroy's cheap old bull away from my young cow." Everything Louis said he emphasized by striking the ground with the latigo strap.

Annie was at the door, squinting, flat-faced and small-eyed against the sun as he walked up from the corral. "Louis, are you whipping those boys?"

Louis had never whipped them in his life. He clenched his fist with the latigo overhead. "You hear me, I tear the hide off those boy if they bulldog my fine cow. Now, ol' woman, go inside and cook one big breakfast for your husband, make him strong, do much work. Fix fence, fix shed. Cut hay for winter, fix ol' mowing machine. Ol' woman, you like to ride into town, buy a new dress?"

At breakfast he got on the subject of Pomeroy again, naming him a thief and a rustler, recalling all the early stories about old Max Pomeroy and his partner Clyde McOmber, and how they had started with one old lineback steer, a long rope, and a running iron, and had ended with their brand on half the cattle north of the Missouri River.

"Don't be a fool," Annie said, pouring tea for him. "Billy Pomeroy will not steal your cows."

"Oho! How about my horse the bay gelding? And how about old Two-Step?"

"He will not steal your cows," she said placidly.

"No, but it would be one of his tricks to get his cheap bull with my cows so next year my calves—"

"His cheap bull he paid twenty-eight hundred dollars for at Great Falls?"

He muttered, "Well, anyway, I will build that good strong fence."

After breakfast Pete and Little Joe hitched up Two-Step with a roan bronc and set off with a wagonload of tools, poles, and tangled scrap wire. The sun was warm then, and Louis decided to sit down for just a little while. He dozed and watched the wagon roll, rickety and wheel-sprung, up the hummocky hillside, following a trail that switchbacked through rock and pine. It took a long half-hour for it to reach the ridge crest and drop from sight. He fell asleep and awoke two hours later when Annie spoke to him from the door. A beaten-up Model A Ford had crossed the creek and was just jouncing up across the yard.

He stood to see who it was, and Annie said, "That no-good Walt Stephenpierre! And look who is with him—Connie Shortgun. They should have the United States Marshal after them."

Louis was already striding across the yard, his arms out. "Stephenpierre, my friend! You have come to share your Louis' good fortune?"

The Model A had no brakes, so Stephenpierre brought it to a stop by ramming a heap of firewood. He reached through the glassless window to open the door by means of the outside handle. He got out, a tall and angular six foot three, and limped around, hip-sprung, getting the kinks from his legs. He was about thirty-five years old, a halfbreed with a high hooked nose, large ears, and

cheekbones that terminated in lumps looking almost like
carbuncles—a trait not uncommon among the Assiniboin
breeds of that area. He had donned for the occasion a
new flame-red shirt and a thirty-dollar Stetson hat. The
hat was chocolate brown with blue, white, and pink bead-
work around the crown in the forms of leaves and rosettes.
There was a woman in the front seat, momentarily out
of Louis' view because of the plywood which filled the
window on that side, but he knew it was Connie Shortgun,
with whom Stephenpierre had been living. Hanging dangerously from the open windows of the back were two
little girls about eighteen months and three years of
age, filthy and smeared with chocolate.

The two men clasped hands and embraced and slapped
each other on the back, all the while shouting a noisy
Coyote-French. In the meantime Connie Shortgun, a
slatternly fullblood no more than half of Stephenpierre's
age, got out and started for the house. She wore high heels
that kept buckling under her, making her look more
spindly-legged than she actually was. The little girls
screamed, unheeded, to be let out of the car.

Annie was no longer in sight, and the radio was up to
its top level, drowning out the voices of her visitors. It
made Louis apprehensive. Annie had threatened more
than once to send the government police out to Stephenpierre's on Croft Coulee, where he and Connie and his
wife, Mae, and Dub Red Eagle were all laying up together—and there was Dub, no more than eighteen, while
Mae Stephenpierre was forty and a floozie to boot.

"Wait," said Louis to Connie. "Come and see my cows."

"What do I care about your damn cows?" Connie asked with a shrill giggle. "I'm going up to the shack and listen to the rádio."

Louis supposed she had a request coming up on the Melody Wrangler's Hit Parade over KGFM in Great Falls. Every day she had requests—"The Fat Squaw Boogie" for Louise Horse Chaser, or "Loaded Dice and a .38" for Morrie Roque and Nellie Beaverbow; both appearing to be just innocent requests to the Melody Wrangler, but loaded with significance on the reservation. Connie was not even above mailing requests with forged signatures, and "Tobacco-Chewing Baby with Your Juicy Kind of Love" for Eleanor Laney from Boob Dugan had been one of her major triumphs.

There was no way Louis could stop her, and he watched with some trepidation as she went inside the house; but Annie received her well enough, and in a few seconds the radio was switched over to KGFM and he heard the sirupy strains of the "Rose Petal Waltz." Louis exhaled, feeling better; but now a second car was coming—a massive old Hudson sedan, its rear very low on broken springs.

He watched it turn in at the gate. It dropped to the creek ford, settled there like an overweighted duck, and churned, its rear bumper in the mud. After a while the car was shut off, and a woman and two men clambered out by means of the front fenders. The woman was Mae Stephenpierre; the men were Dub Red Eagle and Bill Artois.

Mae, a loud, skinny, slatternly woman with pinkish hennaed hair, came with young Red Eagle in tow. She looked older than forty, while Red Eagle, a dull-looking Assiniboin fullblood, looked even younger than eighteen. Bill Artois was a good-looking breed of about twenty-five; he was Connie Shortgun's former husband, and the father, it was believed, of her eldest child. The fatherhood of her second child had been denied by Artois as well as by everyone else in and around the reservation. Although the second child had been conceived while he was still married to Connie, Bill Artois bore no ill will toward anyone and had recently been shacked up with the Stephenpierres.

"By gare," said Louis, more apprehensive than ever at the sight of Mae Stephenpierre, "this is fine thing, all my old friends come out to see me."

"Where's the beer?" Mae asked. She had had too much beer already. She had one arm around the dull-witted Red Eagle and tried to get Louis with the other, but he fended her off. She pretended to pout and said, "Sweetheart Louie! Don't you like your Mae any more? Louie, haven't you got a bottle of beer for Mae?"

"Oh, beer!" He was embarrassed and looked at the house—not from guilt, for he had never had anything to do with the likes of Mae Stephenpierre. "I don't have beer in long tam."

She stepped back, miffed at his not wanting her arm around him. She looked at Louis and then all around the yard, only just realizing that no one except her crowd had come. "What the hell kind of a celebration is this? Where is everybody? Say, for chrissake, you mean we're the only ones here?"

"Well, yes," said Louis.

"Ain't you going to have no dance, no rodeo, whoop-up?" Mae smelled and looked as if she had been drinking since the night before, but she hadn't had anything for a while; the beer was wearing off, and the feeling made her mean. She stepped back, forking her stringy pink hair away from her eyes. "What the hell's got into you folks anyhow? Maybe you don't want us around here. Sure, you got yourselves a little bit of dough, and now your old friends aren't good enough for you."

"Mae!" said Stephenpierre. "Keep your mouth shut."

She paid no attention to Stephenpierre. She swaggered in her old rayon rag dress and her wrinkled stockings, and said to Louis, "Sure, got yourselves a few cows, won't have anything to do with the Injuns off the reservation."

Louis, with his hands out, pleaded for reason, but Stephenpierre, coming with long steps, said, "Mae, keep your mouth shut or I'll knock some teeth out."

She now took notice of her husband. She turned to curse him, and he swung at her. She retreated out of reach and managed to avoid the first blow, but he clipped her along the neck with the second, and the force of it sent her backpeddling. She managed to stay erect for six or seven wild steps before her body outraced her legs and she sat down with a clatter in a heap of rusty fenders and spring leaves, around which scrub rose bushes had grown. She was jolted and popeyed for a second; her hair was knocked over her face, and her mouth was open. She tried to get up, but the rose thorns had hold of her dress and she couldn't make it. She sat down with a second clatter. The sight of her struggling around in the old iron was very funny to Stephenpierre and Bill Artois, and after a long dumb look Dub Red Eagle decided it was funny too. Mae responded with a stream of obscene names. When they still laughed, she screamed, "You sons of bitches!"

Louis said, "Wait, you let ol' Mama hear you talk lak that, she'll get out shotgun, by gare, she will."

"What the hell do I care about her?" Mae, weeping and cursing, managed to tear herself free from the rosebushes. "What makes her so high and mighty all of a sudden? She's just a goddam tepee Injun, and a quarter Gros Ventre to boot, raised on gut meat and turnips. So who in hell's she just because she's got a daughter working in the bank, snorting around with the white people? Egg in a glass for a country lass, I know about that stuff. You don't need to tell me about that stuff. I been around, and by the God I'm not a squaw either. I'm white so you can tell—"

She looked up and saw Louis standing rigid with his fists closed, and it made her stop.

"Don't you talk about my Mary one more tam!" he said.

She was on her feet. Her dress was torn. She pulled it up and looked at her leg. The rose thorns had cut the inside of her thigh, and it was bleeding slightly. The blood made her skin seem very white and gave it a soft, curdled look.

"Let's get to hell out of here," she yowled to Stephenpierre.

"Go on up to the car. Get yourself a beer."

"I want to hightail. I'm not staying where I'm treated like dirt. This cheap, chippy——" She could think of nothing as cheap as she thought Louis to be. "Come on, can't you see he wants to entertain *white* people?"

Stephenpierre shouted, "You want to go, go ahead. There's your damn car."

She grabbed Dub Red Eagle by the arm and led him back to the Hudson. He started the engine, got the car in gear, and raced it forward and in reverse, but the bumper guards only worked deeper, holding like anchors, while the engine roared, pounding loose connecting rods, and the rear wheels showered mud and water.

Mae leaned out, shouting. "You sons of bitches, come give us a push."

When no one moved, she got out herself. Standing in the creek, she put her fragile weight to the task, pushing by means of the door handles. Dub raced the engine without rocking the car more than an inch or two either way.

"Go around back!" Dub shouted.

She did, getting part way up the bank, bracing herself low against the right rear fender.

"Okay?" called Dub.

"Okay."

He gave it all it had, in low, and the wheels volleyed mud that plastered her from her head to her knees.

"Push, push!" called Dub.

Blinded, she retreated, trying to wipe the mud from
her eyes and mouth. She smeared it in a sticky black
mask all over her face. She staggered along the creek
bank. At a point where it took an abrupt two-foot drop
she lost footing and did a perfect bellyflop into six or
eight inches of water. She sat up. The creek had diluted
the mud slightly. She coughed water. Dub kept racing
the car forward and back, digging it deeper into the
creek. Stephenpierre and Artois had their arms around
each other so they would not fall down from laughter.
Louis laughed too. Even Grandpere, standing bowed
over his diamond willow walking stick, was laughing.
Annie had come outside. She was not laughing. She ran,
holding up her full skirts, going to Mae's assistance.

"You leave her alone," cried Annie.

"Old squaw boogie, ug! ug!" sang Stephenpierre, doing a war dance to the tune which that week was number
six on the Melody Wrangler's hit parade.

"By gare," said Louis, "this is pretty good. Maybe I
will drink a bottle of beer one tam."

Stephenpierre had cans of Schlitz scattered through-
out the Model A. They were warm, and the vibration of
the car had made them wild. He punched them open, one
after another, with a rusty screwdriver, holding his
thumb over each hole until somebody was ready to grab
and drink. In ten minutes all the beer was gone.

A wagon had turned in from the road, an Indian in
sombrero and feathers on its high spring seat, his squaw,
very big and solid, sitting in the wagonbox with her

back toward him. The Indian was John Bull Shield. He
maneuvered his wagon past the stranded Hudson and
drove up, sitting straight, his eyes on the empty beer
cans.

"*Meyo!*" he said, lifting his hand in a sign that beer
was good.

"Goddam," said Louis Champlain with embarrassment. "It is every drop gone." He shaded his eyes and
looked far off down the road. "Where those boy? I send
those boy of mine to town for whole damn wagonload of
beer, treat my friends. Where those boy now?"

"You want beer," said Stephenpierre, "I fetch 'em."

He was waiting for Louis to give him money, but
Louis, with his hand in his pocket found nothing but a
jackknife. He shaded his eyes and looked down the road
again, saying, "Those boy! Why don't those boy of mine
hurry up, bring beer from town?" Old John Bull Shield
was thirsty and staring down on him. Louis, after an
uncomfortable moment, said, "You wait. I got plenty
money in the house."

Mary had given Mama ten dollars about a week ago,
and he knew that most of it was still in the cracked teapot. He went inside, without saying anything, took down
the teapot, and looked inside. It contained a five-dollar
bill, three silver dollars, a nickel, and some pennies.
Mama entered in time to make a grab as he stuck all but
the pennies in his pocket.

"What are you going to do?"

He retreated, one hand on his pocket, making jerky
gestures with the other. "My friends, they come, visit

all satisfied. "That's a boy's drink. Come on, you've
tasted my whisky, how about a big one?"

Although Loren took a drink now and then, it was
generally in a highball of the sort known in that locality
as a "ditchwater," and he misjudged the power of an
equal amount of raw whisky. The big drink immediately
unsteadied him and kept him from reasoning clearly. Joe
kept hold of him, introducing him to this fellow and
that, each of whom seemed to have a bottle to stick in his
hands. He wanted to escape, at least say no to the bottles that were coming toward him, but he could not.

"Don't leave me, Loren," Joe said every few minutes, keeping a tight hold on his arm. "I need you to
keep me out of trouble. Watch and see that damned
Chug Hockering doesn't hit me from behind."

So many things happened that Loren lost track. His
new acquaintances became a jumbled mass in his memory,
together with the awareness that he was drunk. At suppertime someone gave him scalding coffee to sober him up, but
Joe, unseen, had already spiked the coffee with more
whisky. "Let's have another cup of coffee, Loren," said
Joe. "Nothing like coffee to get a man on his feet."

Then Joe said, on the quiet, to Bronc Hoverty, "You
go ahead and dance with Mary. Show my sister a good
time." And to Mary, "I guess that boy friend of yours
shouldn't be drinking with the men. I have had to put him
to bed."

"Where is he?" she demanded, furious with Joe.

"In my car. I've been thinking I should drive him
back to town. After all, I feel sort of responsible for the

poor kid. You go ahead and have a good time, ride to
town with Bronc."

"You deliberately got him drunk."

"Me? Since when have I worried about getting whisky
for anybody except myself? That boy is over twenty-one;
he should know when to stop drinking."

Mary was angry with Loren too. She shared a prev-
alent contempt for men who could not handle their liquor, and she was on the point of saying go ahead, take
him to town—but she reconsidered, knowing that Joe
did not ordinarily have that much charity.

"I'll go along."

But when she had got her wraps and gone downstairs
Loren, Joe, and the Buick were nowhere to be found.

"Take me to town," she said, finding Bronc.

"Let's dance a couple of times first."

She decided she was being selfish, spoiling Bronc's
good time on account of Loren's failure, and she danced
with him. Bronc had a bottle in the station wagon, and
she had a drink with him too. Back upstairs, she forgot
about Loren while dancing with Bronc and half a dozen
other men. Then it was three a.m., and the orchestra
closed down for the night. The two Cristy girls had
been left stranded by their escorts, so, at Mary's sugges-
tion, Bronc drove them to their ranch, which was only
five miles away. On the way back across the Cristy
hayfields, with the stars beginning to dim and a gray of
dawn in the east, Bronc turned off the road and stopped
in the heavy shadow of some cottonwoods.

"Mary!" he said, putting his arm around her.

"Oh," she said, "let's go home."

She did not fight him off, though her body was stiffly unwilling against him. She let him kiss her. It wasn't anything; she didn't dislike Bronc. Then he said, "Mary!" again, and his tone, rather than his hand on the inside of her thigh, frightened her.

She twisted, wiry and strong, opened the door, and got away outside. He did not follow. He sat, leaning over in the seat, staring at her, his face in shadow, his eyes looking white—and at that moment he strongly showed his Indian blood. She did not generally think of Bronc as being anything but white, and now he frightened her, for she knew how often rape occurred among her people.

"What's the matter with you?" she cried.

After a few seconds he answered, "I'm sorry. I didn't mean anything. I've always been crazy about you."

She knew that was true; she had known when she started out with him. She wasn't angry with him, just a little bit scared. "I'm going back to Cristys'," she said, not really intending to.

"No. Don't do that. Come on, I'll behave myself."

"Well," she said, and got back in. She waited for him to start the car, but he just sat and looked at her.

"Why'd you kiss me?" he asked.

"I didn't."

"You did. You—"

"You kissed me. I just sat here. For the love of Mike—"

"Why'd you let me if you don't like me? Don't you know I'm crazy about you? I always been crazy about you."

"I'm sorry, Bronc."

"You hate me."

"Of course I don't. Just behave yourself, I think you're a swell guy."

"Do you?" He was almost pleading now. "Do you really, Mary?"

"Sure."

"Let me come and see you sometimes, will you, Mary? Will you let me take you to the show sometime?"

"All right." She wanted more than anything to get going. She was still apprehensive, and it seemed that giving him hope was her best assurance that he wouldn't start tearing her clothes off. "But don't grab a girl like that. Use some sense. Now let's get started back. I have to work tomorrow."

# Chapter IX

He had to drive slowly to keep from high-centering in the ruts, and dawn was making things bright when they reached the county road. Bronc made no more passes at her. Sometimes he made his hip bump against hers, but that wasn't so bad; and he looked so good-natured, so young and hell-and-be-damned, with his shock of brown hair pushing his sombrero back, that Mary felt ashamed of herself for being frightened of him. He still did not drive fast, only a pleasant forty an hour, through the pine fragrance of the mountains to the arid sage fragrance of the bench country. Then the sun came, bringing out in shining white rectangles the buildings of Big Springs twenty miles away and below, a faultless miniature.

Bronc said, "Tonight how would you like to go to Havre with me, see a show?"

She put him off. She put him off again and again through the next couple of weeks. Joe began calling for her, using a pretext to get her somewhere; and each time,

who would show up but Bronc Hoverty. Once Joe even
told her that Mama was ill and asking for her, but when
she got to the ranch Mama was the same as always, and
Bronc Hoverty was standing with Louis looking at the
horses in the corral.

Mama was furious when she found out about it. She
shouted at Joe, "When your sister has a nice fellow in
town, good job, good friends, you want her to step out
with that no-account bronc rider? I am warning you
now, stop meddling with Mary, getting her in bad with
her friends."

Joe was incensed and said, shaking his finger under
her nose, "You mean that pipsqueak Loren Hankins?
One-two drinks, and who had to carry him out and put
him to bed? Me, that is who." Simulating weakness,
Joe leaned forward, hollow-chested, with his arms dangling, eyeballs rolled back in his skull. "One-two drinks,
this is how he looked. How do you think I feel, having
all my friends laugh at me because my sister goes out
with that skinny nobody? Do you think I would let her
get stuck with him for a husband?"

"Go away and leave her alone."

"Eh?"

"Yes, go away and leave all of us alone. Get in your
big car and go back to Madison Square Garden."

"You are running me out of my own home?"

"Get out! Get out!" Mama shouted.

When Joe did not move, Mama grabbed the broom.
She put it back and, turning, looked for a better
weapon. Her eyes fell on the stove poker, a rod of heavy-

gauge steel, three feet long and bent like a golf club at the end. All in one movement, she seized it and swung overhand at Joe. Reflex took Joe back with his hands up. The poker was deflected by the low ceiling, and, bounding down almost out of Mama's grasp, it struck Joe on the muscles where his neck and shoulder met.

He tried to get through the door, but the blow staggered him; he rammed the casing and rebounded from it, and Mama, this time swinging horizontally, hit him full in the middle of the back. Joe took a long step—too long. He put his weight on a loose board, his boot bent under him, and he fell headlong. He rolled over in the dust with a bellow of pain. He got to his feet, eyes rolling, and stared back at Mama.

"Mama, stop! You have gone crazy?" cried Louis, running up from the corral.

"Ow!" groaned Joe. "She has broken my back."

Mama, in the door, waving the poker at him, cried, "Stay away from this house. I tell you I will knock out your brains if just once more you put your foot in my house."

Joe staggered to a distance, holding his back. He held his back with one hand and his neck with the other. Then he took his hand away from his neck to make a fist and shake it at Mama. "You old squaw, I will fix you sometime. Sometime I will forget I am a gentleman, and then there will be one old squaw with a jaw broken in two places."

"What happened?" Louis asked.

"What happened? She sneaked up behind me with

a stove poker and tried to kill me is what happened. No wonder your daughter acts like she does. I try to find her a boy friend she does not have to be ashamed of—"

"Joe!" His father silenced him. "I think it would be better if you went to Callahan's for a bottle of beer."

When Joe had gone, Louis tried to reason with Mama; but, with the poker still in her hand, waving it at the dust of Joe's car, she said, "Keep him away. Next time he comes in my house I will brain him, that good-for-nothing."

That night Joe slept in the shed, and the following morning, disheveled, with bits of hay clinging to his hair, he came to the porch, where he stood, favoring his wounded foot, sniffing breakfast, until Mama advanced to the door.

"What do you say we call it quits?" Joe said.

"Stay away." Mama had the poker. "Stay away, Joe, or I will chop you up like stew with this stove poker."

Joe sat outside, watching Grandpere eat his breakfast. At last he got up and left, driving slowly across the yard, across the creek, past the Hudson, to the road, where he stopped and sat looking at the house for a long minute before driving on to town and borrowing six bits breakfast money from Mary.

At the Sunshine Cafe he told Tommy, the Japanese cook and proprietor, all about them—how they were using his land, the six hundred and forty acres that was his allotment from the government, to graze their stock, and doing it free, without one cent of rent and not even a thank you; no, not a cup of coffee in the morning or a plate of cold stew. And to sleep in the barn, that was good enough for him. And that wasn't all; anybody who wanted to look could see the bruise on his neck where she had sneaked up behind him and tried to kill him with the stove poker; and he should have her arrested, because Uncle Sam would have something to say about using a veteran like that. "I tell you," said Joe, his mouth full of ham and hot cakes, "it is getting to be a hell of a country, and no gratitude anywhere."

His stomach full, a toothpick cocked in his mouth, Joe returned to the bank to borrow more money from Mary. There were others ahead of him at the teller's window, so he got in line and was waiting when Hy Slager called him into his office.

"How much money you borrowed off that girl since you got home?" Slager asked.

"Oh, I don't keep track, pay it right back."

"Like hell you do," Slager said, looking him cold in the eye. "You never paid back a cent in your life. If you need money, why don't you borrow it on that new car?"

"All right," said Joe, his back up. "Lend me one hundred dollars."

Slager laughed around the panatela cigar he kept scissored in his teeth, and said he knew better than to lend anything to a ward of the government, because his agreement was not valid in a court of law. "Look at the money you borrowed on that section of land five or six years ago. Who was it gave you that mortgage—the Milk River Land Company? Good God, you taught them a lesson. I'll bet they never collected a nickel off you."

"My credit's good all over."

"Not here it isn't." Slager got his riding boot down from the drawer and sat forward in his swivel chair—a long tall man, seventy years old, but with a backbone still as straight as a Winchester barrel. "Now don't forget this, because I'm telling you only the once—I don't want you hanging around. That goes for your pal, that bronc-fighter Hoverty, too. You tell him to keep away from Mary, or, by the God, I'll open him up so the wind will blow through."

Joe said, "How about lending me just twenty-five dollars on the car?"

Slager opened the zipper on his wallet and gave Joe a five.

"You want me to sign something?" Joe asked.

"Hell no," said Slager, waving him out of the door.

As Joe walked past the post office, Bob Lewis, the RFD mail carrier, hailed him and gave him a letter from The Great Falls Time Credit Corporation, which Joe put in his hip pocket without opening.

"Save me stopping at your dad's place," Bob said. "Hey, don't you even open your mail?"

"All say the same thing," Joe said. He walked all over town, looking for excitement, but Big Springs lay dead quiet under the late summer sun. He got into the Buick and drove to Callahan's. There he saw three cars in the yard—Bronc's station wagon, Stephenpierre's Model A, and the Chevrolet which Boob Dugan had just bought at a used-car lot in Havre. The jukebox was on. Joe drove

down and looked inside. Boob Dugan was dancing with
Connie Shortgun, Stephenpierre with Lizzie Bird Looking, and Bronc with Mamie Callahan. Callahan, dressed
up in slacks, white shirt, and an apron, was tending bar.

"All right, goddam you," Callahan said to Joe
when he saw him at the door, "how about that thirty-five
dollars—or do I have to swear out a warrant?"

"You mean that check?"

"Yes, that check!"

Joe came in, laughing. "You know, I've been trying to figure out about that check, why it came back
marked 'no funds.' Now I know—that night when I
asked for a blank check for the Milk River bank, you
made a mistake and gave me one on Big Springs."

"I don't know anything about that. I just know you
wrote me a bum check."

"Now wait," said Joe, his elbows on the bar. "Did
I or did I not ask you for a blank on the Milk River
bank? Right here I stood and said Milk—River—bank."

As he tried to remember back, it now seemed to Callahan that Joe had. "I don't think you got a dime there
either."

"Call them up. Call Havre. There is the phone; go ask."

"I'm not spending four bits more—"

"Bet you five dollars." Joe slammed down the money
Slager had given him. "There, that will give you your
four bits back—and four-fifty besides, clear profit, *if*
they say I don't have money in the bank."

Callahan knew better than to believe him, but everybody had been laughing about the Cadillac Joe had left

in Great Falls too, and next thing he'd showed up in a
four-thousand-dollar Buick, and then they didn't laugh
any more.

"To hell with you," said Callahan.

"Come on, everybody, have a beer. Tear the check
up. I'll write you another one. Goddam, you got me in
a fine mess, giving me the wrong check blank. Mama,
Slager, Mary—everybody raising hell."

He wet an indelible pencil on his tongue and laboriously wrote a check on the Milk River National Bank for
seventy dollars.

"Oh, no!" said Callahan, seeing the amount.

"Why, of course. Pay up my bill and get a few bucks
to spare. Don't you think I want to treat my friends?
What the hell, Callahan, since when did you start turning away cash business?"

Callahan looked at the check against the light—as
though that would prove anything—and decided to ring
it up. With the till open, he figured up all of Joe's old
charge slips and handed him twelve-forty in change. Joe
did not question the amount. If that suited Callahan, that
suited him. He bought everybody a drink, including Callahan. He danced with Connie Shortgun, Lizzie Bird
Looking, and Mamie, stopping after each number to treat
or be treated by somebody else.

"Where's Glenda?" he asked.

Callahan told him she had been in Great Falls, visiting
her sister, and was coming in on the six-o'clock bus. In
fact, he would have to close the place in another ten minutes and drive to Big Springs after her.

The announcement was greeted with dismay. "No wonder," said Joe, "you are always going broke in the saloon
business. The best crowd you had all week, and you close
up."

With money coming in at a good clip, Callahan was
loath to go, but he knew he couldn't leave the place in
Mamie's charge, or they would drink everything and not
pay a cent.

"There's no sense in you losing this business," Joe said.
"I'll tell you—just because we are so friendly again, I
will go after her in the Buick."

Callahan reluctantly consented. It was hours before
Joe returned with Glenda, and she was flushed and very
high. Callahan was angry, but she got her arm around
him and coaxed him to drink with her. They sat in the
booth, having ditchwater highballs, and Glenda, patting
his cheek, said, "Daddee! It's just like a second honeymoon!"

Callahan had had several drinks already, and the ditchwaters on top of them put him in a mood to dance. He
danced with Glenda, doing the new steps, and then with
Connie Shortgun. Exercise gave him steam. There he was,
dancing around in his white apron, forgetting all about
the saloon business, until he happened to look over and
see Big Joe behind the bar, passing out liquor right and
left, saying, "Come on, everybody, have a drink on your
good friend Callahan's second honeymoon."

"Get away from behind my bar!" shouted Callahan.

"Go on and dance, have a good time," said Joe. "I don't
mind to bartend for a while."

Callahan got hold of Joe's arm and tried to drag him from behind the bar; but Joe pushed him away with a force that sent him staggering halfway to the door. Callahan got himself stopped; he crouched with his hands out and came in a bulldog rush. They struggled, without advantage, in the small area behind the bar, ending wedged among cases of empty Coke bottles between the back bar and the refrigerator. There Callahan swung short rights and lefts, but Joe, who had the advantage of height, held him at arm's length. Everyone was around, shouting advice to Callahan, who slugged himself purple and winded without being able to reach farther than Joe's shoulder.

At last Callahan stopped and said, panting, "All right, let me go."

"You be good scout? You promise to have a drink on the house?"

"All right."

Joe released him. He staggered away. He held to the bar. He pretended that he would have fallen had it not been for the bar. He moved along, hand over hand, knowing, without looking, where the shotgun stood. When he got close enough he turned and reached, getting it with the first grab—an old Damascus double with three-quarter barrels.

Callahan started up with the gun as Joe went, long-legged, for cover, but Bronc Hoverty had been watching from the other side of the bar; he reached over, grabbed the gun with both hands, and jerked it away from Callahan.

Callahan, at a run, pursued Bronc around the room, while Bronc, toreador fashion, holding the gun like a cape, avoided him. When Callahan showed signs of slowing down, Bronc called him a shanty Butte Irishman and made him come on again.

Finally Callahan could go no farther. He sat down. "You son of a bitch." He wheezed. "You dirty Injun son of a bitch."

"What's the matter?" said Bronc, feigning amazement. "Did you want the gun? Well, why didn't you say so? Tell you what I'll do. I'll divide up with you." So saying, he pulled the forepiece off and disjointed the barrel from the stock. "Here. Which half do you want?"

Callahan grabbed the barrel and was on his feet again, trying to get Bronc cornered to brain him; but, as before, Bronc was too nimble for him. Callahan got so tired he fell down on the floor. Puffing, blowing, calling them everything he could lay his tongue to, he crawled, got inside a booth, and sat with his head on the table.

Finally able to lift his head, Callahan said he needed a drink. Stephenpierre tried to give him a can of beer, and Callahan flung it back at him. "Not this Injun stuff. Give me the whisky."

He sat, trying to recuperate on whisky—although whisky was his chief trouble. "Glenda," he said. "Take care of the joint. I got to go to bed."

Glenda was nowhere around. He locked the till, looked briefly for Joe, could not see him, and, steadying himself on bar, chairs, and wall, went through the living quarters to his bedroom—only to find the door bolted. He beat the door with his fist, demanding to be let in, but nobody responded. At last he went on down the hall, outside, and stood in the cool night, thinking of how they had wronged him.

Yes, Joe was in bed with her. He had been three or four hours driving her from town too. Every time Callahan went to the mine Joe sneaked around to be with Glenda. He would kill Joe if he had a gun. His mind foggily sought other means of revenge. He saw the Buick darkly gleaming in the moonlight, and went to it. He walked all around it. Then, working with the slow, determined purpose of the very drunk, he let all the air out of the tires.

Joe did not notice how his car hugged the ground when he half fell into the front seat and started for home. It had no pickup, and steering it took all his strength. "Wahoo!" shouted Joe, leaning from the front window, fanning the car with his hat. He kept it wide open in second gear. The flattened tires roared and hammered on the gravel road and tore themselves to shreds, but nothing could stop Joe, armed with the mighty Buick. It almost stalled in the creek beside the derelict Hudson, but the water had sunk to a trickle, and momentum carried it up the far side and across the yard, until it stopped with a crash of twigs in some buckbrush near the house. Joe then noticed the smell of burned rubber and got out to see what the trouble was.

"Joe?" called Louis from the window. "Is that you, Joe? What's the trouble? I could hear you coming for a mile."

"Had a puncture." Then Joe, with the yard steepness

Louis Champlain, wish him good luck. I must treat them all like old tam."

"Not with that money."

He tried to get around her, but she planted herself, strong and wide, blocking the door.

He said, "Ol' woman, your husband is soon big rancher. Eight, ten, twelve dollaire what is that? Soon, poof, we will throw away ten-twelve dollaire."

"How will I buy sugar? How will I buy lard?"

"Since when don't you treat your old friends?"

"Friends!" she said bitterly.

"Yes, my friends. They say, 'There is Louis, he has had good luck, let us go down and tell him how ver' happy this make us.' That is what my friends say. So by gare, Louis Champlain will set up big treat."

"I will cook them a bean stew."

"Fine. We will feed them everything in this damn house. And also I will buy beer."

"Beer for that Connie Shortgun, and her sleeping like a dog with everyone?"

"Oh, phoof! this gossip. Maybe one-two tam with Walt Stephenpierre."

"And Bill Artois!"

"Well, he was one tam her husband."

"And how about Frank Knife and Jiggs Rock Medicine and Morrie Roque? And your own boy, that no-good Joe, before the army sent him to Korea? It's too bad they don't leave that Joe in Korea."

Joe was coming home soon, and she had been brooding over it. Last month, after he sent the postcard from

Fort Worth, showing himself in chaps and big hat, riding a Brahma bull, she had gone for half the day without speaking a word.

"Ho, not my Joe!" Louis said, laughing it off as too ridiculous. "Joe would have nothing to do with that Connie Shortgun. She's maybe sleep with Stephenpierre two-three tam."

"Whose baby has she got? Stephenpierre's? No. Red Eagle? No. Artois? No. *Just now* she told me. I said, 'Connie, does that baby look like her father?' And what did she say? 'How do I know if she looks like her father? It was too dark to see.' This is your friend you would use Mary's money to buy beer."

"How about Bull Shield, he is maybe no good too?"

Bull Shield was a fine old man, and Annie's friend from Fort Belknap reservation even before she had met Louis. She was left without an answer. Grandpere had come to the door and stood supporting himself with both hands folded over the knob of his walking stick.

"*Watche!*" he said in a croaking voice, failing to get above the racket of the radio. He cursed it and swung his stick back and forth trying to bat off its dial. "*Watche,* turn off the devilbox! *Watche,* I, Chief Two Smokes, will talk!"

Grandpere was in a great temper when he referred to himself as Chief Two Smokes. His stick had turned the dial enough to muffle the rackety beat of Roy Acuff and his Smoky Mountain Boys. He said, "Once, in old days, my father, he had four Sioux scalps, he came back from great hunt. All alone he shoot and drag home two

buffalo. *Watche!* It was spring, with the wet snow still
on the ground, and hunger had walked the village so
that some men had died and some had boiled and eaten
their tepees. But now what did this chief, my father, do
with his buffalo? Did he eat them himself like a white
man and leave his friends to starve? No. He called out,
'Come, and we will all forget together the hunger of the
cold moons.' Ay-ya! It was better in the old days."

"Gran'pere," said Louis, "please go outside, make
welcome my old friends." He drew out the money and
looked at it in great sadness as he prepared to return it
to the teapot. "But I feel very bad for my old friend Bull
Shield."

Annie grabbed the teapot before he could put the
money in it and said, "All right, then buy your beer."

Stephenpierre drove Louis in the Model A to Callahan's place five miles down the road. Callahan was a
six-cow rancher with a coal mine which he operated in-
termittently during the cold months, and a large barn
which he had converted into a bar and dance hall. He
had lost his liquor license almost three years before at
the time when he was picked up by federal men for selling whisky to the Indians, but he was still the main
source of supply on that side of the reservation. When
they got there Callahan was out, but his wife, Glenda, a
mousy blonde of about thirty, and Mamie, his seventeen-
year-old daughter by a previous marriage, were sitting
in the kitchen amid the dirty breakfast dishes, drinking
Cokes and listening to *Backstage Wife* on the radio.
Glenda took the money and waved them to the cellar,

letting them carry the beer from the outside stairway
themselves. The entire journey, with Stephenpierre holding the Model A wide open, took no more than half
an hour, but when they got back the crowd in Louis'
yard had increased twofold. The Spotted Wolf brothers,
all five of them, had arrived in their ancient Dodge; and
the Laneys, father, mother, and six children, were by the
creek, pitching a tent.

"By golly, you Laneys come to stay?" Stephenpierre
called, leaning from the car as he plunged it full tilt
across the creek, barely missing the stranded Hudson.
"You think it's sun-dance time?"

"We're going to stay a week!" one of the kids shouted
back.

Another of the kids popped up unexpectedly in the
Model A's path, and Stephenpierre missed him on two
wheels. The car slowed as it ascended the yard, and, as
before, came to a stop against the woodpile.

The last ten yards had been traveled with Stephenpierre's hands nowhere near the steering wheel. He was
holding cans of Great Falls Select beer through the window, calling, "Beer! Who's thirsty for beer?" He got out
and began beating holes in the cans with his rusty screwdriver. "By golly, you come around and drink on Louis
Champlain."

They discovered that, by accident, while Glenda and
Mamie Callahan were listening to *Backstage Wife*, they
had loaded two extra cases of beer. It was needed, for
more people arrived even while Stephenpierre was hack-
ing the cans open.

The new arrivals were Marlene Standing Rattle and
Paul Montclaire, soon to be married, and Dub Red
Eagle's brother Bix, who drove up in a jeep with two
fellows from Fort Belknap, forty miles on the other side
of the Agency.

"By gare," said Louis, "how everybody fin' out I have
this good luck, get cow?"

He learned that it had been on the Melody Wrangler's
program the afternoon before, in the form of a request
from Connie Shortgun.

Said Louis, "I sure do have plenty friend one tam."

One of the young fellows from Fort Belknap said,
"Red Eagle's folks are coming all the way from North
Dakota."

Joe Baptiste and his family, and the Winter Owls,
arrived, Baptiste driving a team and wagon, the Winter
Owls in a fairly new Plymouth.

Then they all stood watching with new interest as a
rider came in sight leading two horses down the long hill
slope from the north. The rider proved to be Pete Brissaud. He was astride a big bay and he was leading his
race horses, a middle-size pinto and a leggy chestnut re-
puted to be half hot-blooded. Brissaud accepted a can of
beer without dismounting and rode around the camp
with the beer in one hand and sixty dollars, all in fives,
in the other, wanting to race and getting more overbear-
ing all the time. Every man there owned at least one
horse which he claimed to be more than a match for the
best Brissaud could offer—but, alas, all those horses were
at home. Only Baptiste and Bull Shield had horses, and

they were work teams. Eventually the talk narrowed down to an argument over the comparative merits of Brissaud's pinto and Laney's buckskin sorrel.

"If I had him here right now," Laney said, "I'd give you one-length start and beat you for a hundred dollars."

Brissaud laughed so hard he almost fell from his horse. He took his black sombrero off and held it in front of his face to keep from laughing so hard. "That buckskin sorrel, he is sixteen years old with two ringbones. Listen, Laney, you could better saddle your old squaw and run races with me."

Everyone shouted on Laney's side, with the result that the buckskin sorrel became faster and faster, a paragon among quarter-horses; but Brissaud showed contempt for all that by yawning, ho-hum, very big, and finally by turning himself away and retying the bits of red ribbon that decorated the ends of his braids. He let them shout themselves out before saying in a hoarse, loud voice, "Ha-ya! you have all, ah, such fast horses *at home!* Since when have you all come to big whoop-up and leave your horses at home?" He was answered that they would have brought their horses, but for coming in cars. "Why do you not put your fast horses *behind* your cars in a trailer? Why? Ha-ya! I tell you why, because you know that Pete Brissaud will be there and do not want to lose your money."

Winter Owl said to Louis, "How about that bay horse of yours?"

"Ol' Two-Step? He's hitch up to team. I don' know

if you get very fast race from ol' Two-Step." Just then
Louis looked across at the ridge and saw the wagon coming, jounce-and-bump, over rocks and grass clumps,
Pete driving and Joe standing braced and holding the
seat. "Goddam, there he come now. You see all day he
pull those wagon."

Laney said, "I don't care if he's been pulling a plow.
I'll bet fifteen dollars he can beat the best quarter-horse
that Brissaud ever owned."

The race was on. Now that he was up against Two-
Step, Brissaud decided to run the part-thoroughbred
chestnut. Amid excitement, with everybody betting what
he had, Little Joe unhitched Two-Step and saddled him.
He mounted to ride. Brissaud himself was on the chestnut. They raced to a cottonwood that stood out on the
flat, circled it, and came back to the finish line; in all it
was slightly more than three furlongs, but the sharp
turn made it two short sprints, and while the chestnut
was faster in the long going, Brissaud's weight was too
great a handicap, and Joe, riding like a monkey over
Two-Step's neck, beating his rump with a willow switch,
came in two lengths in the lead.

Brissaud thirsted for revenge but now he was broke.
He borrowed forty dollars on his saddle and demanded
a rematch with one of the Laney kids riding the chestnut. This time the chestnut won by more than the slather
of his mouth while the argument raged that Louis' horse
had been robbed.

Brissaud now wanted to race the pinto, but old Two-
Step was tired. Suddenly Little Joe thought of the gray

bronc. In five minutes he had him caught and saddled. Joe managed to get the bronc to the starting line, but when old man Bull Shield threw his hat down and yelled, "Hi!" to start the race, the pinto ran, while the bronc bucked all the way to the cottonwood and failed even to finish. His backers felt cheated, and Louis came in for some harsh words.

Rising in defense, Louis said, "This bronc, he is like the antelope. Now he has burn off his vinegar, he will run like hell."

Some of them honored his words by again backing the bronc, but only at two-to-one odds. This time the gray stood doglike at the starting line, waited with his ears down for old man Bull Shield to give the signal, and thereupon ran to the cottonwood and around it and back again as though he had planned the race, shaming Brissaud's pinto by four long lengths.

Brissaud still had a few dollars and wanted to buy the gray bronc, but Louis said, "This horse he is fastest in whole damn countree. With this horse I will race for maybe five hundred dollaire at the fair next fall." But Brissaud would not be turned away. He was determined to get the gray bronc. Nothing could stop him from acquiring the gray bronc. He offered to throw in his saddle, worth at least seventy-five dollars, and when Louis said, "No," he stuck with him, holding to his arm, offering him one thing and another from his ranch. At last he made the grand offer of thirty-five dollars, his saddle, and the pinto, all for the gray bronc.

"You keep the pinto," said Louis craftily, "but give me instead the big chestnut, then I will trade."

"Taken!" cried Brissaud, and it was accomplished.

The enormity of the trade inflamed the imagination of everyone, and beer was needed, but all the beer had been drunk up. Louis gave twenty dollars to Stephenpierre and sent him for more. He walked to the house and with a flourish dropped ten dollars into the teapot.

"Now, ol' woman, what do you think of the gray bronc you would have had me sell to Gus Podonik for ten dollaire? Behold your husband, he has yet money in his pocket, he has on the ground a one-hundred-dollaire saddle, and in his corral one fine half-hot-blooded racehorse. Oh, I fix that Brissaud up good this tam, by gare. Ho ho ho! this new racehorse of mine, he will run the mile. This fall I will make with this racehorse of mine maybe one thousand dollaire!"

# Chapter III

At twilight the house was crowded with women helping to prepare a huge supper of baked beans and biscuits. Stephenpierre had driven steadily back and forth to Callahan's for beer, and Louis had borrowed back the ten dollars from the teapot. Cars kept arriving, leaving, and coming back again. There was a continual honking of horns. Some of the wilder bloods returned from Big Springs with whisky. A mouth organ, guitar, and fiddle could be heard from the old blacksmith shop, and Sylvester Bird Looking, "The North Montana Troubadour," who had already gained local fame through several appearances over the Havre radio station, was singing "Remember Me" in a passable imitation of T. Texas Tyler.

Mary arrived from Big Springs, having been driven out by Loren Hankins, a blond and unassuming young man who sat down on the front step and tried not to look out of place while she was inside helping with the dishes.

Mary was twenty-two, small, and well built. She was

pretty without that about-to-get-slatternly look that
most breed girls have. Her boss, Hy Slager, in at the
Big Springs State Bank, once said that you had to know
Mary for a year or two before you realized how damned
pretty she was. Hy Slager liked to sit in his bank office
with the door open and one riding boot notched on a
drawer pulled out for the purpose, and smoke panatela
cigars, and look at Mary sitting in the teller's window,
and tell everybody that came in how if he was forty years
younger he'd have that pretty squaw for his tepee. When
Harry McCune was paying court to Mary, Hy used to
keep her working until midnight, paying her time-and-
a-half, just to place obstacles in his way; but when
Loren Hankins came up fresh from the engineering col-
lege to be town man for the Montana Power Company,
Hy let her leave work without even balancing the books.

Tonight Mary had on a new outfit and was at her best.
Her hair was not quite jet. It was perfect with her
red dress, which she wore with just enough boldness,
with just enough of her lace petticoat showing. In her
manner she bore a certain resemblance to Louis, none
at all to her mother. Up to her elbows in dish suds, a cigarette in one corner of her mouth, she smoked and talked
in an animated fashion, glad to be home, falling in easily
with these, her own people.

At last, hours later, everyone was fed, the dishes were
all washed, dried, and stacked away in the cupboard,
and Mary got her mother to sit down in her rocking
chair. The sound of music came to them from the blacksmith shop, and some of the older men had gathered for

a ceremonial dance by the light of a bonfire. "Hoy-
ya-ya, hoy-ya!" sang the old men to the thump of a
tom-tom, while in the blacksmith shop Sylvester Bird Looking sang "Loaded Dice and a .38." Then Chief Littlehorse, his squaw, and their daughter, Billie Jo, arrived,
driving up in their new Ford. The chief stopped and
talked to Louis, while his wife and Billie Jo went inside.

Billie Jo was about Mary's age, and they had gradu-
ated from the Big Springs high school together, although at opposite scholastic ends of the class—Mary
first among twenty-two, and Billie Jo next to last.
Billie Jo had a large mouth, and her cheeks were pock-
marked, but, in her brassy way, she was pretty. She had
already been married twice—first at sixteen to Len Hos-
mer, a white boy whose parents had secured an annul-
ment, and next to Pete Shortgun, whom she had left
about eight months before. Since leaving Pete she had
stepped out with any man who would take her, but Pete
complicated things, for he was insanely jealous of her
and had at times armed himself with a .38 caliber pistol
and threatened to kill anybody he caught "breaking up
his home," as he put it. Last spring when she appeared
with Bill Artois at Callahan's barn dance he had gone
so far as to draw and go weaving and threatening
through the crowd before Stephen Franchette and Peter
Old Squaw wrestled him to the floor and got the gun away
from him.

Annie knew that Pete Shortgun was somewhere
around, and the sight of Billie Jo made her apprehen-

sive. She stood up and asked under her breath, "Who did that girl come here with?"

"Only her father and mother," Mary answered.

"Well, she will have a man somewhere."

Billie Jo then tripped in the door. She said, "Darling!" to Mary with a sophistication copied from *Wendy Warren*, a soap opera aired at ten each morning over the CBS station in Great Falls. Midway in the room, where Loren would be sure to see her from his place on the porch, she did a pirouette that made her skirt sail up and reveal a good portion of her muscular thighs as well as the lace edge of panties. While about it, she cast a glance over her shoulder and saw that he was looking. "Oh, dar-ling, is that Loren? Oh, Mary, he *is* cute!"

She turned and waltzed to the door. Music through the night air seemed to carry her. She could not keep her hands or feet or bottom still. She stopped above Loren, smiling archly; she bent over so that the top of her dress sagged to give him a look at her breasts, and he looked. He realized at the same second that Mary had seen him from the door. It embarrassed him, and he got to his feet, too tall and unsure of himself.

"Dar-ling!" cried Billie Jo to Mary. "Aren't you going to introduce us?"

Mary did so, staring holes into Billie Jo's seductive body. She knew that Billie Jo had always been jealous of her and during their high school years had tried by every means at a girl's disposal to exceed Mary in popularity—which, in Billie Jo's mind, was determined by

the number of dates—and in this she had succeeded, with
the result that her name became a byword among the
young men of the community. "Well, there's always
Billie Jo," they'd say with that French-postcard snig-
ger, and commonly referred to her as "Littlewhore" instead of Littlehorse.

"Shame on you, hiding him here," Billie Jo said.
"Let's go dance."

Mary said, "I'd better stay and help."

"Why, Mary! A person would think you were afraid
*somebody* would take him away from you." She linked
her arm in Loren's. "You want to go dance, don't you?"

"Well, I don't know." The whooping and ha-ya mix-
ture of ceremonial and boogie made him feel out of
place and apprehensive; then he noticed the snap of
Mary's eyes and misintrepreted it, thinking she was
angry at him for looking at Billie Jo's breasts, though it
wasn't his fault, they were stuck right in his face, and
he said, "All right," trying to appear enthusiastic. "I'm
game."

There was a big crowd at the blacksmith shop. Men
filled the entrance so that Mary, Billie Jo, and Loren
had to single-file push their way through. The inside
was smoke-filled and hot, dim beneath the light of two
kerosene lanterns. Perhaps a dozen couples were bump-
ing one another, trying to dance. The orchestra was
very loud, chiefly due to the trumpet of Frank Standing
Rattle, who had recently joined the group. After making
it inside, they stood between the dancers and the crowd
along the wall, pushed but not being carried away. Billie

Jo, on tiptoe, was looking around for someone. Her husband was there, but she ignored him as he watched her with a hungry, stunned expression. Presently Frank Knife crowded over and spoke. He was a half- or three-quarter-breed, tall and hawk-nosed, about thirty-five, just home from Deer Lodge, where he had served a two-year term for cattle rustling.

"Frank-ee!" Billie Jo cried, pouting and petting him. "I should never speak to you again." He didn't seem to get what she was talking about, so she shook her finger and said, "Naughty, naughty!" Then, pretending not to notice her husband, she danced away with Frank while Mary danced with Loren. They met when the number was over, and traded partners.

It was very hot. To Loren the dance seemed endless. Billie Jo talked steadily, a long, pointless, giggling account of something involving people he had never heard of. At last the music stopped, and amid the noise and shoving he stood tall and tried to locate Mary. Once he caught a glimpse of her and started toward her, but Billie Jo had tight hold of his right arm with both her hands, and she defeated him. He tried to speak to her, but she kept giggling and talking. Then the orchestra was whanging away again, and he was once more dancing with her.

She danced very close. She kept rubbing one of her small, hard breasts up and down under his arm. She was a good dancer, making every move just as he made it, until sometimes it gave the impression that they were stuck together. She pressed her cheek up against his

neck and got her shoulder under his arm, and clung until
it felt as if she had nothing on. When she bent her right
shoulder inward and down, the while moving slightly
away from him, he could look and see one of her breasts.
He felt sweaty and bored. He wanted more than anything to find Mary and get in the car and drive away
from there. He saw Frank Knife dancing with an Indian
girl and maneuvered close to ask about Mary. Frank,
grinning, leaned over and said into his ear, "You look
out, you get raped right on the floor."

"You son of a bitch," said Billie Jo.

He noticed then that all the stag end of the room was
watching them. He tried to dance farther away from
her, and just then the orchestra stopped and there was
the usual stamping for more.

"Where you going?" Billie Jo asked, hanging on him
when he tried to get away.

"Let's go outside."

She giggled and said, "Sure, baby!"

He tried to pull away and couldn't. He saw Mary
coming, pushing people out of the way.

"You slut!" Mary said to her in Cree.

Billie Jo answered her in the same tongue. *"Utinwuk
pissik-wat-isse-wina!"* She screamed. "Who are you, call
me that? I know you all-time. White man *towee.* Stay late
bank all-time, easy *towee!"*

Mary slapped her flush across the jaw and cheek. It
was a healthy swing that drove Billie Jo backward.
She recovered and reached with both hands, getting hold
of Mary's hair. They fought, tearing each other's clothes

and hair, screaming at each other in Cree. Loren Hankins, not knowing what to do, did nothing.

Mary finally dumped Billie Jo on the floor and got away. She stood, trying to straighten her dress and get her hair back from her forehead. She did not see Loren until he got hold of her arm.

He said, "Let's get out of here."

"All right."

"Let us through," Loren kept saying, trying to push people out of the way. Then the crowd fell apart suddenly, and he saw Pete Shortgun.

Pete was drunk and truculent. He stopped, a short, solid young man in a blue suit that was too small for him. "You wait!" Pete said, pointing his finger at Loren.

Loren did not know he was Billie Jo's husband, or even that Billie Jo had a husband; certainly it never occurred to him that Pete had a gun under his coat.

Mary, suddenly terrified, tried to get between them, screaming, "Pete, go away!"

Pete said, weaving, pushing her aside, pointing his left hand at Loren, his right hand under his coat, "What you doing, dancing all night with my wife? What the hell you think you can get away with, bellyrubbing, think you can get away with that stuff, think I don't know what's going on?"

Loren shoved him. Pete staggered for balance; the rough floor caught one of his riding boots, making it double over, and he fell, landing in a sitting position and leaning on one elbow; then, getting to one knee, he drew the gun.

Loren saw it and acted by reflex, kicking and jumping with both feet. He saw the gun loose on the floor and Pete reaching for it. He tried to kick the gun, but Pete was under him. Terror possessed him. He trod and kicked and kept kicking until he was pulled away. He realized that someone else had the gun, and Pete, with both arms wrapped around his head, was on the floor.

Mary pulled him through the crowd. He stepped down from something and fell. She tugged him to his feet. They were outside, with no one around them, and he breathed, filling his lungs with the cool air, steadying himself, shaking off the nightmare. Mary was talking to him.

"My God," he said, "what was the matter with him? Did you see he drew a gun on me?"

"That was his wife."

"Oh, that—"

"Billie Jo."

"He drew a gun on me. Do you think I hurt him very bad? I didn't know what I was doing. I went kind of crazy."

"He's all right."

"Is he?"

"Of course."

"I kicked him in the head, didn't I? I don't know what come over me."

"It's all right. Come on."

He stopped, looking back at the blacksmith shop, where everyone was still crowded around the door. "You suppose I ought to—"

"No, he's all right." She kept walking, leading him by the arm, around the rough litter of broken wagons and machinery, past the tents that had been pitched by the creek. It seemed very quiet now. They could hear the creek running. She laughed, recovering her quiet manner, and said, "We fought with the whole family."

"Did she hurt you?"

"No. She tore my dress."

"I shouldn't have kicked him like that."

"Oh, they'll all think you're a fine fellow now. They'll make you one of the tribe."

"You're joking."

"No, I'm not joking." They turned and walked back toward his car. "Anyhow, now you know what my folks are like."

"They aren't your folks. Just some crazy drunk—"

"My folks!"

He sat in the car while Mary went to the house, glad for the opportunity to be alone. He had never had such an unnerving experience. He smoked a cigarette. Then she came out and got in the car, and he drove slowly across the creek and up the steep pitch to the road. The dance was going again, with the orchestra beating out the "Fat Squaw Boogie." Then distance washed it out, all except the trumpet, and as he drove slowly with the window down he was aware of the mountain silence and the smell of the pines.

"Your dad carve all those animals around the house?" he asked unexpectedly. "I think he's sort of a genius."

# Chapter IV

It was sunup, and Louis lay in bed listening, but there was no music or shouting, only the sounds of sleeping men and women rolled up in their blankets on the floor. He got up, quietly pulled on his clothes, and, taking long steps over the sleeping forms, went outside. There he warmed himself in the sunshine and looked around. Cars and rigs filled the yard; there were tents by the creek, and tarps stretched from cars and wagons to make lean-to shelters. There was no movement anywhere. Only he was awake. Spread across the little flat on the other side of the creek were his cattle, nineteen heifers and the young bull, grazing the buffalo grass.

"Goddam!" he said.

The sun climbed in the cloudless sky. It promised to be a hot day, but the morning was fine. After an hour there was movement, and by eight o'clock most of the people were up, rusty and yawning, looking for breakfast.

Yesterday they had eaten everything in the house;

46

today they took up a collection and sent Bix Red Eagle, Peter Old Squaw, and the fellows from Fort Belknap to Big Springs for grub and beer. They got back with it before noon, and from somewhere appeared a side of venison. Several cars had left, but more arrived, and then most of those that had left returned again. Indians came from the settlement on Hill Fifty-Seven in Great Falls, and old John and Agnes North Lodge from the Assiniboin reservation at Fort Peck, just under the Canadian border in eastern Montana.

Louis had spent the last of his winnings on beer, there was no grub in the house, and he had to eat at the cookfire, where now another side of venison, together with spuds, carrots, onions, and turnips, was bubbling in a huge brass washboiler.

Seeing Louis dishing into the stew, old Matthew Horse Chaser struck his walking stick on the ground and cackled, "Look! Already the meat of the kettle becomes all bone, like the wolf of the cold moon! Soon Louis, our rich friend, will have to butcher one cow and feed his friends, or else they will starve."

Everyone laughed when old Horse Chaser said out loud what they had been saying on the quiet before Louis came down from the house with his plate in his hand. Louis laughed with a good show of teeth, but when he tried to eat, the food seemed to lodge in his throat.

Louis scraped up four dollars, borrowed six from Stephenpierre, and sent to Callahan's for beer. The cans were empty and strewn on the ground before he was back at the house. Cars shuttled steadily from the ranch to

Callahan's, to Big Springs, and even to Havre, hauling
beer. Car radios and the Philco in the house blared the
Melody Wrangler's hit parade. By nightfall the dance
was going again, and at ten o'clock there was a fight.

It was only a small fight at first. Ron Tilcup, a former
jockey, fifty years old and weighing little more than one
hundred pounds, struggled with big, sixteen-year-old
Humphrey Hindshot, who kept laughing at the little
man's bantam fury and holding him at long arm's reach,
staying safe from Ron's wholly ineffectual haymakers.
Finally, when Humphrey started pushing Ron around,
Boob Dugan tried to stop him, and Frank Knife, misin-
terpreting Boob's actions, pulled him away, doing it too
violently, and was clipped on the chin for his trouble.
Frank got up from the floor, and the battle was on. They
fought brutally, a toe-to-toe slugging match that lasted
without particular advantage for at least ten minutes.
Knife was then so tired he could not lift his arms. He
tried to keep fighting, absorbing rights and lefts until
his legs collapsed and he fell on hands and knees. Boob
was on him with his riding boots, trying to stamp him
against the floor. Knife, his nose and mouth running
blood, got to a kneeling position, and Boob kicked him on
the side of the head. Big Max Beaupre then pulled Boob
off. They fought briefly, Boob retreating to a corner
where he covered up while Beaupre pummeled him. Peter
Buffalo thereupon swung at Beaupre, and Jiggs Rock
Medicine hit Buffalo. The battle spread like flame
through dry straw. In a matter of seconds the entire
room surged with the struggle. Men were down, and men

tramped over them. A bench crashed, and a stool sailed through the air. The battle petered out and then flared again in private fights. Outside, Bix Red Eagle lay like a dead man after being knocked down by Morrie Roque. One of Bix's companions from Fort Belknap, a very tall, skinny youth called Red Rider, ran to the jeep, started it, threw it in second, and raced after the fleeing Roque in a wild S turn with the rear tires showering dirt. Failing to get him by a hair when Roque dived headlong to safety, Red Rider, coming around for another try, forgot about the blacksmith shop and crashed into it, shattering the siding and two-by-fours and killing the engine. Within ten minutes the dance was going again. The jeep was unmoved, its front thrust through the wall, and two old squaws in blankets and moccasins were seated on its bumper, drinking Budweiser from cans, watching the dancers.

By the house Louis watched the near destruction of his blacksmith shop. He was preoccupied with his own problems. His supper had not agreed with him. Even now, with everybody full and having a fine time, he was troubled by the fact that his money had purchased only a fraction of the food and liquor—yet he was rich, with his cattle in full sight whenever anybody looked. It seemed to him that every time he walked up to where people were talking they would stop or change the subject, and it made him feel like an outcast on his own ranch. Then he heard someone behind him, and turned to see Grandpere standing with his hands crossed over the knob of his diamond willow stick, hunched in the

identical posture of old Matthew Horse Chaser at the
stewpot that afternoon. Louis experienced a guilty start,
for Horse Chaser's words had hurt him the worst of anything. He said, "Gran'pere, you should be in your bed."

"In the old days——" Grandpere started, and Louis cut
him off. "Oh, lon la! Always the old days. You were
young in the old days, Gran'pere."

"It was better!" Grandpere lifted his shoulders up
and down, beating the stick on the ground. "I have years
like the chokecherries in September, and I say it was better." He became crafty. "Tell me, my son, have you
eaten tonight?"

Louis knew he had been talking to Horse Chaser or
some of the other old men. "I ate. It is late, Gran'pere.
Better you go to your tepee, get some sleep."

"My father was great hunter. With his knife he kill
buffalo, with his hands he kill deer, with arrow the
grizzly bear. This was in old days. Sometimes my father
traveled far, many sleeps, to the river of yellow water
and beyond, hunting the buffalo. When my father went
out to hunt, the squaws followed him with skinning
knives and fleshing stones, with poles and lines to jerk
the meat. Ai-ai! He was a chief with many cayuse,
*metatut* cayuse, *two-metatut* cayuse. Sometime, after a
great hunt, would come to my father's tepee many
friends, from three-four sleeps—many friends, dance,
sing; and they were big days, strong days, those old
days, you savvy? Did they come carrying their own
meat? No. Did they bring their own tobac? No. My
father, that strong chief, he would have lifted the scalp

of that man who came carrying his own meat like the meat of my father's tepee was not good enough for him."

"You have been listening to that damn old Matt Horse Chaser."

"They were great times when I was young, before railroad, before Ford skunkwagon, before Philco devilbox. Buffalo I have seen on Box Elder flats, many buffalo, as far as I could look, like black spots on prairie, like the ducks that came in autumn in the old days." He lifted the stick in both hands and beat himself on his bony chest, crying, "*Watche!* Grandpere for hundred years has lived, like my people, not in shack, but in tepee, always except in forty-below cold sleeping on the ground. Do I cough blood so the agent sends me away to hospital dying house? No. Grandpere live plenty long. See all white men, devilbox, skunkwagon come. See all white men go too. Pretty soon all white men die. Boom! like devilbox say. Boom! Boom! All white men blown up by bomb." He hopped around, driving his stick to the ground, saying, "Boom! Boom! Blow all white men up like devilbox say. Big bomb kill all white man off, blow 'em up. No house, out in tepee, out in cave, white men die. Boom! Injun live yet, you savvy? Maybe some day great herd buffalo come back."

"No, Gran'pere. You should stay away from the house and not listen to Edward R. Murrow on the damn radio. By gare, those bomb she's cost ten-twenty million dollaire, you think they will drop one on Big Springs, hey?"

He walked with Grandpere to his tepee, actually a wall tent, very dilapidated, blackened from the fires

that the old man liked to build inside, standing beyond
a clump of thorn-apple bushes so Grandpere could sit in
the doorway when he chose and be out of sight of the
house.

Inside, Grandpere still talked, his voice coming from
the tent darkness. "When they came to my father's house
he always had the fattest of all buffaloes for them to
eat. Tallow, like that, on the ribs of the young buffalo.
Over coals of the red willow the squaws would roast the
buffalo, and everyone ate until his belly was full, and
no one brought food to the tepees of my people. That
was in the old days."

Louis had started away but came back and stood,
troubled and thoughtful. "Gran'pere!"

"Uh?"

"They talked about me, Louis Champlain? They are
saying that I am a cheapskate?"

"They say that one night some Scotchman must have
crept into your mother's tepee, that now you are rich and
do not share food with your friends."

"Who said this thing? Matthew Horse Chaser? By
gare, I wish that Horse Chaser was thirty years younger,
I would beat him with my fists. Gran'pere, I do not think
you should be friends with this Horse Chaser—"

"Did I say it was Horse Chaser?"

"Who, then?"

"Ai, it was good in old days, in my father's time, when
the chokecherries hung black and the fat on the antelope was white and thick. Ai, my father was a chief,

many cayuse, many guns. From three-four sleeps came
riders to the tepee of my father . . ."

Louis left the old man still talking, shuffling around,
finding his way into the heap of quilts, deer robes, and
blankets that served as a bed. He walked to the house,
soundless in his moccasins, and stood in the dark near
the back door, looking inside to where Annie and the
squaws were seated around the kitchen.

He spoke. "Ol' woman!"

She came outside. "What is the trouble?" she asked,
having a hard time seeing him.

"I am going to sell one of the cows to Littlehorse."

Annie whispered, "Are you crazy?" and came down
from the step to peer into his face. "Only two days you
have had the cows, and already you want to sell and
spend the money!"

He answered with unexpected fury, waving his arms
out at the ranch yard. "My friends, they are here. From
hundred mile they have come to celebrate with Louis Champlain his good fortune. Do I feed them, do I give them
beer? Only maybe old bean soup. My own stomach I can
feel my backbone through. How do I eat—me, the host?
Do I say, 'Come, have big feast?' No. I, Louis Champlain, go to their fire, carrying my dish, lak bum, lak old
Gros Ventre squaw, saying, 'Please, may I have food, I
am so hun-gree.' In the old days it was not so in my
family."

"You have been listening to Grandpere again."

"I say myself, in the old days it was not so. In the

old days a man did not come and ask his squaw to sell
one cow. In the old days, in a man's tepee was he a chief.
By gare, yes. And now I say, ol' woman, I will sell those
cow to Littlehorse." When she did not answer, but stood
in sullen opposition, he grinned and said, "We still have
plenty cow. Ol' Congréss come around and ask, we tell
him this one cow she's lost in the brush."

"And how long will the money last that you get from
one cow? They will drink it up in one night. Then you
will sell another cow, and another, until pretty soon
there will be nothing left. You know they will stay as
long as there is anything left to drink. They will stay
until sun-dance time."

"I will sell one cow," Louis said doggedly.

After Annie had gone back inside, Louis stood by himself in the dark, still not quite resigned to selling the
cow to Littlehorse. The beat of the dance came plainly
to him—the trumpet blasting rhythmically, Sylvester
Bird Looking, a little more husky and nasal than before,
singing "I Wouldn't Treat a Yellow Dog the Way You
Treated Me." The blacksmith shop was brighter than
before. They had torn some of the loose siding away and
turned on the lights of the jeep, which augmented the
lanterns. Among the cars were couples having private
parties, drinking, and making love. Two of the younger
bloods warwhooped and wrestled. A truck turned in from
the county road and wallowed in the creek, its dual
wheels giving it a hard time as it got past the mired
Hudson. Finally it ground on in compound low, swung
around undecided between the house and the blacksmith

shop, decided on the latter, and rolled to a stop. It was
an orange-yellow Montana state highway maintenance
truck, so Louis supposed the driver must be Clyde Wal-
schmidt, who had married one of the Bird Tracker twins.
There proved to be four persons jammed in the cab of
the truck—Clyde, a heavy, bald man of fifty; his wife,
large with child; a second woman; and a tall, broad man
in a gigantic white sombrero.

Sight of the tall young man brought Louis up rigid
and popeyed. He shouted, "Ol' woman, come quick! See
who has come home from Korea and Madison Square
Garden! It is my boy Big Joe!"

Joe heard his father's voice and waited while Louis
crossed the yard with long, downhill strides. They embraced, and Louis wept. He pulled Joe down and kissed
him on the cheeks, talking French, Cree, and English all
at the same time. The word of Joe's arrival spread, and
the crowd swarmed from inside. They tore Big Joe away
from his father and wrestled with him and called him
strong names, and pounded him on the back. Someone
thrust a can of beer into his hand. Louis kept pushing
them away, trying to keep charge of Joe, saying, "This
is my boy. Goddam, you let me talk to my boy. Two-
three year I have not seen my boy. Joe, here's your papa,
wait long tam."

"Grandpere still alive?"

"Sure." Louis turned to the crowd. "That's my Joe—
always think of the old folks!"

Joe drank his beer, the entire can at one draft, without lowering it from his lips. "Ha!" he said and blew

foam, and wiped his lips on the back of his hand. He kept
glimpsing old acquaintances and shouting to them.
Everyone tried to hand him beer, telling him he was far
behind and had to catch up. He tilted a second can of
beer and drank it without lowering it.

"Look at those Joe!" Stephenpierre shouted. "He's
same old Joe all right."

"I want to see Grandpere," Joe said, tossing the can
away over the heads of the crowd. "Brought something
along for Grandpere."

One of the Laney kids went running to the tent for
him. Big Joe was then on his third can of beer. He tow-
ered above everyone. He was six three or four; an extra
two inches were added by the heels of his riding boots,
and his huge white hat made him seem taller yet. He was
broad and thick through, weighing about two hundred
and ten pounds, with not an ounce of fat on him anywhere. He was slightly bowlegged—not in the hip-
sprung manner of a cowboy, but bowlegged as so many
Indians are, starting with his toed-in feet and ending
in his spread-apart hips. His legs were rather short in
comparison with his trunk, which was very long. He was
more Indian than anyone else in the family—his mother,
Louis' first wife, having been a full-blood Assiniboin—
and his face showed it, being built in the classic lines of
the warlike chiefs, with a low, slanting forehead, very
high cheekbones, a huge nose, and a jaw that was square
and big under the ears. He had a fresh haircut, and his
sideburns were held stiff and comb-marked by pomade.
In addition to the boots and big white hat, he wore Pen-

dleton stockman's pants, a scarlet shirt with decorative
pearl buttons, and a fawn-colored silk crepe neckerchief
knotted like a four-in-hand and held to his shirt-front by
means of a large Navajo silver concha.

Little Joe and Pete, who had been in bed, were now
up and dressed and wriggling through the legs of the
crowd to get to their big half-brother.

"It's Joe, it's Joe!" Little Joe shrilled, getting there
first, pulling himself up by means of Big Joe's free arm.
"Let's have a look at the Cadillac, Joe."

Pete cried, "Can I drive her, Joe? I know how to
drive. I drove the old Chevvy."

"That damn Cadillac," said Big Joe.

Bronc Hoverty said, "Say, how about that Cadillac
you wrote that you'd bought? What you doing hitching
a ride in the highway truck?"

"I brought it all right. Drove from Umatilla to Great
Falls in seven and a half hours. Stopped in Missoula for
grub. You should have seen me hit that straight stretch
this side of Helena. Hundred and eight miles an hour.
Burned out the main bearings. Couple of connecting
rods too. She was hammering like hell when I got into
Great Falls. I left her there for repairs."

"Did you leave the saddle in it?" Little Joe screamed.
"Huh?"

"The silver-mounted saddle you won riding broncs in
Fort Worth."

"Oh, that. I sold that."

"How about the diamond belt-buckle you won bulldogging the steer in nine and a fifth?"

"Hah, I got that around someplace."

Bronc Hoverty, grinning, said, "Here, have another can of beer and tell us all about the Cadillac."

Joe still had half a can of beer, but he took the one Bronc handed him anyhow. He was not in the least bothered when everyone began to rib him about the Cadillac.

"I'll show all you bastards I got a Cadillac one of these days," Joe said.

"Does it say Chevvy on the front of it?"

"I'll drive up here about next week and take all your squaws away from you."

They all jeered and hooted at him, and Joe went on, drinking beer and shouting back, "One of these days I'll come back here and drive my Cadillac right through your tepees. By jeez, you need a hundred and sixty acres to turn that Cadillac around."

Soon Grandpere came, hobbling with his diamond willow stick, and everyone made way for him.

"You are a chief!" Grandpere said, stopping at a distance and peering up with his sunken eyes. He struck the stick up and down. "A chief come home from battle. *Watche!* All my people chiefs, kill plenty Sioux, steal plenty cayuse. When I was young I stood tall, like so. *Watche!* He is a chief like old days."

Joe said, "I brought something for you, Grandpere," and, limping slightly, as though his right boot were too small for him, he walked to the truck and got out a leather-bound canvas bag. He unstrapped the bag, dug down through clothes, spurs, and odd pieces of saddle gear, and came up with a worn manila envelope, which he opened. He took out something wrapped in an old red silk kerchief.

"Smell, Grandpere," he said, sticking it beneath the old man's nose.

Louis said, "Poor ol' Gran'pere, he's smell nothing in twenty-thirty year."

Grandpere steadied himself with the stick leaning against his waist, and, using both hands, unfolded the kerchief, revealing a tuft of black hair attached to a dried and wrinkled piece of skin.

"A scalp!" he said.

"Didn't I promise I would bring a scalp home from Korea?"

The women all pretended to be repelled; they shrieked and crowded to escape, without moving away or making room for the men at the fringe who tried to get in for a look. Grandpere held the scalp overhead and did a jiggly war dance, first on one moccasin and then on the other. "Hoy-ya-ya-hoy-ya!" chanted Grandpere, waving the scalp overhead.

"It is not a scalp!" said Louis.

"Sure it's a scalp!" Joe said, finishing one can of beer and starting the other. "What the hell, nobody's going to tell me it's not a scalp. I took it myself."

"You should not bring it here."

"Why not? I promised Grandpere I'd bring him a scalp, and I brought him a scalp."

"You are a chief!" said Grandpere. "You have taken coup from the Communists."

Everyone wanted to examine the scalp, but Grandpere

would not let it out of his fingers. In a few minutes the
dance was again in progress, but with new fervor, for
Joe was home from the war, and he gave it a patriotic
purpose. The beer was low, and Louis searched for Chief
Littlehorse so that he could sell the one cow; but Littlehorse and his wife had gone home, and no one else had
the cash to buy. So Louis got Big Joe aside and asked,
"You maybe have ten dollaire for beer?"

"Here's *fifty* dollars," Joe said, handing him a bill.

Louis had never before seen a fifty-dollar bill. He carried it in his hands to the house, where he held it out for
the squaws and Annie to see.

"Look here at the money that my son Big Joe has
brought home with him from Madison Square Garden.
Some men have ten-dollaire bills, some twenty-dollaire
—but Big Joe, oho! My Joe has *fifty*-dollaire bills. Look
at those picture on bill. He's ol' U. S. Grant, le général;
he presidenté long tam before your Louis was even
born."

"Joe gave that to us?" Annie asked incredulously.

"To buy beer, drink up, have big tam. Oho, when
those boy treat, he treats, by gare! And in Great Falls,
with burned-out bearings, one Cadillac car! A hundred
and eight mile an hour he drive those car."

With Stephenpierre he rode to Callahan's for beer.
All evening, up until now, Louis had not touched a drop,
but he decided now to celebrate the return of his boy
with just one can. He drank the one, and then a couple,
and then one more. He got to feeling very good on beer.
He stopped the orchestra and made a speech. In French,

English, and Cree, with tears hunting crooked courses down his cheeks, he told them how dear it was to his heart to have Joe, his firstborn, back with him—a hero, with the Purple Heart, and with two toes gone, shot off by the Communists in Korea. And he went on to speak highly of Mary, and of his cows, and of Gran'pere, who was the oldest man in the whole damn country, and yet, though perhaps 105 years old, would sleep in the house only eight or ten nights in the whole year, but sometimes at twenty below zero would sleep on the ground in his tent, showing what kind of men they were in the old days, and the kind of men the Champlains still were, by gare! The Champlains, Louis said, were always strong, big fighters, with many fast racehorses, and he himself when young had one tam danced the whole night through, from sundown to dawn without stopping once, ending with no soles at all on his moccasins, only the tops; but that was in the old days, in Canadá, vive la Canadá!— except for those damn Protestant red-coats police.

Everyone started shouting at Louis about dancing the soles from his moccasins, and he answered back, saying yes, by gare, he could do it yet if only someone would play the old-time tunes like "French Minuet" or "A La Claire Fontaine." So old Jamie Croix borrowed the fiddle and sawed it dissonantly, while Louis, choosing for his partner Minnie Hindshot, did his best on a minuet. But soon the crowd lost interest, Jamie was divested of the fiddle, and the blacksmith shop was filled with the push and shove of a fox trot to the tune of "Sneaking the Alley, Looking for You."

Louis still danced with Minnie Hindshot; then somehow he was dancing with Mary Whitecalf; and next he
was outside, drinking with Connie Shortgun, Nellie Beaverbow, and Walt Stephenpierre.

Grandpere was still around, a can of beer in one hand,
waving the scalp aloft on the diamond willow stick with
the other. It occurred to Louis that Grandpere should be
in his tent, and he went over to say so; but instead he
found himself listening while Grandpere said, "In old
time, long time ago, when war chief return to his village, from far off come tall smoke. Smoke tell 'em, pretty
soon all squaw get ready, make big time, know from
smoke war chief come back, plenty horse, plenty scalp,
you savvy? Pretty soon big feast. Whole damn fat buffalo. Young buffalo bull, you savvy? Fat young bull,
roast on fire all day all night. All this for young war
chief come home safe to tepee, you savvy?"

Grandpere was joined by old Matthew Horse Chaser,
who said in Cree, "If I had a son like that Big Joe I
would butcher a beef for him. I would show all tribe and
white men too what I think of my son."

"By gare, yes!" Louis cried, throwing his empty beer
can as hard as he could throw it. "*Watche*, everybody,
you will see what kind of party Louis Champlain throw.
You will see big whoop-up this tam, by gare. We will
have a fine beef roast on fire just lak in old days."

# Chapter V

It was hot. The sun through the open window had a brassy shine that brought pain to Louis Champlain's eyes. He was sick. Every movement stirred his stomach and nauseated him. He thirsted for water, but he knew that drinking brought only a temporary relief, for soon the water warmed inside him and turned him giddy, and he was worse off than before. The heat made his sickness seem worse. Mama banging pans in the kitchen made it worse; the shouting of Little Joe and Pete at the corral, the passing of a car on the road with its delayed drift of exhaust gas—all made it seem worse. He wished he could die. He tried to sleep, lying very still, eyes closed, but each time he dozed a large, bluish bulldog fly came to rest on his forehead, which was slightly damp from perspiration. Louis tried to kill the fly; he tried repeatedly, missing each time; and each time the movement rocked his stomach and made his head ache.

"Ol' woman!" he called.

She was rattling pans in the kitchen, and she kept rattling them, pretending not to hear.

"Ol' woman, I am very sick. Would you fix me some soda water for my stomach?"

After banging more pans—hurling them, it seemed to Louis' aching head—she came to the door, stolid and solid, and stood looking at him.

She said, "Ask your fine son, that no-good Joe, about soda. Ask him too about the aspirin which he carried out to his friends."

"Where is he now?"

"Gone. Rode off with that Billie Jo Littlehorse. I tell you, her husband will kill him, and he will have no one to blame but himself."

Louis decided to get out of bed. He stood with a hand on the wall, steadying himself, while his head pounded. "I am sick unto die. Beer! Ha, beer! Mama, your husband is a fool."

The admission mollified her sufficiently so that she started digging around in the cupboard until she found a beaten-up Arm and Hammer package from which she scraped a spoonful of soda.

He asked, "What day is this?"

"Saturday."

It was Thursday night that Big Joe had come home. Louis tried to sort out all the crazy happenings of that night, and yesterday, and yesterday night, when the dance had become a drunken brawl and finally, in search of more beer, everyone had left for Callahan's. He jerked his head back, making a dry laugh, showing his large

brownish teeth, and said, "By gare, we eat meat on
Friday."

"Your fine bull."

He stiffened and said, "Eh?"

"Yes, your fine bull."

"They butchered the *bull?*"

"You didn't know?"

He cried, "Of course I did not know! I thought perhaps they butchered one cow."

Mama said wearily, "It was the bull."

"Goddam." Louis looked very ill now. His face beneath its smoky tan seemed translucent, and the spots of
moles showed through. All he could do was whisper again,
"Goddam!"

"You had better go back to bed."

"No, I want to sit outside."

He drank the soda and went to the porch. Grandpere
was asleep, crosslegged, the faded Monkey-Ward blanket
over his shoulders, the huge, undented sombrero shading
his eyes, his diamond willow stick, the tuft of skin and
hair still tied to its end, propped up between his knees.
Louis said nothing. With aching eyeballs he surveyed
the ranch yard, its rusting auto bodies, its scattering of
brightly labeled beer cans shining in the sun. The Hudson was still in the creek, very low, its running boards
awash. Only some trampled spots showed where the tents
had been pitched. Someone had tied a pair of women's
pink panties on the high gatepost of the corral, where
they shook listlessly in the breeze. He could see his heifers in the pasture across the creek, and Pete and Little

Joe chasing one of them on horseback, trying to bulldog her.

"Joe, Pete!" he called in a voice that failed even to reach the corral. "Leave those cow alone."

He sat down. Momentarily the soda had helped him, steadying his stomach. From force of habit he opened his jackknife and carved for a while on a bit of wood, but nothing came of it, and he tossed the wood away. He was sick again, but he resolutely held the soda water and refused to go back to bed.

"Well," said Annie from the door, "what are you going to do about a bull?"

"Ol' woman, keep quiet while I think."

"What is there to think about? You must have a bull."

He shouted, "Of course I must have a bull. I got him one bull, no? Okay, I will get another."

"I suppose you will ask the congressman for another bull."

"No, I will not ask Congréss."

"There is only one thing to do. You must trade one of the cows for a bull."

"*One* cow for a bull! Listen to this old squaw talk! You do not trade one cow for a bull. Do you know what good young whiteface bull cost? Perhaps five hundred dollaire."

"Then you will have to trade two cows for a bull."

"I will trade none of my cows."

"You have found a way of raising calves with no papa?"

"Ol' woman, leave me alone. I will perhaps borrow the money from my son Joe."

She exhaled so he could almost feel the force of her disgust. "That Joe!"

"Yes, that Joe! You saw the money he gave me to buy beer. Fifty-dollaire bill! And Cadillac car. Le grande bulldoggaire! Ol' woman, you listen to your husband Louis Champlain when he say that pretty soon in an hour or two will come driving up the road my Joe, and then I will show you how to get new bull without selling two-three cow."

He dozed, sitting quietly on the step, keeping the soda water on his stomach. Slowly, very slowly, he felt better. Mama was cooking, and it did not nauseate him. She brought him a dish of soup with bits of baking-powder biscuit floating in it, and he was able to eat. Grandpere, the scalp on its stick between his knees, also ate.

A beaten-up old Dodge truck turned in from the road, and Louis sat up, thinking it was Joe; but it was Dub Red Eagle and a second man. They went to work to rescue the Hudson. They tried first to tow it, but the rope broke. Next they tried to dig it out so the rear wheels would get traction, but one of the tires was flat, and the rear end dragged in the mud. They stood looking at the house but did not come near to ask for help, so Louis knew that they were among those who had had trouble with Mama the day before. Finally they got in the truck and drove away.

It was cool now; the breeze carried the fresh odors of pine and sage from the hills. The chestnut race horse hung his head over the top corral rail, looking toward the house—a fine horse, big in the barrel, heavy-legged, a horse that could run the mile when trained for it; and when Louis recalled how he had put it over on that big-mouthed Pete Brissaud, trading the gray bronc and getting something to boot, he felt better. Oho, he would make plenty of money with his chestnut racehorse at the tribal fair that fall.

He rolled cigarettes and smoked, enjoying the slow departure of day, the flame cast up by the disappearing sun, the sunset colors and formations—first bright yellow and gold, then the emergence of the deeper shades, the dull furnace colors, the deep reds, coppers, and violets. Clouds lay in a horizontal bank, their bottoms perfectly straight and solid, but their tops frayed out so he could see in them a line of galloping horsemen, or phantom tribesmen chasing the buffalo of Grandpere's dreams. The pictures of the sunset always appealed to him. Sometimes in the past he had called to Mama to point out some resemblance—a running horse, tepees with smokes, or mountains beyond a fiery sea. But, after looking, Mama would always say something like, "Yes, I think it will be dry weather. You should fix the irrigation ditch." So now he no longer called to Mama or to anyone, knowing that the pictures of the sky were for his mind's eye alone.

Shortly after dark he saw Mary coming in Hy Slager's old Packard car. He got up quickly, before she could see him, and circled the house, keeping out of sight behind Grandpere's brush clump, and then out of sight past the corrals until he could double back to the horse shed. He stood there in the dark, cursing softly to himself, watching through a chink in the logs, surrounded by the warm horse and manure smells, listening as the car door closed and Mary talked to Mama outside the house. Then they went inside, and for a long time it was quiet. At last he was surprised by the sound of a footstep, and his daughter's voice close by the doorway.

"Where are you, Pa?"

He hesitated a second and said, "Yes?"

"What's the matter, Pa?"

"Ho, this damn old hackamore." He pretended to be hanging a hackamore back on one of the pegs. He shuffled to the door, making no sound, the soft corral earth beneath his soft moccasins. "I guess I need light to fix him old hackamore."

She stood very small and quiet, waiting for him, pretending to believe he was only fixing a hackamore. She said, "I heard about the bull. It wasn't all your fault, Pa."

"No, of course not. It was that old Matthew Horse Chaser, all-tam talk, talk, say your father is cheapskate, too stingy to buy grub. By gare, if those old woman there in the house had let me sell one cow to Chief Littlehorse we would still have our young bull. But no—"

"I'd rather you butchered the bull than sell anything to Littlehorse."

He recalled her fight with Billie Jo and said, "Sure. Anyhow, I never said to kill the bull. One cow, I told them. It was that Horse Chaser said to kill the bull. I should have the sheriff after that Horse Chaser, getting them to butcher my bull."

She laughed and said, "Anyhow, you really put on a good old-fashioned whoop-up."

Louis laughed too. "By gare, never in this country has there been whoop-up lak the one throw by Louis Champlain!"

"And Grandpere with his scalp!"

"You were here? You saw him with the scalp?"

"He was just showing me."

"You should have seen him all full of beer doing the war dance with that scalp, while old Dog Walker played on drums. By gare, Gran'pere he's not move around like that in maybe forty years. I don't think it's real scalp, though. Joe just tell Gran'pere that to make him feel good. My Joe wouldn't take off scalp from dead man."

"The dickens he wouldn't!"

"Now you talk like Mama. Have you seen Joe yet?"

"He was in the bank this morning."

"Maybe he go to Great Falls to get his car?"

"I don't know. He borrowed ten dollars from me."

"Eh?" Louis straightened from surprise. "Oh, but maybe he leave his money someplace else. He's come home with plenty money, those boy. Fifty-dollaire bill. Was he alone?"

"No. He had Frank Knife and Bronc Hoverty with him. And that kind of a good-looking fellow who used to be a rodeo rider."

"Bronc Hoverty? And those damn Frank Knife! I

hope that thieving Frank Knife don't get our Joe in trouble."

"Dad, you'll have to get another bull."

"Joe will lend Papa money when he's get home."

"You'll never get any money from Joe."

"Already fifty dollaire!"

"I think I can get Hy Slager to lend you a bull."

"And have him find out we eat those fine bull he's help me get from Congréss? What Congréss say about Louis Champlain when he find out?"

"They're bound to hear—"

"No! If somebody tell Congréss, you say this is damned lie. You don't let anybody find out they butcher my bull. If somebody say I don't have my young bull, you say Chief Shortgun spread stories about me. No, don't you tell to Hy Slager one word."

She tried to argue with him, but Louis had become adamant as quartz. "Tomorrow," he said, "Joe will come. You wait—those boy, he's fix up old Papa. He's big man now, Purple Heart, picture in New York paper, first prize bulldoggaire at Madison Square Garden. Big Joe, he's not forget Gran'pere, he's not forget ol' Papa either, by gare!"

Big Joe did not come that night, and he did not come the next day. Through the open door Mama talked to Louis' back as he sat on the step carving a bear from mellowed pine, telling him he should get a hump about him and go to town and have a talk with Hy Slager like Mary suggested, and tell him everything, because only a fool would try to keep the bull a secret when everyone

knew anyway. That, Mama said, was what a real rancher
would do, one who wanted to make a success of the business; it was what Chief Littlehorse would do, and look
at the new Ford he was driving—all paid for. But Louis
remained solid in his decision, not answering her except
once in a while as he rubbed wood fragments off the
bear and cast a look down the road for approaching cars,
when he would say, "Joe will be home pretty damn quick.
Joe will come home, lend old Papa five hundred dollaire,
buy bull."

"He borrowed ten dollars from Mary!" Mama shouted
in exasperation. "Why would he borrow ten dollars if he
had five hundred to lend?"

"Did I not already say that perhaps he left all his
money in his other pants?"

"When did you know Joe that he had two pair
of pants?"

"Ha!"

"Who said he had money in his other pants? Did Joe
say he left his money in his other pants?"

"Keep quiet, woman. Any fool would know he only
left his money in his other pants."

Joe did not get home that night, nor the next day. On
the third day, about six, he returned, riding with Bronc
Hoverty in Bronc's jeep station wagon. Joe had been
some time without sleep. He still wore the same clothes
he had arrived in the Thursday before, and now they
were soiled and sweat-wrinkled to his body like he had
been sleeping in them, and there was a boot-print on the
crown of his big white hat.

"Hohum!" said Joe, yawning and stretching gigantically. He took off his hat and scratched all through his hair. "Ho-hohum!" yawned Joe. "What's for supper?"

"Beans," said Mama and turned from the doorway.

Louis said, "We think maybe you don't get home at all."

"Been in Havre. Chinook. Been all over hell. Beans, eh?"

"By gare, if I known you were coming I'd have gone down the coulee and shot maybe two grouse."

"Oh, beans are all right if you got catsup. Boy, we sure lived good in the Marines. Plenty of catsup."

Pete and Little Joe ran up from the corral to hang to their big half-brother's legs and scream, "Hello, Joe! Where you been, Joe? Didn't you bring home the Cadillac, Joe? Ain't the bearing fixed yet? Hey, Joe, where's the diamond belt-buckle?"

"Been to Havre," Joe said, stretching some more, choosing to ignore the other questions. "It sure don't look like much of a place after New York and San Francisco. And Tokyo! Ha! you should see all the women in Tokyo!" He looked over at Grandpere, who had hobbled to the corner of the house. "You know, those Jap women would make Grandpere throw his cane away. I bet even Grandpere could go catch himself a Jap woman, they run so slow."

Grandpere shook his stick with the scalp on it, calling Joe, "Chief! Chief!"

Mama, back in the doorway, said to Louis, "Have you asked him yet about money for the bull?"

"You wait," Louis said, and, after preparing himself, got around in front of Joe and said with a deprecating shrug and laugh, "Those old woman, she think you don't have plenty money in your other pants. Of course, what does old squaw know about big money you make bull-dogging steer in Madison Square Garden? How about lending Papa few dollaire—ohh, maybe five hundred dollaire, buy new bull?"

"Ha?" said Joe, rearing straight and staring at him.

"That damn Matt Horse Chaser kill my young bull, roast him over fire. By gare, those young heifers are ver' unhappy without their husband."

"You want me to buy a bull?"

"Well, I saw plenty money, fifty-dollaire bill." It made him nervous to have both Mama and Joe looking at him, and he cried in defensive anger, "You said you the mighty bulldoggaire, first prize in Madison Square Garden, silver-mounted saddle, diamond belt-buckle, great big Cadillac car with the bearings burned out. I guess if you are big shot you don't mind lend ol' Papa five hundred dollaire."

"Oh, sure," said Joe, snapping the fingers on both hands. Contempt for five hundred dollars showed all over his caribou face, but he made no move to produce the money.

"Is it in your other pants?" asked Mama.

"I have been around a little bit. I have found out better than to tell where my money is."

"You think I would steal it?"

"Oh, no!" Joe hurried to say. He sniffed the **aroma**

of beans and biscuits that came from the doorway behind her. "By gosh, that smells good. Did you cook that,
Mama?"

"Of course I cooked it. Who else would cook it?"

He wanted to go inside, but she did not move from
the door, standing her ground, blocking him from the
beans, until Louis said, "Let us eat, and we will talk
money afterward."

Joe, seated at the table with his mouth full of beans,
talking and chewing at the same time, said, "You talk
about five hundred dollars—one time I won five hundred
dollars like that in ten and one-fifth seconds, bulldogging a steer in Fort Worth. In Fort Worth they had
my picture in the *Star*."

"Ai-ai!" said Grandpere, crosslegged in the doorway,
his plate of beans on his knees, his stick with its scalp
propped over his shoulder. "In ten seconds five hundred
dollar!" He jabbed a finger several times at Mama and
said, "Ha-ya, now who makes big talk about young
squaw and her job? Ha-ya, how long your Mary work
for five hundred dollar? Three month—five hundred
dollar! *Watche!* Big Joe, young war chief, make that
much in ten seconds, click-click, like that, five hundred
dollar."

Louis said, "Gran'pere, be quiet."

Mama said, "Yes, but when he needs ten dollars, who
does he go to for it? To Mary. Big talk—saddle, Cadillac car—big talk five hundred dollars! But where is this
saddle, where is this car, where is this five hundred dollars, eh?"

Joe kept chomping, his mouth full. He finally swallowed and said, "You will see."

"I will see! I will see you broke and in jail like last time."

"Mama!" said Louis.

"Yes, I will see him broke and in jail. I will see him shot if he keeps chasing after that chippy Billie Jo Littlehorse. Her husband will shoot him."

"Ha!" said Joe, eating beans.

"Yes, he will shoot *you*. Chasing around with another man's wife!"

Louis said, "Mama, everybody chases around with Billie Jo Littlehorse. One tam, down by corral—" But he decided not to go into it. "That Billie Jo, she would even take out after Gran'pere if there was no other man around."

Grandpere said, "When I was young, plenty squaw, plenty horse."

Mama said, "When you were young the redcoat police chased you out of Canadá. Big talk. All the time big talk." She addressed Joe. "You talk so big, why don't you get us a bull for our cows in place of the one you killed?"

"I did not kill the bull," said Joe.

"It was because you came home the bull was killed."

"You didn't want me to come home. This is what a man gets, fighting in Korea, getting half his leg shot off. Oh, big hero! Wave flag, great guy. Hooray, hooray, go out get shot. But when a soldier comes home all wounded and tired out, then it's a different story." He looked

around, his head back, his eyes staring out on both sides
of his massive nose. "Oh, yes, it is a different story then.
Then they say, where is your money, where is your big
car, where your saddle? That is what they say."

He had finished his second plate of beans. Now he
placed biscuits on his plate, cut them in quarters, and
poured Karo sirup over them—all in silence, while they
looked at him.

"Of course I wanted you home," Mama said grudg-
ingly.

Joe said, "You need a bull? Okay, then I will get you
a bull."

Mama said, "Give Louis the money. Let him buy the
bull."

"No, I will get the bull myself."

"Where?"

Joe ignored the question, while eating his biscuits.

Mama said, "When will you get him?"

"Tomorrow."

"See?" said Louis. "I told you those boy he's get bull
all right. Now we have nothing to worry about."

Joe was still sleepy in the morning; he got up only for
breakfast, and then went to bed again to sleep until
noon, when Bronc Hoverty drove up for him.

"Bring back the Cadillac!" Pete shouted, chasing the
station wagon in his heel-bent riding boots, and Joe,
leaning from the window, gave assurance with a sweep
of his hand.

"Cadillac!" snorted Mama. "Maybe he will bring the
bull in his Cadillac!"

All the next day Louis sat on the front steps, keeping watch for the bull while carving an elk being stalked by timber wolves. The bull did not arrive; Joe did not return. That evening Mary came out with Loren Hankins and brought word that Joe had gone to Browning to compete in the bulldogging and calf-roping at the Blackfoot roundup.

"When is he coming with the bull?" Mama demanded of Louis.

"He will bring us a bull like he said."

"Ha!"

"You will see," Louis said placidly, once more at work on the elk and timber wolves.

Grandpere said, "When he promised me a scalp, no man believed it would be so, but see now on my medicine stick! Ha-ya, old squaw, you will get your bull."

The following night the state news broadcast from KGFM reported that Joe had won first money in bulldogging. Louis was jubilant. "He will have plenty money in *both* pair of pants now, ol' woman!" he said to Mama.

But at eleven on the following Monday morning Joe walked into the Big Springs State Bank and tried to borrow ten dollars from Mary. She lent him five. Waiting for him outside in the station wagon with its back seat full of bedding and saddle gear, were Bronc Hoverty and Jiggs Rock Medicine. They left by the reservation road, stopping at Callahan's, where they spent the rest of the day drinking beer and dancing with Glenda and Mamie until Callahan locked them out at one in the

morning. The three then drove on to Louis', their car
radio going full blast, and got out and whooped and
wrestled until Mama put a stop to it.

In the morning Joe got up, looking rusty and mean;
he was still sleepy after going outside and pumping
water over his head. When he was seated at the table
Mama asked, "Well, where is the bull?"

Joe closed his eyes tightly and opened them. "Bull?"

"Yes, the bull you promised to have here four days
ago."

"Hasn't it come yet?"

"No, of course it hasn't come yet."

Joe started to eat and said, "That damned Charlie
Bowers. He said he would send the bull out next day."

Bowers was a partner in the livestock commission
yards in Havre. He might easily have a bull that he
would be willing to lend out for a while; furthermore, he
and Joe had been in the marines together during World
War II. It was so reasonable Mama almost believed him.

"Well, he isn't here," she said, softening a little.

"I'll go down to Callahan's and call him up on the
telephone. You lend me one dollar. I left all my money
in Havre in the safety deposit box."

"Ho, ol' woman!" cried Louis. "You hear that? *Those*
are his other pants, by gare!"

# Chapter VI

Joe saddled Two-Step and rode to Callahan's. He stopped at a distance and waited in the brush along a cutbank until Callahan, as was his daily custom, drove off along the coulee road to his coal mine, where he had a man at work screening the sandrock out of some old waste heaps, getting stoker coal ready to sell at Big Springs as soon as the cold weather set in. When Callahan had gone, Joe rode down and went inside the bar, grinning and flipping the dollar in the air. Glenda was sitting on a high stool, smoking a Pall Mall and reading a movie magazine.

"You got your nerve, big boy," she said, giving him an arch smile. "Once Pat gets on the prod—"

"That pipsqueak husband of yours! Sometime he'll talk too loud, and I'll break his neck." Joe walked through the bar and looked down the dim length of the dance hall, shouting, "Callahan!" as though he expected the proprietor to be there and not three miles distant at the mine. "Callahan, come out here, you shanty-Irish cheapskate!"

"He's gone to the mine."

"Luck for him. One of these days he'll talk too much, and I'll tie knots in his neck like I did those steers at Browning. A fine thing, threatening his customers with a shotgun just because they run out of money."

With a big flourish he jingled the dollar down, and Glenda got two cans of beer and gave him fifty cents change. "Let's sit down," she said, carrying the beer around to one of the three booths built against the wall.

"Here you do all the work," said Joe, "and what does that Callahan do at his mine? I'll bet he is sleeping in the shade now. If I were you I'd run that Callahan out."

"Pipe down," said Glenda with a tilt of her head, indicating the door that led to the living quarters. "Mamie's in there, and you know how she peddles things."

"She don't give a damn about her old man."

"Well, pipe down anyhow. I have to live with them. It's just as easy to get along."

Mamie Callahan came to the door and stood, combing her hair, looking at Big Joe. She was about seventeen, rather pretty, thin and sag-shouldered, a burlap blonde. In a way she resembled Glenda, and strangers naturally assumed they were mother and daughter, which irked Glenda a great deal, for there was only twelve years' difference in their ages; but, all in all, they got along quite well for stepmother and daughter.

Mamie, still combing her hair, said to Joe, "I heard

your name on the radio. You won the bulldogging, didn't
you?"

"Sure," He banged his empty beer can on the table.
"Need another. Need another one over here."

Mamie, in her droopy manner, went around behind
the bar and got one for him. "You want one too?" she
asked Glenda.

"He's got four bits, hasn't he? Well, let's get it away
from him. I can see, kid, that you got a lot to learn about
the saloon business."

Joe drank the second beer, burped, and said, "Now
how's about the house setting one up?"

Mamie, without question, got more beer from the
refrigerator.

"Lay off that free stuff," her stepmother said.

"Why?"

"You heard your noble father sounding his horn this
morning, didn't you? Do you want him to come back and
blow his guts all over the place?"

"I didn't think it would hurt to set up just one."

"He counted the beer and he checked the till. Draw
your own conclusions."

Mamie stood with three cans of beer in her arms and
stared blankly through the open door at the coulee road
that wound white and deserted through the midmorning
sunshine.

Joe called to her, "Hey, I'm thirsty. What the hell,
I'll buy the beer. Didn't you hear I won first money, bulldogging at Browning?"

"Okay then," said Glenda. "I didn't know you had any more money."

Mamie opened the cans, carried them to the table, put them down, and waited for Joe to produce, but he didn't.

"Pay the lady," said Glenda.

"Huh? Oh, I didn't mean I had the money right here. Pretty soon I'll get it out of my other pants."

"Where are they?"

"Home."

"Well, here we go again. Seven beers gone, and only a dollar in the till. What'll we tell Callahan when he gets home?"

"To hell with Callahan," said Joe, getting angry and rearing his back straight, the heels of his palms planted on the table. "Put it on the tab. Isn't my credit good, all the money I spend in this dump?"

"You're into him ten bucks already. If you'd pay something on that—"

"All right, I'll pay the dollar on the old bill. Now is my credit good again?"

"I don't care how you do it," Glenda said, drinking her beer. "It's only a lousy dollar, no matter how it's figured."

Joe said to Mamie, "Go ahead, put it against my bill. Now I owe only nine dollars."

"What should I do?" asked Mamie.

"Put it against his bill if that's what he wants."

While they were arguing, Mamie went to the till, got out the slips, found Joe's, and changed the total. She figured it several times and with a troubled expression put the slips back. She then opened the till again, took out a dollar, and brought it around to Joe.

"*Now* what the hell?" asked Glenda.

"It's what you told me to do."

"It is not."

"You said to put the dollar against the bill. He paid cash for the drinks, didn't he? Well, then I put it on the slip. If I keep the dollar he'll be charged for the same drinks twice."

"Ow!" wailed Glenda. "Listen, you rummy-dumb blonde—"

While they caterwauled at each other, Joe took possession of the dollar. When he finished his beer they were still arguing, so he got up, very big and tall, and limped on his old battle scar to the jukebox, where he read through all the records. He frisked himself for a nickel and, finding none, went around the bar to the tin can where Callahan dropped the slugs when he fished them out of the machines. He selected one, fed it into the slot, pushing it on when it refused to slide easily, and the machine gave forth with a Dixieland band rendition of "Muskrat Ramble."

Joe couldn't keep his feet still, the music was so good. "Let's dance," he said.

Glenda drank beer without appearing to notice, so Mamie got up, saying, "Okay, I'll dance."

But Glenda headed her off. "Go over and straighten out the till," she said, placing herself in Joe's arms.

They danced around the room a few times, Joe holding Glenda very close and Mamie watching from over the bar with a slack-jawed expression of longing. When "Muskrat Ramble" came to an end, Glenda saw her standing there and said, "Well, Miss Einstein, did you get it all added up?"

Mamie went to work figuring the slip, and the jukebox started "Muskrat Ramble" again.

"What the hell?" said Glenda, looking inside the machine. "What did you put in it?"

"Nickel," said Joe.

"You did like hell. You put a slug in it. My God, I'll bet it was the one that Callahan fished out last Sunday, and if it is it'll hang up and play all day."

"So what?" said Joe, grabbing her and fox-trotting her. "When we get tired of it we can just pull the electric cord."

They danced to "Muskrat Ramble." It ended again and started again. Over and over the jukebox played "Muskrat Ramble."

"Holy hell," said Glenda. "I don't want to dance again. I'm thirsty."

"Beer, beer," said Big Joe, rapping the dollar on the table.

"That same dollar!" said Glenda and got to giggling.

Mamie came over, carrying three beers and Joe's charge slip. She stood with the slip until Glenda got her breath from laughing and said, "What's wrong, kid?"

"Look and see if this is right."

Glenda took the pencil and started to explain how it was. "Now, look. He came in here owing ten bucks, right? Well, it says here ten twenty-five. Okay, add the dollar

for the first round of drinks. It comes to eleven twenty-
five, doesn't it?"

"But he paid for those drinks."

"Sure he did, but then you gave the dollar back to
him." She said to Joe, "She shouldn't have let you have
that dollar. Give it back to her."

"Why should I do that? It's already marked down on
the slip."

"Why, you cheap—"

"I don't care about the dollar. Ha! Dollar, what's
that? It's the principle of the thing. I won't have that
damned cheating Callahan getting the best of me."

"Don't worry, he won't get the best of *you*."

"Let her figure it out. The kid is doing fine. Come on,
let's dance."

Glenda said, "I'll bet he makes that dollar last all
day," and got up to dance with him. They went on drinking beer and dancing to "Muskrat Ramble." It was one
o'clock before they realized it, and Callahan, in his
truck, was coming from the coal mine.

"Here he is!" cried Mamie.

The women dashed around, getting rid of the empty
beer cans and stacking the full ones to the front of the
refrigerator so that it would not be readily apparent
how many were missing.

"Turn the switch on the jukebox," Glenda said.

"I don't know how."

"Well, get in the kitchen and open a can of soup. I'll
disconnect it."

Joe said, "Let's have some pretzels."

Mamie stopped to get him a bowlful, and he was in the booth, munching them, when Callahan came in.

Callahan was about forty-five, somewhat under average height, but thick through and powerful. With his sloping shoulders and his sidewise way of moving, he looked like a has-been pug, and he was fat the way pugs get when they go out of training on the bartending circuit. But aside from a couple of four-rounders he had never been in the ring. In his young days he had worked underground in Butte, and later he had tended bar. He had come to the Big Springs country eight years before to ranch and get away from liquor. However, the saloon business had an attraction for him that he could not overcome, and he kept running places and going broke and ducking prosecution for selling whisky to the Indians and promising to go on the water wagon for good, the while drinking his quart a day.

"Oh, you," Callahan said, looking at Joe. "Don't forget what I told you last night. I meant every word of it."

Joe, his mouth full of pretzels, said, "You lay off me or after this I'll take my business to Big Springs."

Callahan laughed derisively and went to the washroom, where he could be heard pouring water to wash coaldust off his hands and face. He emerged, rubbing the back of his neck with a paper towel, saying, "Listen, you big ape, you couldn't buy a drop in at Big Springs."

"The hell I couldn't."

"For how much? That's the point—how much? I'll

tell you—four bits a can and call for it at the back door.
Don't tell me about those joints in at Big Springs, because I know what their Injun price is."

"I'm a vet, don't forget that. A vet is allowed to buy
all the beer he wants. In Korea, Uncle Sam himself
hauled beer over and sold it to me."

"Well, Callahan isn't selling you a drop until you
pay up your bill."

"I already paid some on account."

"How much?"

"Dollar."

Callahan cursed. He threw the towel away; it was
black-smeared from coaldust. "Why don't you work it
out?"

"How?"

"Shoveling slack over at the mine. Pay you a dollar a
ton."

"A dollar a ton! Work all day—maybe ten dollars. In
Browning, one day I made almost two hundred dollars."

"Well, that may be, but you didn't show up here
with much of it." Callahan sat down in the seat across
from Joe and said, "Well, how about it? Take the job?"

"No. I'm not shoveling any coal."

Callahan cursed and took the bowl of pretzels away.

"What the hell?" said Joe, rising.

"Go on, get out."

Crouched and baleful, Joe advanced toward Callahan,
and Callahan retreated, backing across the room with the
bowl ready to swing in self-defense.

"Get out, stir the dust under you, Injun," Callahan

said. "I'm still capable of running my own place. I'll not put up with you coming here, wrecking the joint, running your face for booze."

He was behind the bar, and Joe knew he had a shotgun there within reach, so he made a pacifying gesture and said, "Haven't we always been friends? This is a hell of a way to treat a vet just come back from Korea, had half his toes shot off."

"We been through that before, and your toes don't buy anything in this place. Why don't you borrow money from your old man and pay up your bills? He's got plenty at the expense of us poor taxpayers."

"You'll get paid. One day I'll drive up here in my Cadillac car. I'll show you if I have money or not. Now bring me one Budweiser."

"You'll not get another cent of credit from me."

Joe banged down the silver dollar, saying, "Beer! And bring me my change."

Callahan said something about putting it on the bill, but he got sixty-five cents out of the till and brought it over along with the beer.

Joe would not touch the money. He said, "I have seventy-five cents coming back."

Callahan shouted, "Thirty-five cents is the Injun price for beer, take it or leave it."

Joe took it. He put the sixty-five cents in his pocket and truculently drank the beer. Callahan carried the dollar back to the till, where he saw the slip. He took it out and said, "I thought you paid a dollar on this."

"Sure."

"Why's it say eleven dollars? Whose writing is this
—Mamie's? Mamie!" She came to the door of the living
quarters. "Did you get a dollar from him?"

She looked dumb and said, "Uhuh."

"You should have subtracted. That makes nine twenty-
five."

"Bring back the pretzels," said Joe.

While Callahan was eating his lunch, Joe left, rode
down the road until the brush hid him, and waited there
until he heard Callahan start up the truck and drive
back to the mine. He went skulking back then, looking
to make sure, and came up to the kitchen door. Glenda
and Mamie were seated among the dirty dishes, listening to *Backstage Wife* on the radio. Remembering his
promise to Mama, Joe walked through to the saloon,
where he cranked the wall phone for the Agency.

"Who you phoning?" Glenda called, suspicious.

"The Agency."

The Agency could be called without charge, but, un-
heard by Glenda, Joe had the girl out at the Agency
ring on to Havre, which bore a toll of forty-five cents.
He talked to Bowers at the Livestock Commission yards,
and Bowers said yes, he would send out a bull next time
one of his trucks was picking up cattle in the vicinity,
provided an old lean bull came in, and also provided
Joe would put the bull on good grass so he would have
some weight to show for it next fall. This Joe agreed to
and hung up. He then connected the jukebox, which
started right out again on "Muskrat Ramble."

"Come on and dance," he said, grabbing Glenda and

lifting her from the radio, holding her tight with one arm against the small of her back, forcing her to synchronize her movements with his whether she wanted to or not.

"You big lug," she said, fighting back but liking it very much.

He danced her down the hall and into the bar. They danced and opened beer and danced while drinking it.

"Why don't you dance with me once?" asked Mamie from her roost on the barstool.

"Keep your eye out for Pat," Glenda said. "I'll do you a favor sometime."

Mamie kept watch through the door, up the coulee. She watched for Callahan, and watched her stepmother, who now sat in the booth. She went out into the yard to investigate a noise, which proved to be only a pickup rolling away toward the Agency, and came back to find Glenda and Joe gone and the jukebox playing unheeded. She walked around, looked in the dance hall and in the washroom, and finally went into the living quarters and stopped at a closed door. She listened with one ear close to the panel. She gently tried the knob, but the door was bolted on the inside.

"Glenda!"

After a moment Glenda answered, "Yes?"

"What are you doing in there?"

"Joe took sick. Go back and watch for Callahan. You know how he'll raise hell, him and his suspicious mind."

Mamie listened for a while and then went out again to watch the coulee road. She gave herself a finger-wave and let her hair dry in the sun. She saw the truck coming a mile away and went back to give warning. She found her stepmother sitting in the booth across from Joe, drinking beer.

"Ain't you sick?" she asked, looking at Joe with blank perplexity.

"Me? Oh, sure, but medicine fix me up, feel fine."

"Papa's coming."

"Well, get a move on," Glenda said to him. "Go on, get to hell out. I don't want to have any trouble with him."

Joe went out the rear door and kept the building between himself and the truck until brush hid him. He found his horse and rode off. The movement of riding made him belch beer. He reached in his pocket and found that he still had the sixty-five cents. He rode on, cursing Callahan. That shanty-Irish Callahan would go too far sometime, threatening Big Joe with a shotgun, charging him thirty-five cents for beer. No wonder he couldn't make a living in the beer business and had to run a coal mine on the side. Yes, by the good gods, said Joe to himself, if it wasn't for Callahan's wife being such a good scout he would stop trading there and take his business where it was appreciated.

"Bull all fixed up, get him next week," he said to Louis when he dismounted at the house. "What's for supper?"

# Chapter VII

When a week had passed and the bull had not arrived from Havre, Joe telephoned Bowers again. Bowers had forgotten all about his promise, but he had no bulls anyway. Joe returned with the news, saying not to worry, because he had fixed it up with a friend of his in Great Falls so Louis could trade two cows and secure for them a fine young pedigreed bull, son of Fielding Domino XII, with blue ribbons all over him from the fat stock shows. Ordinarily, Joe said, four—yes, five or six—cows would have to be traded for such an animal; but Joe could get him for only two, showing what a good thing it was to have served in the Marine Corps along with big men who had pull. Mama held back stubbornly, insisting that they stop fooling around and buy a bull from Hy Slager, but Louis and Joe derided the idea— with the result that two days later Joe and Bronc Hoverty set out for Great Falls in Hoverty's station wagon, with two heifers in a stock trailer behind.

Joe was gone for four days and returned behind the wheel of a huge new emerald-green Buick sedan.

Without getting out of the car, he honked the horn. The clear, trumpet-like sound echoed from the far hills as Joe blew in steady blasts, looking neither one way nor the other. Louis had stopped whittling and was on his feet. Grandpere brought his eyes slowly to focus, saw who it was, and said, "Chief! Chief!" shaking the scalp on its diamond willow stick.

In the doorway, Mama said, "Louis, see what he has done? He has traded our two cows for a new car."

"Eh?" said Louis. "He would not do that."

"Then where is the bull?"

"Bronc Hoverty in his trailer would have the bull."

"I see no Hoverty with a bull!"

Louis shouted over the clarion of the horn, "Of course Hoverty has the bull. Any fool would know Hoverty was coming with the bull."

But no one was coming. Far away he could see the winding white ribbon of road, and no movement anywhere.

When his father approached, with his toed-in moccasin walk, Joe waved an arm carelessly and said, "Little old Buick car, new model. Traded the Cadillac for it. What you think?"

Louis shouted back at Mama, "Aha, you see, ol' woman? He traded the Cadillac for this Buick." And to Joe—laughing hard at such a ridiculous thing—"That old squaw would have me think that you traded our two cows for this Buick."

"Hah!" said Joe.

Mama, coming forth, shouted, "Then where is the bull? Is Bronc Hoverty coming with the bull?"

"Pretty soon," said Joe, getting out of the car and pulling his stockman's pants down from his crotch. "You will see the bull." They were new pants. His scarlet shirt and white sombrero were also new. On his boots of three-tone leather were chrome and brass spurs that none of the family had seen before. "Yes, by golly, pretty soon you will see the finest damn bull in the whole country."

"When?" thundered Mama.

"Oh, couple-three days."

"You didn't even buy a bull. You spent the money on good clothes and that car."

"Of course I bought a bull."

"Let me see the receipt."

Joe leaned inside the car to look in the glove compartment but did not find anything. He frisked all his pockets, but he could show no receipt. He said, "Oh, maybe I left it in my other pants. Pretty soon I will find the receipt."

"If you bought the bull why didn't you bring him with you?"

Louis said, "Haul a bull behind this beautiful new car? Ol' woman, you do not use such cars to haul bulls around with."

"Ha-ya!" cried Grandpere. "You are a chief. You have come with the greatest of all skunkwagons."

Mama was not to be diverted from the bull. "Why didn't you bring the bull today?"

"All right, I'll tell you why. Because he is still in Colorado, in Pueblo, at the fat stock show. Third place, white ribbon, that bull won at the fat stock show. Get here two-three days, maybe a week."

Louis said, "Hear that, ol' woman? A white ribbon our young bull was won. By gare, I cannot wait to see the face on Littlehorse when he hears our bull has won the prize."

"White ribbon, hah! You will get no bull. That lazy no-good son of yours has stolen our two cows and bought *that*—that car."

"One of these days," said Joe, "you will be very ashamed of yourself that you said those things about me."

She stormed at him, forcing him to retreat around the car's massive chrome-plated bumper. "I will see you in jail. Do you hear me? If you have taken our cows I will swear out a warrant and see you in jail."

"Mama!" Louis pleaded, holding her.

"Sure," said Joe, "that is just what a man gets when he tries to do somebody a favor, drive two hundred miles, take time off."

She shouted, "From what? Time off from Mrs. Callahan?"

"I went to Great Falls, didn't I, at my own expense? Made long distance calls, asked favors from my friends. Didn't I? And what thanks do I get for it?"

Louis said to him gently, trying to make him understand Mama's position, "Mama only wishes that she could see the bull today. She does not really mean the things she says."

Mama yelled, "I mean he is a thief. A lazy, no-account, good-for-nothing thief."

Joe was really angry now. He stood tall, his head and shoulders reared back, a scowl on his caribou face. "You listen to what I say. If you don't get your bull I will give you this car. What do you think of that?"

"What do I want of your car?"

"Sell the car and buy a bull. Buy two or three bulls with the price this car is worth."

Slightly reassured in spite of her common sense, Mama looked at the automobile; its magnificence made the whole ranch seem inconsequential. She said, "Hah, big talk."

Louis said, "That car, she's worth two-three thousand dollaire?"

"Four thousand dollars!" thundered Joe.

"You hear that, ol' woman? Four thousand dollaire! I guess two thousand dollaire apiece would be a good price for our cows, no?"

That night Mama could not sleep. After tossing for hours, she got up and looked from the door at the Buick dull-gleaming in the moonlight. When Louis asked her what the trouble was, she said, "I was thinking that Joe, with his broken Cadillac and our two cows, would have just about enough to buy that Buick car."

The days passed as Louis and Mama waited for the bull to arrive. A couple of times they woke up and found

Joe in bed with the two boys, but most days they would
get only a glimpse of him as he raced past in the Buick,
an arm lifted in greeting from the window, his scarlet
shirt aflutter, the car around him filled with young men
and girls from the reservation. The horn would sound its
long trumpet, and Louis would stand to wave his knife
blade, but by that time the car would be nothing but a
rolling drift of dust over box elder and jackpine.

"There goes your young bull," Mama would say from
the door each time.

Then a week passed and they saw nothing of Joe. He
had driven to Lethbridge to compete in the rodeo. Mary
rode out with Loren Hankins and tried to convince Louis
that he should after all see about getting a bull from
Slager, but Louis said no, that he had paid for one bull,
and one was enough.

Joe came home finally, his clothes wrinkled, his eyes
glazed from lack of sleep, unable even to hear the questions they asked of him. After pulling off his boots he
fell face forward on the bed and snored straight through
from five that afternoon until nine the next morning,
arising only when Mama smacked the bottoms of his feet
with her pancake turner.

"Get up, get up, you lazy nothing!" Mama shouted
at him. "Where is our bull?"

Joe arose with a vinegar temper, muttering about his
wounded foot.

"Where is our bull?"

"The bull?" It took him a while to remember anything
about a bull. "Oh, isn't he here yet?"

"You know he is not here. Go out and get us our bull, or else I will have your car attached."

Outside, Joe had Pete pump water over his head. Little Joe hopped around him and begged, "Can I drive the car, Joe? I know how to drive a car. I drove the old Chevvy. Please, Joe, let me take a drive in your car."

"Pretty soon," said Joe. He stood with his hair sticking to his scalp, his shirt sticking to his body, and water running in a trickle from the end of his heroic nose, as Louis walked up.

Louis said, "Joe, where is the bull?"

"Goddam the luck, they promised me that bull would be here a week ago. The only thing I can do is drive to the Falls and—"

"I have to have a bull. You should just go listen to those poor cow—moo, moo! All-tam stand and look over the fence for their husband."

"Well, if you will give me a day or two—"

"Already four-five week, no bull, nothing but talk-talk. Do this, do that—but no bull."

"Well, I'll go down to Callahan's and phone Bowers. I'll see if I can get a bull by tomorrow."

Louis spread his hands, indicating "all right," but he was still not satisfied.

Joe said, "As soon as I have breakfast I will call him."

"Go now." When Joe held his stomach and looked weak, Louis cried, "Behold your big car, go past one hundred miles an hour with five squaws and ten chippies, so you are not too hungry to do this thing for Papa right now."

Joe went. He returned in the evening to tell Louis that Bowers was in St. Paul, but that as soon as he got back he would surely keep his promise and send the bull.

"No," said Louis. "I will sell two-three more cow, see if I can buy one range bull from Slager."

"Don't!" said Joe. "I have an idea."

Joe was very complacent about his idea, but he would divulge it to neither Louis nor Annie. He sat at table, eating a huge supper of rabbit stew, his face stolid against all their questions, except once in a while, when he swallowed and reached for another biscuit and said, "You will see."

That night Joe and Bronc Hoverty drove over the ridge in Bronc's four-wheel-drive station wagon, let down the fence on the south side of the pasture, and car-herded the cows so they would drift to the Cliff Creek drainage, which was the summer pasture of Pomeroy's Lazy Y outfit, and where by accident they might become acquainted with some of the pedigreed Hereford bulls which Billy Pomeroy was always buying for a thousand or two thousand dollars in at the Great Falls auction. Mama, hearing of the maneuver from Little Joe next day, stormed at Louis, demanding that the cows be brought back immediately, and saying that Billy Pomeroy would sue him for damages; but Louis was content to sit on the steps and carve the figures of three wolf-dogs pulling a toboggan, and wait for developments.

"Billy Pomeroy will shoot those cattle," Mama said to him, and he answered, "Then I will sue him for ten thousand dollaire."

"He will sue *you*."

"Hah, let him sue. If that Billy Pomeroy had all his friends in the whole country together there would not be enough for one jury. Haven't you already heard how the Pomeroys got their money, old Max Pomeroy branding everyone's cows? Ask Gran'pere about old Max Pomeroy."

"What does Max Pomeroy have to do with it, dead fifteen years? The point is you have let that Joe turn your cows in Billy Pomeroy's field."

"Well, when he finds it out, maybe in two-three weeks, let him drive them back, but next spring we will have whiteface calves, by gare."

Louis secretly hoped that his cows would graze the remote Cliff Creek country for the rest of the summer without being detected, for Pomeroy was short-handed and most of his men were occupied in cutting alfalfa on the irrigated fields below the home ranch. But it was not yet ten the next morning when Billy Pomeroy arrived, driving his Ford pickup hell-bent through the creek past the mired Hudson, and across the yard, as if intent on carrying Louis and all his property before him.

"Get your damned cattle out of my field!" Billy Pomeroy shouted, skidding to a stop, with his head thrust from the cab window.

Pomeroy did not look like the scion of a millionaire family who, ten years before, had studied for the bar in an Eastern university. He was a red-headed man of thirty-two, gaunt from hard work, dressed like one of his own field hands.

"Eh?" said Louis, standing, but not moving from his place.

"I said get your cattle out of my field."

Louis approached the car deferentially, without being sneaky about it—with a French courtesy, making apologetic gestures with his hands. "Sometam, you see, I don't speak English so good. French, all-tam French, my people speak, in Canadá, you savvy? You say sometheeng? *My* cattle in your field?"

Pomeroy shouted at Louis, although Louis was now only three or four steps away. "Yes, goddam it, I said they were in my field. You get 'em out, or I'll drive 'em so far you never will find 'em." Billy had been saving it, and now he had blown himself out. He took a breath and felt a bit foolish at losing his temper. He then said in an easier tone, "They're over on Cliff Creek near the lower springs. Go over and drive them home, will you?"

Louis, staring hard at Pomeroy, said, "One tam, two-three year ago, you told me nevaire, nevaire set one foot on your land again."

"Well, yeah, I know, but you go over and get them." Pomeroy sat in his mud-spattered Ford pickup, looking at the Buick. Its size and magnificence in contrast to the state of everything else seemed to fascinate him. Joe was not in sight—he was still asleep.

"Whose car?" asked Billy.

"My boy Joe. He's drive home from Madison Square Garden in Cadillac, but he trade off and buy little ol' Buick. Diamond belt-buckle, silver-mounted saddle, these things he have in safety vault in Havre. Bankroll"—

with his fingers Louis circled an area as large as a
man's throat—"lak so, fifty-dollaire bills. Korea, two
toes shot off, my Joe, while all-tam *some* young men sit
at home with their family."

It was true that Billy Pomeroy had used a hernia and
his agricultural occupation to escape service in the big
war, and they hadn't even thought of him for Korea.
Beneath his red tan he went pale from anger. He was
suddenly all atremble, but there wasn't a thing he
could think of to say. He took it out on the car, fairly
tearing its transmission out as he jammed it into reverse
and raced in a backward U turn, clankety-clank, over
the old iron that strewed the yard. Then he stuck his
head out and shouted, "Get those cows out by tomorrow
or, by the God, *I*'ll drive 'em out, and maybe you never
will see 'em again."

Louis, cupping his hands, shouted back, "Those are
very good cows of mine. I hope none of my cows get near
your bulls. In town the other day I heard those Great
Falls fellows cheated you with one bull that had Holstein
blood."

Louis walked back to the house, cursing Pomeroy and
his ancestors who had been rustlers—branding everybody's calves in the country. He sat down and whittled
with angry jerks of the knife, saying over and over how
he would rather be broke than have money given to him
by a thief like old Max Pomeroy.

Mama, who had been listening inside the house, said,
"You see now what a mess your Joe has got you into?"

"Keep quiet, ol' woman. It was not Joe's fault. Why

wasn't that lazy Pomeroy over helping his men cut alfalfa? What was he doing on Cliff Creek, spying on my
cows? I tell you, you will hunt the country over and not
find one man as sneaking as that Billy Pomeroy."

That afternoon Louis sent Pete and Little Joe after
the cows, but it was late by the time they reached Cliff
Creek, and they returned with only five. Louis sent them
again the next morning, and they again returned with
five, leaving seven unaccounted for. The third day Louis
went with them, riding until dark along the brushy, dry
coulee and its tributaries, finding only four of them. He
searched again two days later, riding all over the main
thirty-thousand-acre pasture of Pomeroy's ranch without finding one of his cows among the thousand that
were grazing there. When evening came he did not return home but rode on to the Pomeroy home ranch, where
he found Billy in slacks and sport shirt, with his wife
and a couple of guests, enjoying the fine July evening on
the front porch of the big old house.

"Oh, hello, Louis," said Billy, pleasant enough, getting up and crossing to the carriage path where Louis
had reined in his horse. "What can I do for you?"

Louis had been saving it up. "My cows! All over your
ranch I look for my three cows. What have you done
with them?"

His guests were listening, and Billy was embarrassed.
"Why, they were on Cliff Creek like I told you. I was
there yesterday and didn't see them, so I naturally supposed you'd driven them home."

"Fourteen I drove home. What have you done with my other three cows?"

"Fourteen was all there were. I counted them myself the evening before I saw you."

Louis was almost in tears. "Seventeen! What have you done with my cows?"

"Damn it—"

"You have driven them off like you said you would do. You said I would never see my cows again, and now, by gare, it is true. There you are, big man, four or five thousand head cattle, ver' rich, big house, these things you have. But how about me, Louis Champlain, not even citizen of the United States, not citizen anywhere, even though we were here long tam before there was one Pomeroy. Live in shack, goddam. And now you have driven off this poor man's cows, the only thing he have in the world."

Under other circumstances Billy would have been at no loss for an answer, but the guests, who listened with fascinated interest, were friends of his wife from Ohio, and he didn't want them to go back and tell everybody that Connie Lou had married a cattle rustler.

"Louis, get your wits about you. You know damned well I didn't steal your cows."

"Ha, no! Oh, lon la! You would not steal cows. Who ever heard of a *Pomeroy* putting his brand on another man's cows?"

Billy controlled himself, saying, "Go down to the mess house and tell Charley to give you some supper. He'll lend you some blankets, and you can sleep here. Tomorrow I'll get a couple of the boys to ride out and help you."

But the Pomeroy cowboys could not find the cows either, and Louis rode home convinced that Billy had driven them off.

After supper, with the boys out of the way, Mama said to him, "I think it was Joe and Bronc Hoverty stole your cows. Why else were they gone in that station wagon all night?"

"Oh, ha, they are always gone all night."

"Where is Joe getting his money to stay drunk all the time?"

"You heard him say, in safety deposit box, fifty-dollaire bill!"

"Talk-talk, big talk!"

When Mary came to visit, Louis told her that surely Billy Pomeroy had driven off his cows, and she carried his suspicions on to Hy Slager, who immediately got in touch with Billy by telephone and asked for the truth. The interest of Slager moved Billy to greater efforts. He used three of his riders, badly needed elsewhere, to ride the brush and the rough country—a three-day task that led to the discovery of a spot on Stud Horse Coulee, near the old Edgar mine, where a car had driven in and several cattle had been dressed out, but whether they were Louis' or his own he could not tell.

The sheriff drove out from Havre, but nothing came of it. All day Louis sat on the steps, carving wooden animals, keeping watch for the young bull that never

came. At last he said he was ready to sell more cows to
buy a bull from Slager; but Joe, very earnest and even
admitting to partial responsibility for Louis' predica-
ment, announced that he had talked to George Staples, a
friend with a ranch south of Chinook, who was willing as
a favor to Joe to lend Louis eight hundred dollars at
interest of only ten dollars a hundred for the season,
provided four cows were left as security. The cows, Joe
explained, would be sent to the Staples ranch, and Staples' eight hundred dollars could be used to buy a good
bull Joe knew about. Of course, said Joe, when the bull
came from Colorado they would sell that second bull for
all they had paid, and more besides, for Joe knew where
he could get a very good deal. Then, he said, with their
eight hundred dollars back, they could get the cows from
Staples—but that wasn't all, for the cows would all that
time have fed on another man's grass, thus saving the
pasture for winter, and leaving Louis in very good
shape with all his remaining cows, for it would look bad
otherwise if Congréss should come around and ask to see
how he was coming along.

To this Mama objected violently, and the argument
rocked the house for days; but one morning, after listening to her for an hour, Louis said, "Ol' woman, there
is no use of talking, for those cows are already on their
way to Staples' ranch, and Joe will be here tonight with
our eight hundred dollaire."

Mama threatened to get the sheriff, for Joe would
never come home with the money; but that night he
rolled up in the Buick, with his hand out the window,

waving a check. The check was for seven hundred and sixty rather than eight hundred dollars, because Staples had demanded half his interest in advance. Mama took possession of it, darkly hinting that it would come back from the Chinook bank marked "no funds." But she was wrong; it cleared without incident.

Joe said they should turn at least half the money over to him, for hadn't he already spoken for the bull, and could he expect it to be delivered before he put a few dollars down? But Louis had deposited the money with Mary at the bank, and he kept tight hold on his checkbook, saying, "First you will show me this bull with my own eyes. Then, if I like him, maybe I will give you some money."

"Very well," said Joe, "I will go out tomorrow and get the bull."

He was true to his word. Next afternoon a truck from the Havre livestock yards was driven up to the corral, its rear chute was dropped, and through the combined efforts of the driver and his helper a bull was prodded into an unwilling descent.

The bull was a massive creature, stolid and ill-tempered from age, unwilling to move. It was a three-hour job for Little Joe and Pete on horseback to goad him to the pasture.

When Big Joe came home that evening Mama was waiting for him. "Do you expect us to pay out seven hundred and sixty dollars for that old bull?" she asked.

Joe stood with his head up, his big shoulders filling the cabin door. With a grand flourish of his right arm he said, "Did I say, 'Give me seven hundred and sixty dollars?' No. I did not say give me one cent. That bull my friend in Havre lent me for nothing." He walked on, his limp a symbol of his injured pride, and sat down at the table, where there was as yet no food. He looked at Mama. "What is more, I am going to get you a younger bull from another friend of mine, and he will not cost you one red cent either. What's for supper?"

A letter had come for Joe from the Great Falls Time Credit Corporation. He opened it, glanced at it, said "Ha!" and thrust it, wadded, into his pants pocket. After eating, he was off again in the Buick. It was still light, so Louis sent Pete and Little Joe to the pasture to report on the bull. They came back with word that he was sleeping in the fence corner.

"He has had a hard day, riding around in that truck," said Louis. "Wait until tomorrow, when he has had a good look at those heifer."

Mama said, "He is an old bologna bull. That bull should be run through a meat grinder."

Louis laughed and patted her shoulder. "Mama, you do not like Big Joe, and so you say this thing. You wait, we have a bull now, everything will be all right."

In the morning Louis saddled old Two-Step and rode to the pasture to see how things were coming, but the old bull stood off by himself, his great shaggy head down as if it had grown too heavy for him to carry, his eyes glazed by years. Louis shouted, "Hi-ya!" striking the bull's rump with a quirt, but the old bull was moved only to a reluctant jog as far as the fence corner, where he turned and swung his head and pawed dirt over his shoulders—and there he stood as long as Louis could see him while he headed back to the house.

"He is very old bull, all right," he said to Mama, "but pretty soon maybe he will rest up."

Louis sat on the step, carving a bear from tough juniper wood, keeping an eye cocked for Pete and Little Joe. Each time they came within shouting distance he said, "Boys, ride up and see what the bull is doing now." Coming back, they reported each time, "He is standing in the fence corner"; and Louis said, "Goddam!" and went on carving the bear.

That evening Joe drove up in the Buick and said, "Well, what do you think now? I guess *now* you know who can find you a bull."

"Oh, sure, he's very big, strong bull," said Louis, not wanting to appear ungrateful. "Of course if he was few years younger that might not be bad either. All day he just stand in the fence corner, not once did he look at those young heifers."

"Give him time," Joe said, yawning and sniffing to see what was on the wind for supper.

"By gare, he's had two days already. Even Gran'-pere don't need two days."

"All right, he's an old bull. What the hell, he didn't cost anything."

"What we need is a *young* bull."

Joe was irked. He stood with his shoulders thrown back, looking down from both sides of his moose nose.

"Goddam it, didn't I say I got him for nothing? What do you expect for nothing?"

Louis talked, gesturing at times with the knife blade. "Listen, I will tell you how it is with an old bull." He tapped his forehead. "Old bull has big ideas up here. 'Hoho!' he says before he gets up in the morning. 'Feel pretty good this morning. I think I will have one cow.' But old bull, he is very lame in the knees, and his back aches. So he says, 'First I will eat some breakfast and then I will have one cow.' But breakfast makes him very sleepy. So what does this old bull say? He says, 'Ho-hum, I think I will take nap and digest my hay; *then* I will have one cow.' But when he wakes up from his nap it is very hot, and he lays there, chewing his cud, and he has forgotten all about that poor cow. So you see how it is with the old bull. But *young* bull, oho! Listen, I will tell you about the young bull. Young bull, he's wake up ver' earlee. 'Hoho!' he's say, this young bull, pawing dirt all over. 'I feel fine this morning. Bring me three cow so I can get good appetite for breakfast.' Then this young bull say, 'This make me ver' hongree, bring me whole bale alfalfa hay.' So he's eat that hay, does the young bull take a nap? No. 'This hay has made me ver' strong. Bring me *five* cow.' That is what the young bull say."

"I know all that," Joe said. "But I got him for nothing."

In the doorway, with folded arms, Mama said, "And he is *worth* nothing!"

"What the hell, I find you a bull free, not even any charge for the truck, and what thanks do I get?"

"What we should do is send that bull down to Callahan's with you, and then maybe he would get an idea what he should be doing."

"Leave Glenda out of this."

"*I* will leave her out of it, but will Callahan leave her out of it? Do you know what Callahan told John Bull Shield?"

"I don't give a damn what he told that old liar Bull Shield."

Mama shouted right on, blowing Joe back from the door with the force of her voice. "Callahan told Bull Shield that sometime he would catch up with you sneaking around his wife every time he drove to the coal mine."

"You see, what did I tell you? That Bull Shield has been carrying lies to Callahan about me."

"Callahan will shoot you sometime."

"Ha!"

"And do you know what Pete Shortgun said? He said he would fix you up good if you tried any more breaking up his home."

"Ha!"

"And do you know what Baptiste Lafontaine said, if he caught you one more time sneaking through the window into Jennie and Arline's bedroom? He said—"

"Yah-yah, all this talk, gossip, trying to ruin a man's reputation. You should listen at church on Sunday at what that priest says about ruining a man's reputation."

"You will get shot and have no one to blame except yourself."

"Hoha, I am laughing my pants loose, these people shoot your Joe. In Korea five thousand men with guns, and there is your Joe, all alone, crawling on his stomach with wounded feet, get out okay. One or two guns, do they worry me?"

"Korea, Korea—big talk. Wounded foot. Pooh-pooh wounded foot. What did the medical report say about wounded foot? *Frozen* foot, amputated toes. You don't fool me. Outside of a barroom lying drunk is where you got your wounded foot."

In rage Joe said, "You should be in Russia with an iron curtain around you. In Russia you say those things about a hero medically discharged with the Purple Heart, you would be sent to the salt mines."

"*You* are the one who will be sent away—to Deer Lodge Penitentiary for writing bum checks at Callahan's."

"Who said I wrote a bum check?"

Mama realized that she should not have mentioned the check. She muttered, "Never mind. I know."

"Did Mary come from the bank and say I wrote a bum check?"

"Of course she would not carry stories from the bank."

Joe stamped back to the Buick, got in, and, leaning from the window, shouted, "I am looking into this. If that Hy Slager says I wrote a bum check on his bank, I will sue him for fifty thousand dollars."

Mama came out of the door, saying, "Don't you go around there making trouble for Mary—" But Joe had ripped the car into gear and swung in a careening half-circle, with the big rear tires flinging dust. He drove wide open in second, downhill across the creek, laying a solid sheet of muddy water over the deep-settled Hudson.

"Why did you say that to him?" Louis asked. "Now he will maybe make trouble for Mary."

Deep in her throat she said, "I will brain him with the stove poker if he makes trouble for Mary."

"He did not write a bum check."

She shouted, "He wrote a bum check! Mary said he wrote a bum check! For thirty-five dollars to Callahan."

"Did Callahan see the sheriff? Then why hasn't the sheriff been looking for Joe?"

"Callahan did not see the sheriff."

"Then of course it's a mistake."

"How would Callahan dare complain to the sheriff to collect a thirty-five-dollar bad check for whisky? He would be sent to the federal jail for selling to the Indians."

"Hoho!" said Louis, opening his eyes very wide. "That Joe, he's a smart one all right. By gare, Callahan would have to be out of bed all night to get ahead of my Joe."

"Ha, smart! Thief."

"Oh, Mama! Don't say this thing. So he writes one bum check, what is that? Every time I carve bear is it a good one, eh? Is every time your pancake turn out right? This bad check could happen to anyone. Maybe even Rocke-

feller make mistake, write one-two bum check. What the
hell do you know about checks, ol' woman?"

After she had gone inside, slamming the warped screen
door behind her, Grandpere rapped the end of his stick
and said, "Hi-ya! She had better look out for Joe,
that squaw. He is a war chief. With his Buick skunkwagon he will drag her through the crick on lariat ropes.
When I was young——"

"Hush, Gran'pere." Louis saw the boys ride up to
the corral and shouted, "Joe, Pete! Have you been to
the pasture? What is the old bull doing now?"

"He's just laying there," said Pete.

"Goddam!"

# Chapter VIII

Joe drove until he could see Callahan's from the road, and, seeing that Bronc Hoverty's car was in the yard, blew his horn steadily for almost fifteen minutes until Bronc heard it and came.

Bronc Hoverty was a well-built young man, almost six feet tall, and good looking. He was a quarter-breed, though nobody would ever guess it from his sandy hair and medium complexion. Bronc grinned, leaning in the window, and said, "What's the matter? Why didn't you come on in?"

"I'll come in one of these times, don't you worry. He'll threaten me one time too many and get that shotgun tied like a necktie around his neck. But first I'm going to fix that goddam bank, going around telling people that I write bad checks."

"Did Slager shoot off his guff?"

"Mary. My own sister. Told Mama, made big trouble for me at home. I'm going down there right now and tell that Mary a thing or two."

"You mean it?"

Joe struck the steering wheel with his fist and shouted, "Yes!"

Bronc thought of something that made him go slightly pale, and there was a change in his voice and manner that Joe did not notice. He said, "Okay, let's go."

The truth was that Bronc had long had a secret yearning for Mary, and he saw now a chance to go along and bring Joe under control, and in that way enhance himself in her eyes. So before Joe could change his mind Bronc started away in the station wagon, motioning for Joe to follow.

In a quarter-hour they were at Big Springs, a small town sitting on the flat prairie. It was chopped north and south by the Havre-Butte branch of the Great Northern railway, and chopped again, at a slightly different angle, by the paved highway for which the Lion's Club had diligently worked, and which now allowed the chain stores of Great Falls and Havre to take the town's business away. Big Springs was a fairly planless scatter of white frame houses, most of them remodeled in recent years, and a business section of old false fronts built in the nineties, and a couple of brick veneer that had gone up during the 1912 land boom. One of the brick buildings housed the Big Springs State Bank, and there Hoverty pulled to a stop with Joe on his tail.

Leaning from the car window, Joe shouted, "Too late, all closed up. Let's go down to the Elkhorn for beer."

The bank was indeed locked, and a curtain saying

CLOSED was pulled behind the door window; but Mary was still at work, and all anybody had to do to get in was rap hard at the side entrance. This Bronc knew, and he tried to convince Joe, but Joe would not get out of the car, stubbornly insisting it was too late; so they drove to the Elkhorn, parked in the alley, and went to a back room where the management favored the reservation trade.

"Lose your guts?" Bronc asked him over beer.

"Ha!"

"You're a hell of a guy, afraid of your little sister."

"Pretty soon I'll show you if I'm afraid of Mary or not. I'll hunt her out and give her a good piece of my mind."

Bronc kept needling him as they drank beer—one glass after another. When they got too loud, Chuck Wesser, the bartender, came back and said, "All right, you Injuns, do you want the feds down on us?" That quieted them for a while. Thus a couple of hours passed. Then they heard the high-pitched giggling of women, and Joe peeped from the hall to see who it was.

"It's Bernice Red Eagle and Littlewhore," Joe said, calling Billie Jo Littlehorse by her common name. For some reason the federal officers took less interest in the alcoholic habits of Indian women than in those of Indian men, with the result that Billie Jo and Bernice were able to make the rounds of Big Springs using the front doors. "What do you say we take them out for a ride?"

Bronc had become very nervous, fingering his empty glass. "Joe, do you know what I wish you'd do? I wish you'd fix me a date with Mary."

"My sister?"

"Yeah."

"Sure," said Joe, as though it was the smallest thing in the world. "So you like Mary, eh?"

"Yeah."

"Okay, this is Friday night, how about that dance at McGee's barn? You take Mary, and I'll take Billie Jo."

"Do you think Mary will go with me?"

"Sure, I'll tell her to go, she'll go all right."

Bronc ordered some breath deodorizers and ate half the package. He used the time in trying to calm himself and not show the tumult inside him. It was the first time he had ever told anybody how he was about Mary, although *she* must have guessed—all the times she had turned and caught him staring at her at dances, on the street, or through the bank window. Bronc had been that way about her for years. When she was a kid in high school, spending her summer vacations at home, Bronc used to drive over at night, hide his car, sneak up from the creek to lie in the buckbrush that grew close to the house on the side uphill from the bedroom window, and wait for her to undress. Every night she put the lamp down and pulled the shade, but he could see her silhouette when she bent and took her dress off over her head, and sometimes he glimpsed the naked flesh of her body through the narrow opening where the ragged shade failed to reach the window casing. Then one night he came when Louis, Annie, and the boys had gone somewhere—to the Winter Owls, perhaps—and Mary was alone, except for Grandpere in his tent. That night, after hiding his car in the brush a quarter-mile upstream and coming around by the hill path, Bronc had barely reached his hiding place when Mary came into the room and put down the lamp. This time she did not pull the shade. He did not realize that she was already undressing until, unexpectedly, she stepped into full view, wearing only a brassiere and garter belt. She stood fooling with the garter belt and slid out of it. Bronc was prone, without breath, only a dozen steps away. She took off the brassiere and stood naked, examining her nipples, the little mole on her left shoulder, and a place on her hip where the garter belt had rubbed. At last she wandered off, put on her nightgown, and blew out the lamp.

Bronc lay staring at the blackened window. He kept saying to himself, "Her folks aren't home. You got to go in there while her folks aren't home." He forced himself to walk to the house, while all the time he wanted to run away. He stopped at the front door and looked into the blackness of the house. He could smell her perfume. He went inside, groping his way. He struck a chair with his thighs. He put the chair aside, reached, and touched the wall. He felt along the wall to Mary's door. He tried to speak her name. The door was ajar, and it swung a little, making a sound, and Mary's frightened voice came from close in front of him. "Who's there?

"Who's there?" Mary called again, sounding as if she was ready to scream. He heard her get out of bed. "Mama!" she called, and he knew she *was* ready to scream. All his resolve left him. She was coming toward

the door, and he slammed it, holding it while she twisted
the knob, trying to hold it or force it open—Bronc was
never sure which—while she screamed, "Grandpere!
Grandpere!"

Bronc let go of the knob and ran. Outside he fell
headlong down the steep drop by the old root cellar; then
he was running again, blindly, around the corrals,
through brush, against a barbed-wire fence that cut his
thigh, to his car, which he drove crazily toward the reservation.

It caused a lot of talk—who was the man in Mary's
room? And that was why he never asked her to dance,
and pretended not to be in the least interested in her—
for fear people would guess. But she was with him a
thousand times in the dark of night. Even when he was
with other women he would for an instant be once more in
the bushes, seeing Mary—her legs thin and wide-set on
her hips, not like you'd expect, seeing her with her clothes
on; her small sharp breasts with their large brown nipples; and her abdomen, very round, and the way the garter belt slid over it, making him sick and sweaty in
an ecstasy of want. Bronc had thought of lying in wait
for her in the dark shadows by Baker's garage, when
sometimes she went home late from the bank. He had
thought of it, and he'd got drunk for fear he would do it
—and the next day he'd think of it again, and think of it
in other ways too. But now Joe had promised to get
him a date with her, and it took the load off him; he felt
he would never do such a thing after they had actually
gone places together.

"Don't tell her I asked," he said to Joe.

"Okay. You beat that damned electrician's time. The boy-scout son of a bitch, he's nobody for Mary to be running around with."

At McClure's big two-story house, where Mary roomed and boarded, Bronc Hoverty's nerve almost failed him, and he stopped short of the porch while Joe climbed and rang the doorbell. No one responded. A phonograph was playing, and it drowned out the chimes.

"Let's get the hell away from here," whispered Bronc.

"No, she's in there. I can see her," Joe said, craning to see inside. He opened the door and called, "Mary, it's Joe. Can I come in?"

She answered, "Yes," and Joe turned to see why Bronc did not follow. "Come on," he said. "What are you waiting for?" So Bronc followed him.

Mary and that tall young Montana Power man, Loren Hankins, had been seated on the floor, listening to a record that slowly revolved on a long-playing turntable.

"You know Joe, don't you?" Mary said to Loren, and Joe, grabbing the young man's hand, bore down deliberately, trying to make him wince.

"Sure," said Joe. "Why don't you come around sometime, drink beer with the men?" He looked startled as a clear, high soprano voice split the air. "What the hell is this?"

Loren said, "That's the 'Waltz Song' from *Romeo and Juliet*. I just bought it."

"You *like* it?"

"Oh, it's pretty good."

"It sounds like old squaw laid an egg in the haystack to me."

Bronc stood in the archway of the living room with his hat in his hands, now wishing desperately that he had escaped while he had the chance.

"Hello, Bronc," Mary said.

His voice sounded strange when he forced out, "Hello," and he stared at her like he'd been shot.

"Come on in. You know Loren Hankins."

Joe said, "Why don't you play something good like 'Sneaking the Alley, Looking for You'?"

Mary said, "Oh, for gosh sakes, keep your mouth shut."

"Eh?" He reared around in his bull-moose manner. "I like snappy music. What's wrong with that? I'm *hep*—you know what that is?"

"You're drunk."

Joe had a good laugh about that. "One-two drinks of beer, that doesn't make *Joe* drunk." He was close to Loren and rammed a nudge into Loren's ribs, almost knocking him down. "How about it, Loren? Do you think I'm drunk?"

The blow had paralyzed Loren down one side, leaving him unable to get his breath. He turned away so as not to show the pain. He didn't want to, but he had to take hold of a chair to stay on his feet.

"Joe, you fool!" said Mary. "Loren—"

"I'm all right. He didn't mean anything."

"Eh?" said Joe, pretending a baffled innocence. "What's wrong?"

Mary was furious. "Why didn't you use your fist?"

"What are you talking about? Oh, did that little nudge hurt you, Loren? Maybe I should call a doctor, give you vitamins, make you strong."

Loren was about as tall as Joe, but he was a beanpole, and his heavy-rimmed glasses made him look physically helpless as he faced Joe and said, "All right, lay off. What you got against me?"

"Nothing."

"Well, don't come roughing me around because—"

Mary said, "Oh, Loren, don't pay any attention to the big ox. That's his idea of being funny."

Joe said, "Sure, sometimes I don't know my own strength."

Loren turned off the phonograph and put *Romeo and Juliet* back in its folder.

"Maybe you got the 'Fat Squaw Boogie'?" said Joe.

"Joe," Mary pleaded, "go back over town."

Bronc said, "Yah, let's get out of here."

Mary had forgotten about Bronc; now she saw him standing there, ill at ease, and felt a twinge of remorse. Many times she had turned unexpectedly and found him watching her—and she had an idea what was on his mind too—but she did not dislike him, and it had never occurred to her that Bronc was the man who had sneaked into the house that night. Besides, she didn't want him going back to the reservation and telling everyone that her own people were no longer good enough for her.

So she said, "Joe, why don't you behave yourself like

Bronc? He knows enough to act like a gentleman.
Come on in and sit down, Bronc."

He did—very nervous, lowering himself to the edge
of an overstuffed chair, where he carried his weight more
on his boots than on the seat of his pants. Then he looked
around the room, not meeting Mary's eyes but only
looking at her when she looked elsewhere.

"Why don't you come along to the dance with us?"
Joe said to Mary.

"Where?"

"At McGee's barn."

McGee's was forty-two miles back in the mountains.
Mary laughed and said, "Are you crazy? I have to
work tomorrow."

"Oh, what the hell? Meet your old friends, have good
time. Marlene Standing Rattle will be there, Connie Beaupre, Lola Whitecalf. All your old friends you went to
school with."

Joe had named the favorites among her old companions—without any idea whether they would actually at-
tend the dance—and he noticed with satisfaction that she
didn't say no right away but shot a glance at Loren
first.

"No, I got to work."

"What's forty-two miles? Just forty-two minutes in
that Buick."

"That's what I'm afraid of."

Joe said to Loren, "You don't want to come along
—okay, you don't care if I take my sister."

Loren did not know what to say, except that it was all right with him.

Mary said, "Go back over town. I don't want to go to McGee's."

They wrangled, making considerable noise, and Mrs. McClure came to the head of the stairs and called down, "Is something the trouble, Mary?"

"Oh, me and my drunken relatives."

Joe, in deep truculence, pulled his hat down, motioned for Bronc to follow, and stalked out. In the yard he said, "It's that damn electrician. Sometime I'll tie knots in his neck."

"She wouldn't go with me anyhow," Bronc said.

"Who the hell said she wouldn't?"

"She doesn't like me."

"Of course she likes you. Why don't you push that Hankins' face in and say, 'Come along to the dance'? That's the way a woman likes to be treated."

"Not Mary."

"Ha!"

"She wouldn't go with me."

"She likes you. She talks about you all the time."

"You're kidding."

"No, I'm not. All you have to do is shove that fellow out of your way—that nothing, that pipsqueak." He coughed hollowly, holding his stomach, imitating Loren, "Oh, I am sick. You bumped me with your elbow, I am sick to die. Please get me some Lydia E. Pinkham's Vegetable Compound or I will fall in my phon-

ograph. Ha! How would it make you feel to have your
sister hanging around with a nothing like that?"

They went back over town and ordered T-bones at
the Stockman's Cafe. Bronc, after a silence, asked in
a tight voice, "Does she really talk about me?"

"Of course she does."

It was then that Loren Hankins walked in the door.
He saw them and hesitated, wishing he had gone elsewhere; but it was too late then, so he sat down at the up-
per end of the counter and ordered pie and coffee. He
bolted the pie and drank the coffee scalding hot, trying
to get away before Joe started anything; but Joe got
up, big and casual, wiping beefsteak grease from his lips,
and sauntered up, saying, "Loren, old pal, why don't
you go ahead and take her out to that dance? All the best
people will be there; Billy Pomeroy and his friends go all
the time."

"You heard her. She said she didn't want to."

"Oh, she *said* that, sure, but you know why. She
thought you didn't want to go."

"I said I'd—"

"She has the idea you don't want to have anything
to do with her Indian friends."

"That's not true. I—"

"Well, maybe, yes; but you know how girls are.
Haha on their face and go home and cry all night. Poor
little Mary. Sometimes I feel very sorry for my sister." He laid a hand on Loren's shoulder. "Loren,
you're a good scout. I am sorry I wrestled you around

and made all that trouble. I'd like to be your friend. Me, Joe, you know how it is with me—never went to school much, ride broncs, sleep in any old barn, tepee maybe; bulldogger, Marines in World War Two and Korea both, toes shot off. You don't learn much about classical music, crawling through snowdrifts in Korea." He tapped his heart. "But here I am not such a bad fellow. I talk loud but I would give you the shirt off my back."

Loren believed him. Besides, he felt a secret guilt that, as an electrical engineer, he had been deemed too essential to be picked up by Selective Service; and Joe's talk about Korea, and his exaggerated limp on his wounded foot, gave the whole thing a patriotic cast.

"Sure, Joe. No hard feelings. I think it'd be fun going out to McGee's."

"Good boy!" said Joe, slapping his shoulder. "Strong boy!"

"Of course, she has to work tomorrow at the bank—"

"Short day, close at noon, sleep all afternoon. You go up there—don't tell about me, you take all the credit, make yourself good sport."

"I'll call her up," said Loren, and he did.

With almost silent power the Buick raced up the mountain road, its headlamps finding the distant curves, making a bright surface-shine on rocks and pines, giving depth to the shadows beyond. The country seemed very big at night; the gulches became canyons, and the low mountains, yellow-green-brown by daylight, became a

towering fastness deep in mystery. But to Joe the
mountains were only obstructions standing between him
and McGee's barn, and he kept the speedometer at sixty.

"Slow down," Mary said from the back seat.

"Okay," Joe said and eased off to fifty-nine.

The speed was about fifteen miles an hour too fast
for the road, but Joe was a masterful driver, never touching the ruts when there were ruts, utilizing the last degree
of bank that had been engineered into the curves, apply-
ing power at just the right split second. Behind him,
Bronc Hoverty kept close in the station wagon.

"I should have brought my car," Loren said, on the
quiet, to Mary. "He might want to stay a week."

"I'll make him get us home," Mary said firmly.

They reached McGee's an hour before midnight, when
the dance was in full swing. The men each paid a dollar
at the door and had their hands stamped with indelible
ink. They climbed to the loft floor, where the dance was
proceeding to the music of a five-piece orchestra—young
punks from Havre, with a bass drum bearing the name
"Rumba-leers." The crowd was about equally divided
between ranchers and reservation folk, but everyone
mingled freely; a couple of pretty halfbreed girls were
the most sought-after partners there.

Big Joe immediately grabbed one of them, a tall,
vivacious girl named Clarice Beaudry, and danced with
her straight through the next two numbers, keeping her
for himself even when she made wild but undetermined
efforts to escape—giggling so that everyone would notice, for it is a fine thing to be young and popular. Her

escort for the evening, a thick-necked young cowboy named Chug Hockering, finally became incensed to the point of grabbing Joe by the shoulder and pulling him away.

"Go on, you're bothering us," said Joe, trying to elbow him back into the crowd, and Chug grappled with him.

They struggled, tearing each other's shirts, and ended against the wall, where Chug had a headlock and Joe kept him rammed with a shoulder. They were in that position when the management broke it up, telling them to settle it in the yard—a thing which both principals promised to do, with talk of terrible mayhem; but there was no move for the stairs until one of the spectators said, "Shake hands," which they did.

"That drunken brother of mine!" Mary said. "Everywhere he goes—"

Loren said, "I thought the other fellow started it."

"Oh, that girl Clarice, she ought to know better too. She and Chug are engaged to be married, and Joe, big shot, he has to dance with her three times in a row."

While Bronc Hoverty was dancing with Mary, and Loren was having a smoke, a young cowboy came up and said somebody wanted to see Loren downstairs. Loren hesitated for a moment, thinking it might be Pete Shortgun, out for revenge after that fracas at Louis'.

But it was Big Joe. He pulled a quart of blended whisky from a manger and said, "Hey, boy, come on, drink 'em up, big stuff. We're friends all the time now, eh?" He watched Loren take a small nip and was not at all satisfied. "That's a boy's drink. Come on, you've tasted my whisky, how about a big one?"

Although Loren took a drink now and then, it was generally in a highball of the sort known in that locality as a "ditchwater," and he misjudged the power of an equal amount of raw whisky. The big drink immediately unsteadied him and kept him from reasoning clearly. Joe kept hold of him, introducing him to this fellow and that, each of whom seemed to have a bottle to stick in his hands. He wanted to escape, at least say no to the bottles that were coming toward him, but he could not.

"Don't leave me, Loren," Joe said every few minutes, keeping a tight hold on his arm. "I need you to keep me out of trouble. Watch and see that damned Chug Hockering doesn't hit me from behind."

So many things happened that Loren lost track. His new acquaintances became a jumbled mass in his memory, together with the awareness that he was drunk. At suppertime someone gave him scalding coffee to sober him up, but Joe, unseen, had already spiked the coffee with more whisky. "Let's have another cup of coffee, Loren," said Joe. "Nothing like coffee to get a man on his feet."

Then Joe said, on the quiet, to Bronc Hoverty, "You go ahead and dance with Mary. Show my sister a good time." And to Mary, "I guess that boy friend of yours shouldn't be drinking with the men. I have had to put him to bed."

"Where is he?" she demanded, furious with Joe.

"In my car. I've been thinking I should drive him back to town. After all, I feel sort of responsible for the

poor kid. You go ahead and have a good time, ride to
town with Bronc."

"You deliberately got him drunk."

"Me? Since when have I worried about getting whisky
for anybody except myself? That boy is over twenty-one;
he should know when to stop drinking."

Mary was angry with Loren too. She shared a prev-
alent contempt for men who could not handle their liquor, and she was on the point of saying go ahead, take
him to town—but she reconsidered, knowing that Joe
did not ordinarily have that much charity.

"I'll go along."

But when she had got her wraps and gone downstairs
Loren, Joe, and the Buick were nowhere to be found.

"Take me to town," she said, finding Bronc.

"Let's dance a couple of times first."

She decided she was being selfish, spoiling Bronc's
good time on account of Loren's failure, and she danced
with him. Bronc had a bottle in the station wagon, and
she had a drink with him too. Back upstairs, she forgot
about Loren while dancing with Bronc and half a dozen
other men. Then it was three a.m., and the orchestra
closed down for the night. The two Cristy girls had
been left stranded by their escorts, so, at Mary's sugges-
tion, Bronc drove them to their ranch, which was only
five miles away. On the way back across the Cristy
hayfields, with the stars beginning to dim and a gray of
dawn in the east, Bronc turned off the road and stopped
in the heavy shadow of some cottonwoods.

"Mary!" he said, putting his arm around her.

"Oh," she said, "let's go home."

She did not fight him off, though her body was stiffly unwilling against him. She let him kiss her. It wasn't anything; she didn't dislike Bronc. Then he said, "Mary!" again, and his tone, rather than his hand on the inside of her thigh, frightened her.

She twisted, wiry and strong, opened the door, and got away outside. He did not follow. He sat, leaning over in the seat, staring at her, his face in shadow, his eyes looking white—and at that moment he strongly showed his Indian blood. She did not generally think of Bronc as being anything but white, and now he frightened her, for she knew how often rape occurred among her people.

"What's the matter with you?" she cried.

After a few seconds he answered, "I'm sorry. I didn't mean anything. I've always been crazy about you."

She knew that was true; she had known when she started out with him. She wasn't angry with him, just a little bit scared. "I'm going back to Cristys'," she said, not really intending to.

"No. Don't do that. Come on, I'll behave myself."

"Well," she said, and got back in. She waited for him to start the car, but he just sat and looked at her.

"Why'd you kiss me?" he asked.

"I didn't."

"You did. You—"

"You kissed me. I just sat here. For the love of Mike—"

"Why'd you let me if you don't like me? Don't you know I'm crazy about you? I always been crazy about you."

"I'm sorry, Bronc."

"You hate me."

"Of course I don't. Just behave yourself, I think you're a swell guy."

"Do you?" He was almost pleading now. "Do you really, Mary?"

"Sure."

"Let me come and see you sometimes, will you, Mary? Will you let me take you to the show sometime?"

"All right." She wanted more than anything to get going. She was still apprehensive, and it seemed that giving him hope was her best assurance that he wouldn't start tearing her clothes off. "But don't grab a girl like that. Use some sense. Now let's get started back. I have to work tomorrow."

# Chapter IX

He had to drive slowly to keep from high-centering in the ruts, and dawn was making things bright when they reached the county road. Bronc made no more passes at her. Sometimes he made his hip bump against hers, but that wasn't so bad; and he looked so good-natured, so young and hell-and-be-damned, with his shock of brown hair pushing his sombrero back, that Mary felt ashamed of herself for being frightened of him. He still did not drive fast, only a pleasant forty an hour, through the pine fragrance of the mountains to the arid sage fragrance of the bench country. Then the sun came, bringing out in shining white rectangles the buildings of Big Springs twenty miles away and below, a faultless miniature.

Bronc said, "Tonight how would you like to go to Havre with me, see a show?"

She put him off. She put him off again and again through the next couple of weeks. Joe began calling for her, using a pretext to get her somewhere; and each time,

who would show up but Bronc Hoverty. Once Joe even
told her that Mama was ill and asking for her, but when
she got to the ranch Mama was the same as always, and
Bronc Hoverty was standing with Louis looking at the
horses in the corral.

Mama was furious when she found out about it. She
shouted at Joe, "When your sister has a nice fellow in
town, good job, good friends, you want her to step out
with that no-account bronc rider? I am warning you
now, stop meddling with Mary, getting her in bad with
her friends."

Joe was incensed and said, shaking his finger under
her nose, "You mean that pipsqueak Loren Hankins?
One-two drinks, and who had to carry him out and put
him to bed? Me, that is who." Simulating weakness,
Joe leaned forward, hollow-chested, with his arms dangling, eyeballs rolled back in his skull. "One-two drinks,
this is how he looked. How do you think I feel, having
all my friends laugh at me because my sister goes out
with that skinny nobody? Do you think I would let her
get stuck with him for a husband?"

"Go away and leave her alone."

"Eh?"

"Yes, go away and leave all of us alone. Get in your
big car and go back to Madison Square Garden."

"You are running me out of my own home?"

"Get out! Get out!" Mama shouted.

When Joe did not move, Mama grabbed the broom.
She put it back and, turning, looked for a better
weapon. Her eyes fell on the stove poker, a rod of heavy-

gauge steel, three feet long and bent like a golf club at the end. All in one movement, she seized it and swung overhand at Joe. Reflex took Joe back with his hands up. The poker was deflected by the low ceiling, and, bounding down almost out of Mama's grasp, it struck Joe on the muscles where his neck and shoulder met.

He tried to get through the door, but the blow staggered him; he rammed the casing and rebounded from it, and Mama, this time swinging horizontally, hit him full in the middle of the back. Joe took a long step—too long. He put his weight on a loose board, his boot bent under him, and he fell headlong. He rolled over in the dust with a bellow of pain. He got to his feet, eyes rolling, and stared back at Mama.

"Mama, stop! You have gone crazy?" cried Louis, running up from the corral.

"Ow!" groaned Joe. "She has broken my back."

Mama, in the door, waving the poker at him, cried, "Stay away from this house. I tell you I will knock out your brains if just once more you put your foot in my house."

Joe staggered to a distance, holding his back. He held his back with one hand and his neck with the other. Then he took his hand away from his neck to make a fist and shake it at Mama. "You old squaw, I will fix you sometime. Sometime I will forget I am a gentleman, and then there will be one old squaw with a jaw broken in two places."

"What happened?" Louis asked.

"What happened? She sneaked up behind me with

a stove poker and tried to kill me is what happened. No wonder your daughter acts like she does. I try to find her a boy friend she does not have to be ashamed of—"

"Joe!" His father silenced him. "I think it would be better if you went to Callahan's for a bottle of beer."

When Joe had gone, Louis tried to reason with Mama; but, with the poker still in her hand, waving it at the dust of Joe's car, she said, "Keep him away. Next time he comes in my house I will brain him, that good-for-nothing."

That night Joe slept in the shed, and the following morning, disheveled, with bits of hay clinging to his hair, he came to the porch, where he stood, favoring his wounded foot, sniffing breakfast, until Mama advanced to the door.

"What do you say we call it quits?" Joe said.

"Stay away." Mama had the poker. "Stay away, Joe, or I will chop you up like stew with this stove poker."

Joe sat outside, watching Grandpere eat his breakfast. At last he got up and left, driving slowly across the yard, across the creek, past the Hudson, to the road, where he stopped and sat looking at the house for a long minute before driving on to town and borrowing six bits breakfast money from Mary.

At the Sunshine Cafe he told Tommy, the Japanese cook and proprietor, all about them—how they were using his land, the six hundred and forty acres that was his allotment from the government, to graze their stock, and doing it free, without one cent of rent and not even a thank you; no, not a cup of coffee in the morning or a plate of cold stew. And to sleep in the barn, that was good enough for him. And that wasn't all; anybody who wanted to look could see the bruise on his neck where she had sneaked up behind him and tried to kill him with the stove poker; and he should have her arrested, because Uncle Sam would have something to say about using a veteran like that. "I tell you," said Joe, his mouth full of ham and hot cakes, "it is getting to be a hell of a country, and no gratitude anywhere."

His stomach full, a toothpick cocked in his mouth, Joe returned to the bank to borrow more money from Mary. There were others ahead of him at the teller's window, so he got in line and was waiting when Hy Slager called him into his office.

"How much money you borrowed off that girl since you got home?" Slager asked.

"Oh, I don't keep track, pay it right back."

"Like hell you do," Slager said, looking him cold in the eye. "You never paid back a cent in your life. If you need money, why don't you borrow it on that new car?"

"All right," said Joe, his back up. "Lend me one hundred dollars."

Slager laughed around the panatela cigar he kept scissored in his teeth, and said he knew better than to lend anything to a ward of the government, because his agreement was not valid in a court of law. "Look at the money you borrowed on that section of land five or six years ago. Who was it gave you that mortgage—the Milk River Land Company? Good God, you taught them a lesson. I'll bet they never collected a nickel off you."

"My credit's good all over."

"Not here it isn't." Slager got his riding boot down from the drawer and sat forward in his swivel chair—a long tall man, seventy years old, but with a backbone still as straight as a Winchester barrel. "Now don't forget this, because I'm telling you only the once—I don't want you hanging around. That goes for your pal, that bronc-fighter Hoverty, too. You tell him to keep away from Mary, or, by the God, I'll open him up so the wind will blow through."

Joe said, "How about lending me just twenty-five dollars on the car?"

Slager opened the zipper on his wallet and gave Joe a five.

"You want me to sign something?" Joe asked.

"Hell no," said Slager, waving him out of the door.

As Joe walked past the post office, Bob Lewis, the RFD mail carrier, hailed him and gave him a letter from The Great Falls Time Credit Corporation, which Joe put in his hip pocket without opening.

"Save me stopping at your dad's place," Bob said. "Hey, don't you even open your mail?"

"All say the same thing," Joe said. He walked all over town, looking for excitement, but Big Springs lay dead quiet under the late summer sun. He got into the Buick and drove to Callahan's. There he saw three cars in the yard—Bronc's station wagon, Stephenpierre's Model A, and the Chevrolet which Boob Dugan had just bought at a used-car lot in Havre. The jukebox was on. Joe drove

down and looked inside. Boob Dugan was dancing with
Connie Shortgun, Stephenpierre with Lizzie Bird Looking, and Bronc with Mamie Callahan. Callahan, dressed
up in slacks, white shirt, and an apron, was tending bar.

"All right, goddam you," Callahan said to Joe
when he saw him at the door, "how about that thirty-five
dollars—or do I have to swear out a warrant?"

"You mean that check?"

"Yes, that check!"

Joe came in, laughing. "You know, I've been trying to figure out about that check, why it came back
marked 'no funds.' Now I know—that night when I
asked for a blank check for the Milk River bank, you
made a mistake and gave me one on Big Springs."

"I don't know anything about that. I just know you
wrote me a bum check."

"Now wait," said Joe, his elbows on the bar. "Did
I or did I not ask you for a blank on the Milk River
bank? Right here I stood and said Milk—River—bank."

As he tried to remember back, it now seemed to Callahan that Joe had. "I don't think you got a dime there
either."

"Call them up. Call Havre. There is the phone; go ask."

"I'm not spending four bits more—"

"Bet you five dollars." Joe slammed down the money
Slager had given him. "There, that will give you your
four bits back—and four-fifty besides, clear profit, *if*
they say I don't have money in the bank."

Callahan knew better than to believe him, but everybody had been laughing about the Cadillac Joe had left

in Great Falls too, and next thing he'd showed up in a four-thousand-dollar Buick, and then they didn't laugh any more.

"To hell with you," said Callahan.

"Come on, everybody, have a beer. Tear the check up. I'll write you another one. Goddam, you got me in a fine mess, giving me the wrong check blank. Mama, Slager, Mary—everybody raising hell."

He wet an indelible pencil on his tongue and laboriously wrote a check on the Milk River National Bank for seventy dollars.

"Oh, no!" said Callahan, seeing the amount.

"Why, of course. Pay up my bill and get a few bucks to spare. Don't you think I want to treat my friends? What the hell, Callahan, since when did you start turning away cash business?"

Callahan looked at the check against the light—as though that would prove anything—and decided to ring it up. With the till open, he figured up all of Joe's old charge slips and handed him twelve-forty in change. Joe did not question the amount. If that suited Callahan, that suited him. He bought everybody a drink, including Callahan. He danced with Connie Shortgun, Lizzie Bird Looking, and Mamie, stopping after each number to treat or be treated by somebody else.

"Where's Glenda?" he asked.

Callahan told him she had been in Great Falls, visiting her sister, and was coming in on the six-o'clock bus. In fact, he would have to close the place in another ten minutes and drive to Big Springs after her.

The announcement was greeted with dismay. "No wonder," said Joe, "you are always going broke in the saloon business. The best crowd you had all week, and you close up."

With money coming in at a good clip, Callahan was loath to go, but he knew he couldn't leave the place in Mamie's charge, or they would drink everything and not pay a cent.

"There's no sense in you losing this business," Joe said. "I'll tell you—just because we are so friendly again, I will go after her in the Buick."

Callahan reluctantly consented. It was hours before Joe returned with Glenda, and she was flushed and very high. Callahan was angry, but she got her arm around him and coaxed him to drink with her. They sat in the booth, having ditchwater highballs, and Glenda, patting his cheek, said, "Daddee! It's just like a second honeymoon!"

Callahan had had several drinks already, and the ditchwaters on top of them put him in a mood to dance. He danced with Glenda, doing the new steps, and then with Connie Shortgun. Exercise gave him steam. There he was, dancing around in his white apron, forgetting all about the saloon business, until he happened to look over and see Big Joe behind the bar, passing out liquor right and left, saying, "Come on, everybody, have a drink on your good friend Callahan's second honeymoon."

"Get away from behind my bar!" shouted Callahan.

"Go on and dance, have a good time," said Joe. "I don't mind to bartend for a while."

Callahan got hold of Joe's arm and tried to drag him from behind the bar; but Joe pushed him away with a force that sent him staggering halfway to the door. Callahan got himself stopped; he crouched with his hands out and came in a bulldog rush. They struggled, without advantage, in the small area behind the bar, ending wedged among cases of empty Coke bottles between the back bar and the refrigerator. There Callahan swung short rights and lefts, but Joe, who had the advantage of height, held him at arm's length. Everyone was around, shouting advice to Callahan, who slugged himself purple and winded without being able to reach farther than Joe's shoulder.

At last Callahan stopped and said, panting, "All right, let me go."

"You be good scout? You promise to have a drink on the house?"

"All right."

Joe released him. He staggered away. He held to the bar. He pretended that he would have fallen had it not been for the bar. He moved along, hand over hand, knowing, without looking, where the shotgun stood. When he got close enough he turned and reached, getting it with the first grab—an old Damascus double with three-quarter barrels.

Callahan started up with the gun as Joe went, long-legged, for cover, but Bronc Hoverty had been watching from the other side of the bar; he reached over, grabbed the gun with both hands, and jerked it away from Callahan.

Callahan, at a run, pursued Bronc around the room, while Bronc, toreador fashion, holding the gun like a cape, avoided him. When Callahan showed signs of slowing down, Bronc called him a shanty Butte Irishman and made him come on again.

Finally Callahan could go no farther. He sat down. "You son of a bitch." He wheezed. "You dirty Injun son of a bitch."

"What's the matter?" said Bronc, feigning amazement. "Did you want the gun? Well, why didn't you say so? Tell you what I'll do. I'll divide up with you." So saying, he pulled the forepiece off and disjointed the barrel from the stock. "Here. Which half do you want?"

Callahan grabbed the barrel and was on his feet again, trying to get Bronc cornered to brain him; but, as before, Bronc was too nimble for him. Callahan got so tired he fell down on the floor. Puffing, blowing, calling them everything he could lay his tongue to, he crawled, got inside a booth, and sat with his head on the table.

Finally able to lift his head, Callahan said he needed a drink. Stephenpierre tried to give him a can of beer, and Callahan flung it back at him. "Not this Injun stuff. Give me the whisky."

He sat, trying to recuperate on whisky—although whisky was his chief trouble. "Glenda," he said. "Take care of the joint. I got to go to bed."

Glenda was nowhere around. He locked the till, looked briefly for Joe, could not see him, and, steadying himself on bar, chairs, and wall, went through the living quarters to his bedroom—only to find the door bolted. He beat the door with his fist, demanding to be let in, but nobody responded. At last he went on down the hall, outside, and stood in the cool night, thinking of how they had wronged him.

Yes, Joe was in bed with her. He had been three or four hours driving her from town too. Every time Callahan went to the mine Joe sneaked around to be with Glenda. He would kill Joe if he had a gun. His mind foggily sought other means of revenge. He saw the Buick darkly gleaming in the moonlight, and went to it. He walked all around it. Then, working with the slow, determined purpose of the very drunk, he let all the air out of the tires.

Joe did not notice how his car hugged the ground when he half fell into the front seat and started for home. It had no pickup, and steering it took all his strength. "Wahoo!" shouted Joe, leaning from the front window, fanning the car with his hat. He kept it wide open in second gear. The flattened tires roared and hammered on the gravel road and tore themselves to shreds, but nothing could stop Joe, armed with the mighty Buick. It almost stalled in the creek beside the derelict Hudson, but the water had sunk to a trickle, and momentum carried it up the far side and across the yard, until it stopped with a crash of twigs in some buckbrush near the house. Joe then noticed the smell of burned rubber and got out to see what the trouble was.

"Joe?" called Louis from the window. "Is that you, Joe? What's the trouble? I could hear you coming for a mile."

"Had a puncture." Then Joe, with the yard steepness

accelerating his momentum, walked with long steps to the shed, where he flopped in the hay, face down, and went to sleep.

About noon Louis came down and said, "Joe, you had better come out and look at your tires. By gare, I think you have ruined the rims too."

Joe went to the pump. On his knees, with his head under the spout, he worked the handle and pumped water over his head. Then, dripping water like a surfaced beaver, he regarded the state of his car. "Goddam," he said. "Four punctures."

"No, somebody took the valve cores out."

One of the valve stems was still intact, and, sure enough, the core was missing.

"That damned Callahan!" Joe said, remembering the big time they had had the night before. "He can't even take a little joke. I wish I had him in the Marine Corps; they would show him how to take a joke."

He walked all around the car, looking at the tires, which were cut to shreds, with rags of cord and rubber sticking out for six inches from the wheels. The sight and the brightness of the sun hurt his eyes. He sat down, cross-legged, on the ground, with his hands over his eyes and his thumbs pressing his temples, and said, "If there is one thing I can't stand it's a man with no sense of humor."

# Chapter X

Joe tried to borrow money from Louis for new tires, but Mama got wind of it, and the answer was a thundering no. The car sat where it was, and Joe rode on Two-Step to Callahan's, where he heard from Glenda that the Havre check had bounced and that Callahan, fortunately now at the mine, had sworn murder.

"Ha!" said Joe, trumpeting through his nose in derision of Callahan's revenge; but he left, nevertheless, and rode on to Big Springs, where he stood around, watching the bank for Mary. It was hardly worth the wait, however, for all she would lend him was fifty cents. He bought a supply of Bull Durham with the money and rode back to the ranch.

Poor and friendless, Joe sat all day in his car, smoking the Bull Durham and playing the radio until the battery went dead. Finally he took the spare tire to Big Springs and sold it, together with the tube, for eighteen dollars. With the eighteen dollars to spend, he dared appear once more at Callahan's, expressing amazement that the check had bounced, and almost convincing Callahan that he should send it through again. Then, because the spare wheel was no good without a tire, Joe sold the wheel for seven dollars. He put the car on blocks and sold the other wheels, one by one, explaining to Louis that one of these days, when it pleased him, he would dig into his savings and replace all of them, because he would want the Buick to be in first-class shape when he started out on the Eastern rodeo circuit. And so the last days of August passed, and Mary came home one evening with a diamond twinkling on her left hand, an excited flush showing through the brown of her cheeks, and announced that she was engaged to marry Loren—the date probably sometime before Christmas, depending on what luck they had in finding a place to live.

Mama, in gladness, wept for Mary. Louis was quiet and thoughtful, hoping that Loren was not such a weakling as Joe claimed; while Joe, for his part, stalked down to the corral and cursed the horses.

"Nobody can say I didn't try my best for that sister of mine," Joe said to old Two-Step, hurling a piece of dried manure at him. "Well, all right, if that is what she wants, then I wash my hands of the whole thing."

Joe was hungry and broke, but he did not go near the house and humble himself for food—nor did he ask for a dollar from Mary. Thank God he still had the Buick, so he took off one of the spotlights and rode to Big Springs, where he traded it for canned corn, sardines, catsup, pre-

pared pancake mix, coffee, and a box of Baby Ruth bars.
In a syrup bucket he made coffee; in a greasy skillet from
Grandpere's tepee he cooked corn and hot cakes; and,
crosslegged on the ground, with his back toward the house,
he ate his meals, not beholden to anybody. He was there
one morning, drinking coffee and smoking Bull Durham,
when Pete came down, hopping from excitement, with
word that Mama had decided on a trip to Havre for the
purpose of buying new furniture for the house.

"They should spend their money on a bull," Joe said.
"Why do they think I drove all the way to the Little Rockies, getting money lent on those cows—to buy
soft chairs? What does that old squaw need with a soft
chair? She has plenty of pillow on her own behind."

He walked to the house, where Louis and Grandpere
were sitting on the step, enjoying the sun after the gray
chill of the September night. Louis was carving a little
pine-bark beaver, trying to get the mottled wood to come
out right so that the beaver's back would be slightly
darker than his stomach.

"I wish your car was running, Joe," Louis said, holding
the beaver up and tilting it this way and that. "You
could drive us to Havre."

"What the hell, I thought your old squaw would be satisfied with her house now that she had put me sleeping
with the horses."

"Well," said Louis, feeling sorry for Joe since things
were going badly for him, "you see, this house is not so
good as the one his people are used to."

"Whose people?"

"Loren's. His mother, pretty soon our mother-in-law. She is coming to visit with Mary."

"Coming *here?*"

"Well, of course she will ask about Mary's mama and papa—and what would she think if Mary say don't come out?"

"Ha!" said Joe in derision.

Grandpere, hearing the sentiments of Big Joe, came to life beneath the Monkey Ward blanket and shook the scalp on its stick. "When I was young man—this was long time ago, you savvy? When I married squaw, did mother-in-law come? No. Pretty soon, one day she send boy to me with new moccasins. Antelope moccasin, plenty beads, you savvy? She have the boy ask can she come to my tepee, pay visit. I say, 'No. You make me also good tobacco pouch, *then* maybe you come to my tepee when I'm not home.' But this was in the old days."

"That's just the point," said Louis. "We are not living in the old days. These times a man has to keep up with the Joneses."

In John White Calf's old Chevrolet, Louis and Mama drove to Havre and came back after dark with clothes for themselves, the two boys, and even Grandpere. In boxes filling the trunk and back seat were curtains, drapes, curtain rods, venetian blinds to fit the front windows, a pink and yellow lace tablecloth, candles and holders, and even an ornate triple-switch electric floor lamp, although the house had no electric power. And that was by no means all, for next day a pickup truck drove out from the Bargain Furniture Mart with a pink frieze overstuffed set, a blond table, six chairs with leatherette seats, and a nine-by-twelve salmon-colored rug.

The davenport was very heavy for Louis and the undersized youth whose job it had been to bring the furniture from Havre; and Louis, blowing while balancing one end of it on his knee, said, so that Joe could overhear, "By gare, I could use one strong man unloading these thing."

But Joe stood munching a Baby Ruth bar, making no move whatever except with his jaw, and said, "I'd help all right, but that old squaw said I could not come in her house."

Joe, standing beside Grandpere, eating his next Baby Ruth bar, said, "I hear that old squaw is going to make you wear shoes and a suit of clothes. Have you tried them on yet?"

Grandpere made the sign "No."

Joe said, "You see what is happening? No longer are you a Cree; you must now be a Swede or something, like that pipsqueak Loren Hankins. In these clothes, your moccasins, blanket, you have been good enough to feed your family, kill off grizzly bears so everybody's safe; but now that you have done all this, your clothes are no longer good enough for them. You are hundred years old. At that age a man should deserve some respect—but no; what do you hear? 'Take off your moccasins; wear these shoes from J. C. Penney; throw away your blanket and put on this white shirt; do all this so old woman from Helena will not know you are Indian.' "

"Ha-ya!" said Grandpere, taking a view of the situation in that light. He beat his diamond willow stick hard on the ground. "When I was young, then were old men great chiefs, make big talk. Grandpere, *my* grandpere, he was hundred years old like me. When he sat by fire everybody waited for him to talk. When he talk everyone listened, for he was wise with years. But when me, *this* Grandpere, talk—ya-ya, they turn on their Philco devil box, drown him out."

"Rug for the floor! The slivers were good enough for my bare foot wounded in Korea, and now, after risking my life for them, I can't even go inside the house."

"*Kinapikwa-iskwao!*" said Grandpere in Cree, shaking his stick at the woman, who, with voice raised, was now giving orders to Louis in the house behind them. "Snake woman! *Muche* snake woman."

"Oh, yes, I am only a Champlain with mother a full-blood Assiniboin. For me nothing. But for her, *her* daughter, things are different. And look what I have done for them. Who was it furnished the pasture for their cows? And this money they are spending for rugs and fancy lamps, where did it come from? I will tell you where it came from; it is the money borrowed for them by me, Joe. Why didn't Mary borrow some money? There she was with a bank full of money, but did she borrow one red cent? Believe me, Grandpere, if I had that job in there with all that money I would say to my friends and relatives, 'Come along, help yourself to a little bit.' "

"Chief, chief!" said Grandpere, beating his stick, showing the esteem he had for his great-grandson.

Louis came outside and said, "Joe, we can hear you in the house. Now don't start any trouble."

Joe went back to his fire by the creek and sat there, hunkered over his blackened coffee can, watching as the stuff was unloaded and put inside. Later the old furniture began to appear through the back door, and the odor of fresh paint drifted to him.

That evening Louis came down, smiling, and said, "Joe, my boy, I wonder if, as a favor to Papa, you would talk to Gran'pere about trying on his new clothes. If they did not fit we promised to take them back tomorrow."

"Did you ask him to try them on?"

"Yes, but you know how Gran'pere is—very proud to be an Indian, always wear moccasin, blanket. But if *you* said something about wearing Army suit of clothes when you got that scalp—well, I think he would say, 'All right.' "

Joe got up and yawned. He walked around, limping on his bad foot. "Fall weather, very hard on wounded foot, sleeping in barn. Well, that's the way it goes; not everybody can sleep in a nice warm house. By golly, I wish I'd stayed at home, learned to be an electrical engineer, instead of going out and getting shot to make this country safe from Communists." Then he yawned very big—"Ho-ho-hum!"—and said, "Well, I have to cook my supper now. Takes a long time to cook supper over an open fire but maybe when I'm through I'll say something to Grand' pere about trying on his new suit."

Later, much later, Joe said to Grandpere, "You had better try on those white man's clothes that squaw bough for you, or she will drive you out of the house just like she did me, your great-grandson, who brought you back the scalp from Korea."

Grandpere shook the scalp in angry defiance, "No, no. Chief don't wear 'em. Chief don't sit at table when big dinner come either. Chief sit on floor. Old squaw goddam. Old squaw go to hell. Both old squaws go to hell."

That night Joe loaded the storage battery into the wagon and drove to Callahan's, where he sold the battery for five dollars and spent the money for beer. He needed more money the next day, so while Louis and Mama painted the interior of the house Joe removed the generator from his car and took it to Big Springs and sold it to the Chevrolet-Buick agent for eleven-fifty. As the days went on he sold other things—one of the side-vision mirrors when he needed only a dollar or two, or the massive rear bumper when he wanted to make a trip to Wolf Point with Bronc Hoverty.

It was raining, a slow, cold autumn drizzle, when he came home from Wolf Point. He had only one blanket, and it was very cold sleeping in the drafty old shed, so he moved to the car and slept curled up in the rear seat. That afternoon, when Bronc came back, Joe had removed the front seat from its moorings, and they hauled it to Havre, where, after they had driven all over town, a body shop operator took it off their hands for eighteen dollars. Now, with a few alterations in the rear seat, Joe was able to sleep stretched out in the car, and it made a fine home, snug and rainproof when the windows were rolled up; and, after setting up a little Sterno stove with a bit of pipe through the ventilator hole, he was able to heat coffee and a can of beans when dampness prevented him from cooking outside.

The pickup truck arrived with more furniture, for Mama had decided to fix up the bedroom too. Joe, in an old rocking chair he had moved into the Buick where the front seat had been, sat and watched as Louis and the delivery boy wrestled the heavy vanity to the porch.

When Louis straightened to rest his back Joe said, "Is that mother-in-law of Mary's going to move in and stay, that you need a new bed for her?"

Louis did not answer right then, but later, after the things were in the house, he came over to say, "Well, you know how women are. Mama doesn't want to have Mary ashamed of the old folks, ashamed of the house she was raised in, you savvy?"

Joe rocked back and forth, his head almost touching the ceiling of the car, looking at the house with stolid indifference.

Louis went on, "The other day, all painted, with that new stuff in the house, those old iron bed looked pretty bad."

"I'll bet you spent all your money?"

"By gare, this stuff cost like hell. I'm buying some of it on the easy-payment plan."

"Well, why don't you just use it once and then let them take it back?"

"No, Mama say we should fix up old house for long tam."

"How about the electric floor lamp? How are you going to connect that up?"

"Well, Mama thinks maybe we could say the fuse burned out, but I think we don't say nothing, only maybe pretty soon we will get this R.E.A. line, have lamp all ready."

The boy came around with a delivery slip for Louis to sign, and drove off toward Havre in the pickup.

Louis said, "Of course if it was me I would say to that Helena squaw, 'This is how we are, we are honest people, we do not steal or kill, we don't have much, but you are welcome to what we have.' This I, Louis Champlain, would say. But women—well, sometam you will be married and see how it is, Joe."

Joe rolled a cigarette and rocked and lighted it. Louis went on, laughing a little. "You know now what she is worried about? That old can down in the coulee. The privy. She says what if Mrs. Hankins has to go to the toilet while she is here?"

"Ha!" said Joe through his moose nose. "If she has to go bad enough she will find out the outside privy works okay."

"Yes, but in cities like Helena everybody has one in the house."

"Ha, that Mama, putting on big show, where did she come from? A Gros Ventre tepee, living on dog meat and turnips, that is where. Her people didn't even have *outside* privy where she was raised. The first damn coulee they come to is what they had."

"Joe, you should not talk that way about Mama."

"Okay, I'll keep my mouth shut. When is this shindig, so I can stay out of sight, not disgrace Mary?"

"Maybe two weeks. Joe, you be good fellow, get along with Mama, tell her you're sorry you raised hell, maybe you come to dinner too."

"Ha! I don't need that house. I got good enough house right here."

"But I think Mary would like it if you were at dinner."

"Let them come around and ask me; then maybe I will think it over."

No one asked him. He traded the car's tail lamps and ashtrays for small beer money. He sold the radio to a bookkeeper from the Agency for twenty-two-fifty. He sold the gearshift and steering column, and then turned his attention to the engine, selling the fuel pump and carburetor, the spark plugs, cylinder head, and oil pan. Then, when the Big Springs garage expressed interest in a transmission, he made a really big dicker, trading the transmission, together with the cylinders and connecting rods, for a Harley Davidson motorcycle in first-class condition.

Once more Joe had a means of rapid transportation. He took off the motorcycle's muffler and enjoyed the full roar of the exhaust. All the way from Callahan's one could hear him racing at eighty miles an hour on the motorcycle. On a Saturday night he insisted that Glenda go with him for a short ride, but once he had her away from the eyes of Callahan he kept going all the way to Fort Belknap, seventy miles distant. They attended the dance there at the school auditorium, then still did not come home but went on to Chinook and Havre, drinking beer and playing the jukeboxes in joints along the way.

Cautiously, the motorcycle quiet as he could make it, with Glenda looking slatternly and haggard on the seat behind him, Joe turned in from the county road and paused for a look at Callahan's. The buildings stood quiet in the September sunlight; a dishtowel fluttered slightly on a line near the kitchen door. There was no other movement; the truck was not in sight.

"Didn't I tell you he'd be at the mine?" Joe said. "Not a thing to worry about."

"Sure, you're all right, you son of a bitch," Glenda said. "You can dump me here and pull out, but *I* have to face him. What'll I tell him?"

"Ha, tell him it was your money that put him in business in this dump after he lost his license. Remind him that it's only good business to go for a ride with your best customer."

"That'll go over but good!"

Joe swung the motorcycle around in the yard and at that instant saw movement though the front door. He had only a glimpse, but it was enough to tell him that Callahan was there and that he had the shotgun.

Joe planted his boots suddenly, half lifting the motorcycle and spilling Glenda to the ground. He gunned the engine and came around, wrestling the machine by its widespread handlebars as he would a steer. The rear wheel, turning full blast, volleyed dust and gravel. Joe was in the seat, bounding across the yard, trying desperately for more speed, when Callahan ran from the door, tossed the gun to his shoulder, and cut loose. Birdshot hit Joe in the back, going through his scarlet silk shirt, stinging like drops of fire. A second charge made a roaring sound as it hit his boot and slapped the earth beneath his feet.

Callahan kept reloading and firing at hopeless range as Joe tore across the bridge and up to the county road. There he paused to feel down his back and look at the blood that had oozed out to make streaks on his hand.

"You Irish bastard," Joe called, shaking his fist at Callahan. "You should be glad somebody is willing to show your wife a good time."

"I'll kill you!" Callahan was screaming. "Next time I'll have a rifle waiting for you."

"Ha, good! You just stick around. I'll be back tonight and have a rifle for you too."

Joe rode to Big Springs, where he had the druggist stick Band-aids over his wounds and told everyone that he would go back that very night and settle with Callahan.

But Joe did not go near Callahan's that night. Next day he sent Jiggs Rock Medicine down to learn whether Callahan was still angry, and Jiggs came back saying that he was and had even exchanged the shotgun for a rifle, which he kept handy behind the bar.

"I am very bad off for whisky," Joe said, although he seldom drank anything but beer. "Tonight at seven o'clock sharp I will be right here waiting, and I wish you would bring me one pint."

That evening, when Jiggs delivered the whisky, Joe was not alone. Men stepped out, one on each side, ordering

Jiggs not to move. He was frightened and wanted to run, but he had no chance, and they took the bottle from him.

"Whisky," one of the men said. "Seal isn't broken. Good old Southern Comfort. Where'd you get it?"

"From Callahan."

"He sell it to you?"

"Yes."

"Pay the money into his hand?"

"Into his cash register."

"Anybody see you?"

"Sure, Pete Buffalo, Jake Spotted Wolf."

The other man said, "Well, that's that. Let's go get him."

They kept the bottle for evidence and, with the warrant all prepared, went down and arrested Callahan for selling liquor to an Indian.

Joe watched this from the darkness outside the door. Then he went inside and looked around as if in great surprise. "Callahan! What's going on here, Callahan? Who are these men? Why are these men taking you away? If they are kidnaping you I'll call the sheriff, Callahan."

Callahan was getting the money from the till. "You ungrateful son of a bitch!" he railed. "It was you that turned me in."

"*Me?* Your old friend Joe? You call on me if you want somebody to testify for your good character."

One of the officers said, "Go ahead and pack your bag if you want to."

"I don't need a bag," Callahan said. "I'll go the way I

am. I know my rights. You got to furnish me clothes in
that place. I might as well get all the good out of the
goddam government that I can."

"That's right," said Joe. "You might as well cash in on
your taxes."

Callahan reconsidered and took a few things from his
room. As he walked to the car between the two federal
men, Joe stood at the door, waving in farewell. "Good-by,
Callahan. I'll take care of things while you're gone, Callahan." But Callahan was too low even to curse him.

After the car had pulled away, Glenda sat disconso-
lately in a booth and said, "Well, that's that. I wonder
how long they'll gow him for this time."

"Aren't they going to padlock the joint?" Joe asked.

"How in hell can they? We haven't even got a license to
operate—no federal license, no state license, nothing.
Technically this is just a private home."

"Well, good, then we can use the front and back doors
both." Joe was already behind the bar, opening beer.

"Say, if you have some half-cocked idea that you're going to drink this place dry just because Pat's out of the
way—"

"Now hold on, what are you going to do, let the federal
men dump all this good stuff in the crick? I suppose that's
your idea of being smart. No, let's save it, drink it up."

Glenda walked wearily to the till, opened it, had one
look, and shut the drawer again. "Sure, didn't leave
a dime!" She turned and patted Joe on the cheek. "You
big lug. I ought to hate your guts, but it does get lonesome when you don't come around."

"Well, lonesome days all over now. You heard me promise Callahan I'd take care of you while he was gone."

"I suppose I'll have to go in and bail him out. How?—that's the question. Think I could mortgage the joint, or would I need his signature?"

"Oh, plenty of time to bail Callahan out. Do it next week. First, what do you say we have just a few friends in for a housewarming?"

Sitting on one of the chrome bar stools, dragging on a long cigarette, Glenda thought it over and said, "Well, I don't suppose there's any point in mooning about the poor bastard. Anyhow, I'll know where to find him when I want him."

Using the telephone, they invited some people, and all night Joe presided as the host of the bar, giving liquor away. Next morning Glenda drove off for Havre in the truck, to see about arranging bail for Callahan. She expected to be right back, but at six she telephoned Mamie to say that things had been held back; some long-nosed judge had set bail at five thousand dollars, her lawyer was trying to get it reduced and needed her around, so maybe she would just spend the night there. Then she asked to speak to Joe.

"Run those bastards out, do you hear?" she shouted at him over the telephone. "I want something left in case I bring Callahan home."

Joe said, "Don't you worry your head about a thing. I'll have them all out, place swept, everything shipshape."

By night, however, the party was going better than ever. The jukebox played full blast, and Joe danced every dance with Mamie Callahan. Keeping Joe near the back of the room, where they could talk above the noise, Mamie lolled in his arms, looked into his eyes with a stunned look, and said, "Joe, let's not wait around for her to get here."

"Eh?" He got his ear down close to her lips so he could hear. "What was that?"

"Let's pull out, you and me. Let's you and me go someplace together."

"You mean in to Big Springs?"

"No, someplace a long way off."

"Run off together? You like me, eh?"

"Ya."

"Well, goddam! Why didn't you tell me your little secret before, kid?"

"I never had a chance. She watched me like a hawk. She said she'd jerk me baldheaded if I made a play for you."

"Well, she's a long way away tonight." Joe held Mamie very close. He got hold of her dress and rubbed it around and around, feeling it slide over her body, making her struggle and giggle. "You're a cute kid."

"Aw, you're just saying that."

"No, I've seen plenty girls—L.A., Dallas, Tokyo, Madison Square Garden, all over hell. You're a cute trick all right. I'll bet you could get on T.V. I'm sure glad Glenda left, so we could get acquainted."

"You mean we can leave together?"

"Maybe."

"Back East? Can I go with you when you make the rodeo circuit?"

"Okay, who can tell?"

"Tonight?"

"Well, not tonight. Can't run out on our friends. What say we get acquainted real good here?"

"Glenda will get back."

"Tomorrow, sure; but what she don't know won't hurt her. We'll keep it secret."

He danced her out of the room, through the kitchen, down the hall, and into the bedroom. He tried to close the door, but she fought with him, saying, "No, she'll get home."

"She's in Havre."

Mamie got away and ran from him, but she let him catch her before she got back to the saloon. She stood against the wall, her feet braced, head down and hair swinging in a long, loose mop, as she wrestled with Joe. She let him kiss her and explore with his hands, but she would not be lured back to the bedroom.

"*When* will you take me to New York?" she asked.

"I told you, pretty soon. I have to get my car fixed up first."

"Joe, you never did take me for a ride in your car."

"Come along, I'll take you for a ride tonight. We'll go on the motorcycle."

"No."

"Sure, come on."

With her head down and her hair swinging, she said, "No, no. Joe, quit it."

"Come on, Mamie."

"No."

"Why?"

"You'll have to marry me."

"Eh?" It brought Joe up, looking at her.

"Don't you ever think of getting married?"

"Oh, sure."

"We'll get married and then start on the rodeo circuit."

"Well, that takes some planning, kid."

"I can just see Glenda's face when she hears we're married! She thinks she's so damned smart."

"Ha!"

"Oh, Joe, I'm so happy."

"Okay, let's go in the bedroom and talk it over."

He could not lure her back to the bedroom, but she was in his arms on the davenport in the tiny living room when Glenda unexpectedly arrived from Havre.

"What the hell goes on here?" Glenda said, turning on the lights. "Or don't you need any light for what you're doing?"

"Just sitting around," Joe said, not in the least taken aback. "Doggone, we were getting lonesome for you, Glenda."

"I'll bet you were!" She looked Mamie up and down. "Listen, you punk, if you think you're going to get in there and pitch while I'm gone—"

"I didn't do anything. He practically drug me in here to sit with him."

Glenda laughed derisively.

Joe said, "Now, girls, don't you fight about me."

Glenda turned on him. "I'll kill you, you two-time me, you son of a bitch."

Mamie, whimpering, **said, "You** two-timed Dad."

"Shut up. I'm getting him out of jail, ain't I?"

"Ya, but—"

"Don't yabut me. If you got a yen, why, take it around to somebody else. Go out and shake it at Bronc Hoverty." She watched Mamie leave the room, stiff-legged and huffy, pulling up her stocking as she went. Then she started in on Joe, but with a laugh he lifted her off her feet and tickled her. She cursed him, but she liked it.

"That's jailbait," Joe said, tilting his head in the direction Mamie had gone. "I don't chase after jailbait. Anyhow, you got her all wrong. She doesn't care anything about me; she just wanted me to get her a knockdown to Humphrey Hindshot. You're the girl for me. Let's keep Callahan in jail a long time, what do you say? Let's run everybody out and have the place to ourselves."

"You big lug! I wouldn't trust you any farther than I could shoot an air rifle." She kissed him, running her hands through his black, pomaded hair. "But don't you try to two-time me for that mousy-haired quiff out there, because if you do I'll come gunning for you. Nobody dumps little Glenda. You hear that? Nobody!"

A couple of days later Glenda went in to have another try at the bail, but those bastards at court had dug up something from ten years before, when Callahan was having his troubles at Coeur d'Alene—a mix-up about the time of a trial, which had made him a technical bail-jumper—and so the bail was kept at five thousand dollars, and nobody could be talked into signing up. When she got back to the joint, Mamie was gone. Immediately suspicious, Glenda drove to Louis' and sat, with the engine running, until Little Joe rode up from the corrals.

"Big brother here?" she asked.

"Nope, haven't seem him since last night. Jeez, you ought to see the new stuff we got. Mary's bringing Loren's old lady up with her so she can look us over."

"Well, buy the old battle-ax a drink on me," Glenda said, slipping him four bits. "And if Joe's in there hiding I'll give you a buck to tell me where he is."

But Little Joe, clutching the fifty cents, stared at her with his quick, black eyes, without answering, so she wheeled around and drove to Big Springs. She cruised the town, looking in the back doors of all the dives, without hearing Joe, and turned again and drove back to the Agency. From the Agency she took the north road and, coming to the Littlehorse place and seeing Billie Jo on the porch, she drove in and learned that Joe was probably attending the big wingding that Stephenpierre was throwing. However, it was almost night then, and Glenda did not know the road, so she kept going on to Havre, had supper there, and, getting back home about midnight, found Mamie in a blue rayon dress and opera heels, rouged and painted like a cut-rate dummy, sitting at the kitchen table eating Vienna sausages and bakery cake.

"Where you been?" Glenda asked.

"Right here."

"You have like hell. I came along at—"

"Well, I went in to Big Springs."

"Who with?"

"I caught a ride with a fellow from the Agency."

"Both ways?"

"Yes!"

"Who was he?"

"I didn't ask."

"Don't lie to me. You were out to Stephenpierre's with Joe."

With voices raised, they called each other names, Mamie insisting over and over that she had not seen Joe, that she had been in at the Paris Beauty Shoppe getting a permanent. She did have a tight new permanent, but Glenda thought it probably came from a Toni kit.

"How's Dad?" Mamie asked, finishing off the cake.

"Happy as a hog in a brewery. Nothing to do but sit around on his big flat all day and play cooncan with a Mexican."

"Can't you find bail?"

"Not with that Coeur d'Alene blackball tied on him. If I thought you were laying up with Joe—"

"I'm not," Mamie wailed. "Why you always picking on me?" And she walked out, having a hard time with the high heels, and locked herself in her room.

"All right, you little bitch," Glenda said under her breath. "Only don't you try to double-cross *me*."

# Chapter XI

Louis was very tired. He sat on the step, the half-roughed-out figure of a bear in his hand, trying to remember what had been in his mind when he began it yesterday. He never had time to finish anything any more. Every time he got started Mama would call for help to mend the glass in the cupboard door or tack down some linoleum or paint the woodbox white and stick decals on it. And now, just as he started to carve the bear's hindquarters, she called, "Louis! Louis, come quick! The stovepipe is falling!"

He ran in and found her moving the heating stove. He grabbed the pipe and said, "Where are you moving the stove?"

"Oh, this old-fashioned stove, nobody in town uses a stove like this, everybody has Heatrolas these days. I'm moving it outside."

It took Louis half an hour to move the stove to the shed. When he came back to the house he found Mama, with soot

on her hands, looking with dismay at the blackened stovepipe hole.

"Now look, Louis, we'll have to get a picture to hang
over the hole."

"Let's hang the calendar over it."

"That bathing beauty?"

"Well, we have one of hunting dogs."

"No, it will have to be a picture."

"Goddam!"

Tired and distracted from days of labor trying to fix
up the decrepit old house, Mama stormed at him. "Don't
you want to make a good impression? Don't you care if
Mary has to say, 'These bums are my people'? What
would that woman say if she saw a stovepipe hole and soot
running out of it?"

"All right, I will get the picture."

"And not horses, Louis. Please not a picture of horses."

"Okay."

"When will you go for it?"

"Tomorrow."

"No, today."

"All right, I'll saddle up and ride in today."

Almost every day Mama wanted him to go to town for
something, and he had learned to put off going so that
maybe he could do two jobs at once, for it was an all-day
journey to Big Springs and back on horseback. Later,
when Mama was not around, Louis slipped inside and
placed an old syrup pail in the stovepipe hole, making it
less conspicuous, and Mama forgot about it in favor of her
chief concern, the outside privy.

Sitting heavily in the new club chair, Mama said, "Oh, it makes me sick, that old privy. What will she think of us?"

"Oh, that privy is not important."

"It is important! If you had your way you would have done nothing. When you heard she was coming what did you want to do? Put your silly wooden bears around on all the shelves! Do you think I wanted her to see how you have been wasting your time?"

"Now, Mama——"

"It makes me sick, that old privy." She held her head in her hands, and her shoulders shook, though no tears came from her eyes. "Not even a sidewalk to that privy —crooked old path, climb up and down the bank."

"Maybe she won't even have to go."

"She will be here all day."

"Oh, come at eleven o'clock, eat at one, go back at four or five. We will have Mary ask her to go to the toilet before she leaves town."

"You fool, how could she ask her to go to the toilet?"

"Well, Mary could say it is a long, rough trip. She could——"

"You don't ask people to go to the toilet. When you just met somebody you do not talk about those things."

Louis, in exasperation, cried, "Well, maybe you would like to have me haul a pot out on the back of old Two-Step."

"Oh, joke, joke, big joke!"

"I only——"

"We still have time to buy a toilet in town."

"Mama, did you ever see how they work? They have to be connected up. They have a pipe at both ends and a handle in the middle—"

"You fool, don't you think I know how they work?"

"You are tired." He patted her on the shoulder. "Come on now, take nap."

"Old privy! And what will she walk past when she goes to the privy? That tepee of Grandpere's! When is he going to move that tepee?" Again gathering force, she sat upright and demanded, "Yes, when is he going to move it? Have you even mentioned it to him?"

"Well, I was thinking, the boys like to play in tent, we could just say it is theirs. Anyhow, behind the thorn-apple bushes, no one can hardly see it."

"She will see the tepee. She will think we *live* in the tepee."

"All right, I will ask Gran'pere can I take it down."

But Louis could not bring himself to mention the tepee to Grandpere. That night Mama inquired, and Louis said he would settle the matter with Grandpere tomorrow. But by then he had something else to think about—the bookkeeper from the furniture mart drove out with word that he would have to have cash for the things they had bought. The bookkeeper explained that they did not themselves handle credits but sold their paper, and that Louis' had been rejected because of an automobile contract that their son, Joseph Champlain, had ignored in Great Falls.

"You mean you'll take the furniture away from us?" Louis asked.

"Unless we can have the cash, I'm afraid that's it. Of course we'll make adjustment for what you've paid."

Louis asked for time and was given the remainder of the week. So they had no choice except to sell two more cows to pay up.

"That Joe, I could kill him, I could kill him." Mama wept. "Everything would have been all right if Joe had not come home; and that Buick he is selling off one piece at a time, and not even paid for. No wonder he was willing to trade the transmission for that old motorcycle. I wish the sheriff would come and get that Joe."

Next day Mary drove out from Big Springs to tell them that a sister of Mrs. Hankins had fallen ill, forcing her to postpone her visit indefinitely; and Mama fell into the chair and moaned at the collapse of her plans, the while experiencing a surge of relief. But two days later Mary came out again to say that the sister was up and around and that Mrs. Hankins would be there on a Sunday, only eight days away.

After her two days of rest, Mama launched herself with new vigor. When Louis would not tell Grandpere that the tent had to be moved, she attacked it herself, using a pickax to pry away the base framework of boards and straw, dragging the tent—canvas, posts, and all—to a place beyond the corrals where three wide-branching box elder trees hid it from the house.

As she dragged the tent Grandpere followed, waving his stick at her, calling her "snake woman" in Cree.

"Keep still to me!" cried Mama, sweating and panting from the effort of moving the tent. "Why haven't you tried on your new blue suit we bought for you? Do you know we paid twenty-nine-ninety-eight for that suit at J. C. Penney's? You think we have got twenty-nine-ninety-eight to throw in the fire? Go to the house and try on your new clothes right now."

It ended with Grandpere in the blue suit, white shirt, and dress shoes, standing bent over, not making a move, held by the straitjacket of the unfamiliar clothes.

Louis pleaded, "Go ahead and walk around, Gran'pere. Look at it this way: it was in such clothes that Joe got you the scalp in Korea."

"The shoes hurt my feet. Ow! My feet!"

Louis said, "Mama, don't you think it would be all right if he just wore the moccasins?"

"No, he will have to look like a gentleman for one time in his life."

"No walk," wailed Grandpere.

She stormed at him. "All right, then you do not need to walk. All you need to do is sit in your chair and say nothing. Do you hear me? All the time she is in the house you are to say nothing!"

Louis, coaxing Grandpere by the arm, said, "Go ahead and sit down in the chair."

Grandpere did, settling into it very cautiously, sitting bent over, still clutching his stick with the scalp attached to it. His face against the contrast of white shirt and bright rayon suit appeared more pulpy and boneless than ever, the long stiff hairs sticking out here and there making him look as much like an ancient woman as a man.

"He can't keep the scalp in the house," said Mama. "Here, give me the scalp."

"No, no!" said Grandpere, swinging the stick at her.

Louis pleaded, "Mama, she is not coming right today. I will get him another stick by the time she comes."

"No one will help me," said Mama. "No one but me cares if the dinner is a success or not."

"Now, Mama—"

"What have you done about that old privy? What?"

"All right, what do you want me to do?"

"Go to town and get a toilet. We can set it up in the shed off the back porch."

"But I told you they have to be connected up. How could we get water here from the creek?"

"You can fill its tank one time with a bucket. Who cares, just so long as we can flush it the once?"

There was no reasoning with Mama. The vision of Mrs. Hankins, in her fine clothes, going out back to the fulsome privy had haunted her daylight hours and caused her to awake in the blackness of night. The new toilet, in her mind, had become the have or have-not of Mary's social success. Mama could just picture Mary visiting the gilded homes of Helena in later years and having people whisper behind their fans, "That is the halfbreed girl I was telling you about, the one whose people have the outside privy."

"I will have to sell another cow," said Louis.

"Sell her—where have they gone already? To buy cars and beer for that Joe."

So Louis, using the Winter Owls' car and stock trailer, took a heifer to the Commission Yards in Havre and returned at suppertime with the toilet and a quantity of sewer tile. For the next two days he worked at installing it, and for good measure he tacked odds and ends of linoleum onto the floor of the shed and enameled the walls blue and white. When he was finished he called Mama and stood awaiting her praise, but she said, "Louis, we should have a bathtub."

He cursed in French and English, ready to weep from fatigue. "Goddam that old woman, why doesn't she stay away from our place if it is not good enough for her?"

"I didn't say anything," Annie muttered. "I didn't say, 'Go get a bathtub.' I only said it was too bad."

On Thursday she began to prepare dinner by cooking cranberries and baking chocolate-bit cookies. On Friday, Louis went to Big Springs and returned with a frozen turkey, sweet potatoes, lettuce, tomatoes, celery, cream cheese, ripe olives, eggs, cake flour, Jello, creamery butter, chocolates, and a special brand of coffee Mama had heard plugged on the radio as "the guest coffee of discriminating hostesses." She cooked and baked and worried herself sick about the turkey's thawing out in time, and then about its spoiling, for she had no icebox. On Saturday night it began to rain—not much, just a slow drizzle. "We would have a bad day!" said Mama. But by dawn the rain had stopped, and by nine o'clock the sun was promising to come out.

An hour later the boys, who had parked themselves up on the road, sighted Loren's car and rode at a gallop to the house, bearing the news.

Somehow Mama had hoped to have more time. "Get off that horse in your new clothes," she wailed. "Where is Grandpere? Does he have his new clothes on? Louis, find Grandpere. Where is he? Where did he go to? Put him in the chair, don't let him walk around. See that he doesn't have that old scalp. Did anybody flush the toilet? Somebody see to it there is a bucket of water in the toilet."

Louis calmed her with an arm around her shoulders. "Mama, be quiet. Take one big, deep breath. You see, everything is going to be okay."

He found Grandpere, who looked like a condemned man in his new clothes, and steered him inside to the chair. Then he went outside in time to meet the car as it rolled toward him across the yard.

"Hello, Louis," said Loren, getting out and holding the door for his mother and Mary. "Mother, this is Mary's father."

Mrs. Hankins was slightly embarrassed when her dress caught on the door handle. She was a graying, medium-tall woman with an erect manner and rimless glasses that made her seem severe. Louis met her with a grave courtesy carried not one bit too far.

"We have been looking forward to this day for long tam," he said. "By gare, the Champlains don't have guests from city every day. It is big occasion, so we fix the place up a little bit, you don't mind?"

Mama, listening unseen by the door, was ready to weep

from frustration. Why, oh, why did he have to say all
those things? Why didn't he let Mrs. Hankins believe
their house was fixed up like this all the time? "Sit down,
sit down!" she whispered, motioning to Grandpere, who
was starting to get up from the kitchen chair. Then she
heard their steps coming and forced herself into sight.

"How do you do?" she said to Mrs. Hankins. "How do
you do, how do you do, how do you do?" she repeated with
intense embarrassment, not knowing what else to say, each
time nodding her head and smiling, almost in tears.

Mary came around to give Mama the reassurance of
her arm. Then everyone was in the house before Mama realized that Mrs. Hankins was in the wrong chair and no
one had taken her coat. Laughing, pleading, apologizing,
all at the same time, Mama said, "Please, that old chair,
you don't want to sit in that old wooden chair. Why don't
you sit here, Mrs. Hankins?"
every time Mrs. Hankins had sat in the new club chair.

Mama had dreamed the scene a hundred times, and
every time Mrs. Hankins had sat down in the new club
chair.

Loren, after looking with momentary surprise at the
unfamiliar house, said, "Oh, don't worry about Mother.
She's a Spartan. She'd have been right at home in a
Shaker community."

"Eh?"

"You know—straight chairs, no springs, no cushions.
Now me, I'd be happy in a ton of feathers." He dropped
into the club chair and tried the springs a few times. "Say,
this is all right."

Mrs. Hankins said, "Loren, give that chair to Mrs. Champlain. I'll bet she's been working all morning, getting dinner for us, and could use some rest."

"Okay," Loren said, hopping out.

"No, no," Mama said. "I thought *you* would like the chair."

"I really do like a straight chair."

"Yes. Well, all right. Let me take your things, Mrs. Hankins."

Mrs. Hankins started to remove her tweed coat and stopped. "I got a little chilly when we drove out. I think I'll leave it on for just a moment."

"This damn rain," said Louis. "I'll build a fire." He looked for the heating stove and remembered that it had been moved to the shed. He laughed and spread his hands. "Goddam, those ol' woman made me move the heating stove out, so I guess it's no fire after all."

Mama was ready to sink from the shame of hearing Louis use profanity and tell that the heater had been moved, thus admitting the extent of the preparations they had made. She tried to laugh and smooth things over and get Louis out of the way, all at the same time.

"Oh, Mama," said Mary, "none of us is going to be very shocked if Papa lets out a damn now and then."

Louis said, "Sure, that's me, always say the wrong thing. I am French, you know. All my people métis, Indian French, from long way back, long tam, French-Canadien, vive la Canadá! You know how it is with French; you can teach Polack, Dutchman, even goddam Irishman almost, speak English in five-six year, but Frenchman—

oho! Frenchman, he never learn notheeng. Look at this
Charles Boyer—movie actor, you know—been in this
country maybe twenty year, can't speak English yet. So,
your poor host, I talk, run out of English, throw in a goddam or two until I think of the right word to say."

Mrs. Hankins herself had dreaded the visit, but here,
to her surprise, was a man whose charm was completely
disarming. Mama, however, could have hidden under the
floor from shame for Louis. She plucked Mary's sleeve
and shushed her into the kitchen, wringing her hands
and pleading with Mary to do something to keep Louis
quiet. "Why, oh, why does he make a fool of himself?"

"He's not. Papa is all right."

She whispered furiously, "He is making a fool of himself!"

Mary laughed, crossed the kitchen with a hard click-
click of her heels, and opened the oven door to peep inside. "Um, turkey. It sure smells good."

Mama was back in the front room, trying to win Mrs.
Hankins' attention away from Louis. But it was no use;
Mrs. Hankins kept looking at Louis, nodding her head,
and laughing. Oh, the fool, the fool, thought Mama; why
doesn't he keep his mouth shut?

Loren got up, looked around in the kitchen, and went
back to ask Louis, "What did you do with all your carving?"

"Ho, that ol' woman made me take them out. You know,
women don't want that stuff sitting all over. Perhaps it's
all right for bunkhouse, but in home—well, they like pictures by big shot like Maxfield Parrish."

"I think he stinks." Loren said to Mary, "Ya, your dad's got Parrish beat. I think your dad's wasting his time. I think he could have an exhibition in New York. When we get married I'm going to have your dad carve us a plaque for the fireplace."

"What fireplace? The rate we're going we'll be lucky to have a hot plate."

"We'll have one."

Louis said, "All my animals are out in shed, in big box. You like to have me bring them in?"

Mama tried to signal him—"No, no!" But he did not look at her, and Loren said, "Sure, let's bring 'em in."

"Oh, dear!" whispered Mama.

Mary said, "Let him bring 'em in."

In a few seconds Louis came struggling in with a huge Wheaties box half filled with a mad clutter of wooden figures and groups of figures. He put the box down in the middle of the room, breathing mightily, and said, "By gare, there's plenty jackknife work in here."

Loren said, "Look, Mother, I want you to see these things."

So Mama stood and watched as the floor and the table became strewn with wooden bears, cougars, buffalo, and horses. "Wouldn't you like some tea and a cooky?" she broke in to ask Mrs. Hankins.

Loren started to say that his mother never drank tea, but she waved him to silence and said, "Why, yes, I would like a cup of tea."

"Where's Gramps?" Mary asked, eating a cooky with chokecherry jelly on it.

Mama experienced a jolt as she looked at the empty kitchen chair where she had left Grandpere. He had not been there since Mrs. Hankins arrived. He had sneaked out while she was on the front porch, and there—oh, my God! There were his shoes.

"He's all right," said Mary. "Forget about him and quit carrying on. Everything is going just fine."

"What if he comes back wearing those old moccasins?"

"Well, what if he does? Where's Joe?"

"I don't know. He's gone most of the time. I don't keep track of that Joe."

"Oh, I thought maybe he was here. I saw his motorcycle parked on the other side of the car."

Mama had many times vowed she would not stand for Joe's being around that day to disgrace them by cooking on his Sterno stove in that car and walking around in his undershirt, scratching. And now it occurred to her that she had not checked to make certain he was gone. Maybe he had come home at four or five o'clock as usual and was in the car, oversleeping.

"The motorcycle is there?" she said.

"Uh-huh."

After giving Mrs. Hankins her tea, Mama got Pete to one side and whispered for him to sneak a look in the car and see if Joe was there. At the window she watched and knew by Pete's expression that her fears were justified; indeed Joe was there. Then Little Joe popped out and stood beside Pete, staring into the car too.

"He's there?" Mama asked, getting Pete back inside.

"Ya!" Pete was fairly trembling with the news he bore

to Mama. "And he ain't there alone, Ma! He's got a *girl* in there with him."

Mama exhaled in pain.

Little Joe shot through the back door, whispering, "Guess what, Ma! Joe's there, and he's in bed with a girl."

"Shush, I know!" she whispered.

"Ya, they're sleeping together," said Pete.

"It's Mamie Callahan."

"Ya, she's sleeping with Joe."

Mama felt like dying. She sat down. She clenched her fists and whispered, "Oh, that Joe, that Joe!"

"They ain't sleeping now," said Joe. "They're awake. I was talking to 'em. I told 'em we had company."

"Did you tell him to hide? Did you tell him to keep out of sight?"

"He asked was it all right for them to come out. He said he didn't want you blowing your top on account of Mary and Mrs. Hankins."

"Oh, thank God he's got that much brains." Mama for once was glad that Louis was talking full steam in the other room. The sun was trying to come out, shining brightly on the Buick's moisture-beaded surface, and through the car's rear window she could see the side of Big Joe's face as he bobbed up to peep at the house. She whispered to Pete, "Go out and tell him to keep out of sight."

The boys shot outside to do her bidding. She could see them talking to Joe through the partly open window, and she could see Joe as he kept stealing looks. "Oh, why doesn't he keep down?" she whispered to herself. "I could kill him, I could kill him."

Mary came in and asked, "What's the trouble?"

"That Joe, he has some whore out there sleeping with him in the car in broad daylight. I could kill him."

"No!" whispered Mary, aghast.

"Yes, he has that little slut of Callahan's."

Mary was furious with Joe too. "What are we going to do?"

"I don't know. We can't let her see them. And that Joe, sticking his head up all the time. She might see him through the door. Quick, Mary, make her sit in the other chair."

"How can I? She likes *that* chair."

"But she can see—"

"I'll close the front door."

Mary went in to do it, but Mama could hear Mrs. Hankins say, "No, I'm not a bit cold now," and then Louis, with his exasperating cheerfulness—"Ol' sun coming out pretty good now. Leave the door open, good fresh mountain air make us feel fine, give us good appetite for dinner."

"The fool, the fool," whispered Mama, weeping and shaking her fists in frustration. "Why doesn't he learn to keep his foolish mouth shut?"

The boys were still talking to Joe. That was another thing—why didn't they quit? Why didn't they get away from the car? Mrs. Hankins would see them and wonder who they were talking to. But they kept talking and *kept*

talking, and every few seconds there would be that Joe
popping his head up. When Mama could stand it no
longer she tapped on the window with one hand and motioned with the other. The boys heard her and turned, but
they couldn't seem to understand what she wanted. Then
there was Joe with his head up. She waved with one hand
for Joe to keep down and with the other for the boys to
come back inside. "Keep down! Come in!" Mama was saying with her lips.

"Oh, hello," said Loren behind her.

He had come in from the other room and surprised her.
She kept on making movements with both hands and said,
"That old fly! Darn those old flies. Trying to kill flies,
trying to kill flies." She would have paid ten dollars spot
cash for even a gnat.

"Oh, what's a fly or two?" asked Loren. He got a drink
from the bucket. "Say, that turkey sure smells good."

"You're hungry!" said Mama. Yes, she thought, I can
serve the dinner now and forget about the apple pie I was
going to bake, and while they're eating Joe and his chippy
will have a chance to make their getaway. "Yes, you're
hungry. I'm going to serve dinner now."

"Oh, no hurry. I'll have one of those cookies like Mary
was eating."

"No, don't spoil your appetite. I'm going to serve dinner right now."

"Mama," said Mary from the door, "maybe Mrs. Hankins would like to see the horses."

Oh, thought Mama, that's no good, because she'd have
to walk right past the old privy. At all costs, Mama didn't

want Mrs. Hankins to see the privy. "No, we will have
dinner now."

The turkey was done—thank God for that. All she had
to do was warm up the sweet potatoes and the rolls.
"Mash the potatoes," she said to Mary.

Loren said, "Don't hurry on my account. I'm not too
hungry—"

"Oh, maybe not, but your mother is starved."

"No, she—"

"She is hungry, of course she is. I am going to serve
dinner now."

Mrs. Hankins came in, carrying one of Louis' groups
showing two cubs up a tree with their mother coaxing them from below. "Isn't this cute?" she asked. "Oh,
may I help?"

"No, no!" said Mama hustling her away from the window so that she wouldn't see Joe. "You come sit down.
Please sit down. Please try the big chair. I would like to
have you try the big chair."

Mrs. Hankins couldn't help feeling pushed around, but
she sat in the chair. Louis, oblivious to everything, was
expounding on bears, mountain lions, horses, and buffalo.

"Now you tak mountain lion, he's big cat and mean
one. He's lay in wait for poor little deer, never make one
sound—just his tail go back and forth. He's real smooth
and ver' strong, this cat. His head I make small like ol'
rattlesnake, with big eyes to see in dark. But bear—oho!
he's not mean. He's don't go creep around. He's don't care
who hear him coming—just bust through woods, eat
honey, have good tam, get fat, and sleep all winter." He

lifted the figure of a slap-happy bear standing erect, scratching his back on a dead tree. "Look, ol' bear, he's like drunk man, fall down without his lamp-post. Mountain lion, he's ol' Hitler, small head, ver' clever. But bear, he's lak this Wallace Beery used to be in movies—big, loud, good for nothing, but you like him just same."

"Yes," said Mrs. Hankins, scarcely listening. It made her uncomfortable to be forced to sit in the club chair. Mary came in and spread the tablecloth, and Mrs. Hankins glanced at her lapel watch; it was not yet twelve o'clock.

Mary said, "Mama is certain you're just famished."

"Oh, no—"

"Well, I think what really happened was the turkey got done too soon."

Mrs. Hankins laughed in sympathy then, thinking she understood Mama's agitation. Half an hour later dinner was on the table, and there had been no sign of life in the Buick, so Mama was almost able to think calmly again.

"Where's Grandpere?" Mary asked. "Isn't he going to eat with us?"

"Oh, let him go."

"I set a place for him."

"I think he would be happier—"

"Well—" Mary was doubtful. "You see, Loren's been telling his mother how he's a hundred and five years old, and she's been looking forward—"

"Oh, all right." Mama whispered to Pete. "Go tell Grandpere that dinner is ready." She remembered the shoes that the old man had left behind and handed them to him. "And tell him to wear these. Tell him not to come at all if he doesn't wear these."

"He says he can't walk in 'em."

"I don't care what he says; he has to wear the shoes."

With everyone now ready to sit down to table, Mama had to stall, waiting for Grandpere. When Pete returned, she met him at the back door and asked, "Did he put on the shoes?"

"He says he won't wear 'em. He says you can go to hell. He—"

"Hush, they will hear you."

"Well, that's what he said."

Mama stepped outside and looked downhill at the grove of box elders that hid Grandpere's tepee, and she saw no sign of him. "Well," she said, taking a big breath, "let him pout and stay away. It is just as well."

They sat down then, and Louis carved the turkey. Mama first worried that it was too done and dried out, and then, seeing the dark juice run from around the thighbone, she worried that it was not done enough. "Oh, my," said Mama after her first taste, "isn't the turkey terrible?"

"Why, it's delicious," said Mrs. Hankins, and it was.

"Sure is," said Loren.

"Oh, I just knew it; the dressing has too much sage in it."

"The dressing is perfect," said Mary.

Mama kept worrying about this thing and that, and

next it was the potatoes, in which she detected lumps. "Those awful potatoes. I just feel sick about these potatoes. I should have put them on longer."

"Light as whipped cream," said Loren.

Mama's piece of turkey really was dry and stringy, for it came from near the end of the breastbone. "Oh, this turkey!" she whispered to herself. "I just feel sick about this turkey."

Louis said, "Ol' woman, keep quiet about the turkey. You know very well that everything is first rate, but how can anybody eat if they have to compliment you all the time?"

Again Mama got to thinking about Big Joe. She wanted to make sure Joe and his girl seized the opportunity to make their getaway. She could not very well leave the table and go herself, and neither could she send Pete or Little Joe. She got up, using the coffee as an excuse, and went to the kitchen, pausing at the door to look out at the Buick. There was no movement. Oh dear, thought Mama, what will I do? They are still there. She wondered if she could sneak out without being seen and have a word with them. But no, Mrs. Hankins might see her go around the house; someone might come into the kitchen and find her gone. Now she wished Joe would put his head up, but of course he didn't.

She brought the coffee to the table, and barely had she sat down when she saw a startled, staring expression on Mrs. Hankins' face. Mama thought first, of course, of Joe; but it was Grandpere. He had come through the kitchen and was now standing in the door, looking down on

the table—and, oh, my God! he had gone and put his old
clothes on.

Grandpere stood hunched over his diamond willow stick
—the one with the scalp on it. He wore his sombrero, the
beaded buckskin shirt that old Minnie Hindshot had
given him at last year's sun dance, his old canvas pants,
and his blackened moccasins.

"Grandpere!" said Mama, getting to her feet, intending to lead him outside; but he struck back and forth at
her with the diamond willow stick.

"Keep away, old squaw," he said in a croaking voice.
"No wear 'em shoes. No wear J. C. Penney suit. Injun
clothes good enough, you savvy?"

"It's Gran'pere," Louis explained in his gentle way to
Mrs. Hankins. "My gran'pere. On mother's side, my
gran'pere. He's full-blood Cree Indian, hundred and five
years old, we think."

Mary said, "Don't hit her with that stick, Grandpere.
What's the matter with you?"

Grandpere had been brooding, thinking how they had
moved his tent, pulling it up by the roots without asking,
and now they wanted him to wear the white man's suit
and the shoes that hurt, and now he was in a fine state of
rebellion. He raised his voice to Mama and Mary both.
"Old squaw, young squaw, go to hell!" Using the stick to
support himself, he vaulted around on it in a sort of hopping dance, chanting in a quaver, "Very old. Me, Chief
Two Smokes, hundred and five years old. Long time been
around. Long time see things go to hell. When I was
young, shoot buffalo. With musket, Sharps rifle, shoot

buffalo. All buffalo long time gone. See steamboat come, railroad firewagon come, skunkwagon, devilbox come. All over now barbwire fence, grass plowed under, country go to hell. Republicans Democrats ruin country. Pretty soon big bomb blow 'em all up. Boom, boom—"

"Gran'pere, stop it," said Louis, pulling him by the arm. "We are trying to have nice polite dinner. How do you come to act like this? Now, look, we have set a place for you, please sit down."

Mama cried, "No, I will not have him at the table in those filthy clothes."

Grandpere turned on her again, jabbing with the stick. "Injun clothes plenty good kill grizzly bear, make country safe for old squaw. Clothes plenty good for—"

"Gran'pere!" cried Louis, and this time his tone commanded attention. "You had better leave."

This Grandpere would have done if Mama had not chimed in, saying, "Go on, get out of my house. Go back to your tepee and stop ruining Mary's life."

"No!" said Grandpere. "Old squaw go to hell!" He advanced with the stick out, the scalp dangling over the dinner table. "Old squaw see that?" He shook the mummified scalp, with its wisp of coarse black hair, at Mrs. Hankins, who recoiled from it. "You know what this is? Scalp! Scalp of Chinese Communist brought back from Korea, by my Joe, my great-grandson, that mighty bulldogger. What do you think of that?"

"Well, by golly," said Loren, willing to humor the old man and admire the scalp. But Louis shouted, "Take it

away! Go outside, Gran'pere." And, with Louis standing,
glaring at him, Grandpere did.

"Oh, dear, dear, dear!" whispered Mama, sinking in
her chair from shame after the old man had gone. She was
so beaten out that she did not even look through the door
when the sound of a motor came to her ears. It was Joe,
she thought, leaving on the motorcycle. "Oh, dear, what
you must think of us!"

Loren said, "He's an old man, you got to humor him.
He couldn't hold a candle to my Great-Uncle Bedloe,
could he, Mother? You remember the time we were enter-
taining the new school superintendent, when Great-Uncle
Bedloe came downstairs—"

"Never mind," said his mother.

"And after all, what's so bad about a scalp? We all walk
around on skin from a dead cow."

The motor had stopped now, and Louis had half risen
from his chair and was looking out the window. His popeyed silence gave Mama an awful premonition that a ca-
lamity even worse than Grandpere was about to befall
them. That fool Joe; it would be like him to bring his
young chippy into the house.

"Excuse me for a moment," said Louis.

A woman had crossed the porch, and, stepping nimbly,
Louis got to the door in time to block her way. The woman
was Glenda Callahan.

"We are having company for dinner," Louis said.
"You're looking for Joe, he's not here."

"Well, little man, you had that answer all ready."

Glenda moved around, trying to get a good look inside. She was not in very good shape. She had missed some sleep; she was bleary from liquor; her hair was in strings; her green silk dress was twisted around her; she wore no brassiere under it, and one breast seemed about ready to pop out. She held a purse against her abdomen; the purse was open, and her right hand was inside it.

"Ver' well," said Louis. "You have now seen for yourself. Joe is not here."

"Well, listen, Mr. Weisenheimer, how'd you get so smart all of a sudden, knowing why I came here? Maybe you didn't notice, but I never even asked for Joe. But there you were with your answer all ready. I'll lay five to three that son of a bitch saw me coming and fixed you up with the answer."

"Please go away. We are having company."

"So I'm not good enough, they can't even look at me. Don't give me that crap—not little Glenda. I know you; you're just a pack of tepee halfbreeds, too poor to feed lice and too lazy to scratch, but the government gave you some cattle, and now you figure you're pretty hot stuff and can lord it all over little Glenda, and that goes for that sonofabitching son of yours. What the hell's he think he can get away with—"

As she talked she wandered off the porch. She tripped over a piece of old iron and half fell. When she stood up her right hand came from the purse, holding a .32-caliber revolver. Louis, thinking she had seen Joe and Mamie inside the Buick, shouted a warning. "Joe, Joe! Look out, she has a gun."

"Oh!" cried Glenda. "So he *is* here!"

She still did not realize they were in the Buick. She looked around the yard, befogged by her long bout with alcohol, holding the gun in one hand, forking her hair back from her eyes with the other. "Where is he? And if he has that mousy little whore with him I'll—"

She stopped. She heard a sound from the far side of the Buick. Joe and Mamie had sneaked out, hand in hand, and, crouched over, were creeping toward the motorcycle. She still could not see them, but she saw that one of the doors on the other side of the car was open, and guessed the rest.

Louis, who could see Joe and Mamie from his place on the step, shouted, "Joe, Joe! She is coming on the downhill side, Joe!"

No longer did Joe waste time. Dropping Mamie's hand, he ran long-legged to the motorcycle, sprang into the seat, worked the controls like mad with both hands, and started tramping on the cranking mechanism. The ignition missed once; then it caught, there was a blast from the exhaust, and Joe, in the seat, was going bumpety-bump down the sloping yard.

"Wait for me!" wailed Mamie, chasing him. She overtook him and jumped on behind. She flung her arms around him and pressed her head against his back and closed her eyes.

Using the parked cars for protection, Joe headed toward the creek, but Glenda had anticipated that and was running around on the downhill side. With the gun at arm's length, she fired as they came into sight, and the bullet ripped a furrow through damp earth in front of the motorcycle. Joe stopped with the aid of both feet and turned the motorcycle back the way he had come. Glenda shot at them as they appeared between the truck and the Chevrolet, and again between the Chevrolet and the Buick. Now, to go farther, Joe had to expose himself on the blank hillside between the Buick and the house. This was plainly suicidal, so he had no choice but to turn back again, and after that to turn back once more, all the time trying to keep a car between himself and Glenda.

"The gun is empty," he heard Louis shout. "Quick, quick, Joe! The gun is empty."

He caught a glimpse of Glenda near the tailgate of her truck, punching empty shells out of the gun. She had more cartridges in her purse, a full box of fifty, but in her hurry she spilled them all over the ground. She was down on hands and knees, picking them up and thrusting them into the chambers, when Joe, with the motorcycle really revved up and moving, roared around the Buick toward the shelter of the house.

Glenda had three cartridges in by then, and she tried for no more. On one knee, she pointed the gun at the motorcycle and pulled the trigger, but the hammer fell, click-click-click, three times on empty chambers before one exploded.

Joe still was not in the clear. A barrier had arisen before him in the shape of Mama's clothesline, which was strung from the house to a couple of pine poles; and beyond the poles was a low cutbank face of whitish clay.

He did not diminish his speed. Gunning the motorcycle,

he swung it boldly around the posts against the slant base
of the cutbank. The bank fell away rapidly toward the
meandering creek bottom, leaving Joe to follow a horizontal path no more than eight inches wide that the kids had
made playing cliff-dweller; but the blessed bulk of the
house had intervened between himself and Glenda. The
tires clung precariously for ten or twelve more feet, then
the friable earth crumbled. Joe felt himself going, and
turned the cycle straight down the bank, plunging deep
into the thorn-apple thicket which until recently had
sheltered Grandpere's tepee.

Joe still did not abandon the motorcycle. With his
head down and poor Mamie hanging to his back, he drove
straight through the thicket, was briefly in the open,
plunged down a second abrupt drop, through a depres-
sion filled with buckbrush, and emerged in the flat area
between the privy and the corrals. Now, taking his big
chance, he swung back toward the road, but Glenda was
not there to intercept him; he had left her behind the
house, and she did not come into view until he was across
the creek, past the Hudson, rolling at fifty miles an hour
through the gate. Then, torn and bleeding from the
thorn-apple barbs, he came to a stop and stood with feet
planted on both sides of the motorcycle, looking back to
where Glenda, in her shapeless silk dress, was small in the
distance.

"Don't you wait up for me, you old biddy," he shouted
at her through cupped hands. "You have made your nest,
and now you can lay a brick in it for all this fellow gives
a damn."

# Chapter XII

When Louis, after watching Glenda Callahan drive off in her truck, went back inside the house, his heart almost stopped beating, for there in the big chair lay Mrs. Hankins, moaning, while Loren, on one knee beside her, rubbed her hands and arms.

Louis' first thought was that she had been hit by a stray bullet. "She is shot?" he cried, making as if to locate the wound; and Loren, to get him out of the way, almost knocked him to the floor.

"No, you fool, she isn't hit, she's having one of her attacks." Mary, on the other side of Loren, was trying to give Mrs. Hankins a glass of water. "No, let the water go. Leave her alone. I think you've done enough already."

"You don't need to blame us," Mary said, almost in tears.

"I said just leave her alone."

Loren's mother found her voice and gasped, "Take me out of here. Don't make me stay here a minute longer. Get me to town. I need an injection."

"Yes, Mother," he said, helping her out of the chair. "Mary," he said, turning to Mary, but she fled from the room, went into the bedroom, and slammed the door. Loren stood, supporting his mother, and asked Louis, "What's wrong with Mary?"

"Let her have her cry out. Think of your poor mother. Let us put her to bed and go for the doctor."

"No, I'll take her to town. The fresh air will do her as much good as anything. Tell Mary I'm sorry."

"Sure, I'll tell her."

With a deep groan Mrs. Hankins said, "Get me to the car."

Mama had been watching all this, standing rigidly by the kitchen door, stunned and speechless. Now that they were leaving she followed with little running steps, saying, "Please, please, Mrs. Hankins, listen to me, it was not our fault. I am so sorry this had to happen, it was all an accident; that Joe, he's no relative of mine, only Mary's half-brother. I think he was shell-shocked in Korea. You must listen and not hold it against Mary for what happened on account of Joe—"

"I'm sorry, Mrs. Champlain," Loren said, turning when he reached the car. "You see, she's in no shape to understand what you're saying."

"Yes, yes!" said Mama, wringing her hands. "Of course, yes, yes, yes."

She watched the Chevrolet roll across the creek, up to the road, and out of sight. Slowly she turned and retraced her steps to the house. She went to the kitchen and sat

down in her old rocker. Staring ahead, not making a
sound, she wept.

Louis patted her shoulder and said, "There, there,
Mama. Everything will turn out all right."

"Always you have said that, but for us nothing turns
out all right."

"He'll be back tonight," said Louis. "We will make him
understand how all this came about."

But Loren did not come back, so at dark Louis rode to
the Winter Owls', borrowed their car, and drove in to
Big Springs. He was not able to locate Loren, but he
found Doc Patterson, redolent of disinfectant, sitting at
a card table with his big stomach off to one side and a
stethoscope hanging out of the side pocket of his coat.

"Mrs. Hankins, she is ver' sick?" Louis asked, at which
Doc laughed in a rough way and said, "Hell, no. She had
what is known in some circles as an acute attack of mal
de mere. You savvy that French, Louis? That's when
mama gets just as sick as is necessary to make a grown-up
son devote all his attention to her." And Doc added in a
growl, picking up his solo hand, "So he drove the old girl
to Great Falls to get some big-city medical advice."

Louis' news concerning Mrs. Hankins proved to be no
satisfaction to Mary. "She was out to get me from the first
minute," Mary said. "Oh, she treated me all right, but
that condescending way of hers. 'Oh, Loren, dear, she *is*
pretty!' —as if she expected me to look like a monkey because I was part Indian. Then she has an attack. Why?
Just to make me look bad."

Mary lay on the bed and wept while Louis tried to re-
assure her. "Mary, it will all blow over. He is only in
Great Falls, he is coming right back. Believe me, you
aren't the first one to have trouble with her mother-in-
law."

Mary said through the pillow, "Oh, I don't want to see
him. I wouldn't be able to face him, not ever."

"Now, now," Louis said, patting her shoulder. "I'll bet
sometam their family put on big fight too."

"No, Pa, not a free-for-all like that. I was a fool to
think I'd fit in there—his family, those people."

Louis did not argue with her. Time, he knew, would fix
things up—for Mary, and for Mama too. And so next
morning he was on the porch as usual, waiting for the sun
to get warm, and roughing a bear out of half-rotted pine.
The pine was quite damp, so it was tough, and its grain
was a richer brown than usual. The wood with its dampness smelled like fall—a different smell than damp wood
of the spring. The fall dampness was everywhere, making
a shine on the frost-tuned leaves of the bushes, giving the
mountain valleys a misty purple cast, turning the pines
a purplish green, and giving Louis a slight pain in the
joints of his shoulders. He did not mind; it was the way of
nature, and soon the sun would grow warm and drive the
pain out of him with a good feeling that he could not get
from donning his old mackinaw. And soon winter would
be there, the long cold, and Louis would trap a little, not
because he enjoyed capturing the wild things of the creek
bottom, or because he expected much profit from the pelts,
but because he and his people had always trapped when

that time came; it was the way of life, like the pain in his shoulders.

"Isn't Mary going to work?" asked Mama from the doorway.

"Is the bank open today?"

"Of course, why shouldn't the bank be open today?" Louis kept whittling the tough wood, and she said, "Louis, mention it to her."

"Me?"

"Yes, she listens to you better than me."

When ten minutes had passed without his moving, she came again to say, "Well, are you going to talk to her?"

"No, ol' woman, we must leave her alone. She knows about the bank. She must decide those things for herself. If she does not want to go to the bank, then this house, it is here for her."

"But her job!"

"Slager can get along without her for one day."

Mama kept coming back and looking at Louis, wanting him to talk to Mary, though she did not mention it again. Then about noon Loren Hankins drove up in his Chevrolet. He was alone.

He got out, long and limber, with his stooped way and the sun reflecting on his thick glasses. "Hello, Mr. Champlain. Is Mary around?"

"Sure, she's in the house."

"Will she see me?"

"Eh, why not?"

"Well, the way I ran out yesterday—didn't finish dinner, you know—it must have looked funny."

"But your mama had her attack. When a woman has her attack, then you must do something, no? Last night I was worried and drove to town, but you were already gone, and old Doc said she would get along all right. She *is* all right, eh?"

"Yeah. That Doc Patterson!" Loren said, looking inside the house for Mary. "Him and his salty manner. Bellowing to my mother that ninety per cent of all ailing women could be cured by a dose of Epsom salts and a kick in the rear. I should have kicked him in the rear. Him a doctor! I don't think he's good for anything."

"I don't know," said Louis with a soft smile. "He has a way with horses."

"He should confine his practice to them. Oh, hello, Mrs. Champlain. Is Mary in there?"

Mama was very nervous, almost wringing her hands. "I don't know. She went someplace."

"Oh?"

"I don't know where."

Louis stood and said, "Why, ol' woman, now what the devil—"

"I said she went someplace!"

Loren, looking from one to the other, asked, "Doesn't she want to see me? Is she mad at me on account of—"

"Oh, no, no. Mad at nothing. Why should she be mad? How is your mama?"

"Okay. I left her with a cousin in the Falls. Mary must be around. She isn't in town, and Slager said—"

"No, no. She's not here. Look in the house if you want to."

"Oh, I believe you." He stood, not knowing what to do. "Well, if she's not here she's not here. You don't know where she went? If she comes back before I see her, tell her how sorry I am about yesterday—running out, you know. Mother and I were both sorry."

"What she must think of us!" Mama said, drying her eyes on her apron. "That awful Joe and those women! You will never know how close somebody came to getting killed—one bullet through the screen door and in the living-room wall, not two feet from where your mother was sitting."

"It was just one of those things."

"I am sick from shame. Tell her—"

Louis said, "You have apologized enough. Those things might happen to anybody."

Loren said, "You're sure she's not around. Well, I guess she'll be at work tomorrow." And he left reluctantly, taking his time in getting back to the car, and more time in looking at this and that in the glove compartment before driving across the yard and slowly down the road.

"Where is she?" Louis asked.

"Oh, I don't know. She went out the back way. I couldn't stop her. You will have to talk to her. You will have to pound some sense into her head."

"If she doesn't want to see him, that's her business. I am not going to say a thing."

Mama raised her voice. "Don't you care what happens to your own daughter, letting her man drive off while all the time you sit there carving your foolish bears?"

"Yes, I care! Believe me, if you had listened to *me* things would have been different."

"How different?"

"Who was it wanted to put on show, pretend to be big ranchers like Billy Pomeroy, that thief? Eh? Not me. Big chair, blond dining-room suite, toilet inside. Go look at that toilet, not even been used once. Trying to appear lak something we are not, and what happens? We are found out, of course. What the hell do you expect?"

"Blame *me*—all my fault, not one word against Big Joe. Big Joe, your boy, no relation of *mine*."

Returning to the bear, Louis said, "I have seen plenty of your relation, ol' woman."

"All right, you're running things. Maybe you would not have invited Mrs. Hankins at all."

"Of course I'd have invited her. To my home everybody always welcome."

"The old dump we were living in—broken-down chairs, mended with jackknife and rawhide? Maybe you would have taken her to Grandpere's tepee!"

"Ol' woman, listen! Yes, keep your mouth shut and hear one tam your husban'. Once—this was long tam ago, in Canadá—I was young man, boy little older than Pete, living, lak you say, in tepee. My father's tepee. He was breed, of course, though he dress lak Cree—moccasin, braids, Indian all the way. So now there came to his tepee a white man, ver' fine looking, twenty-five or twenty-six years old. To my father this young man said he would like to go along in bateau, see him snare beaver, things like that. So for three-four weeks, month anyhow, this young man live with us, sleep, eat with us, on ground in tepee. My little sister Marie, he held her in his arms, that papoose, teach her song. Now wait. Do you know who he was, that man? He was a lord from Mother Country, a nobleman, good friends with king, everyone, all those big people. Yet he was not too good for tepee. And my father's picture—many times he took his picture, and I have heard that in big library, right today, you can find a book written by that young man with my father's picture in it, his very name signed like Cree write. I think sometam it is ver' proud to be Indian."

She muttered, "Is it proud to be Indian like Big Joe?"

"Maybe his white blood make him raise hell sometam."

"Ya-ya-ya," said Mama, who had no ready answer.

"Was that Callahan woman an Indian, so she ran around swearing and shooting with the gun?"

"Talk, talk," said Mama, retreating to the kitchen, where she began hurling pots and pans into place under the cupboard. "Big hero, Big Joe!"

That night Louis said to Mary, "If you would like, tomorrow I could drive you to town in the Winter Owls' car." But Mary said no, she was never going back. Next day Mary kept watch of the road, leaving the house each time a car came in sight; and so she was not there when Hy Slager came in the morning, or when Loren arrived that night. Loren came again and again during the days that followed, but not once did he catch Mary, who had taken to chasing around with her former schoolmates, Corinne Buffalo, Jean Roque, and Nellie Beaverbow.

One night, very late, Mama saw her drive up with Bronc
Hoverty and was waiting for her to come through the
door.

"Where have you been?" hissed Mama, not wanting to
wake up the boys.

"I told you I was going to the dance at Millikin, didn't
I?"

Millikin was a store, post office, and dance hall, away
over on People's Creek.

Mama said, "I won't have you going around with that
Bronc, that no-good."

"Oh, Ma, I can take care of myself. Anyhow, Jean was
with us, and Tom Old Squaw. Didn't you see them?"

"You've been drinking."

"I had two drinks. What's wrong with that?"

"Did you know that Loren was here looking for you
again tonight?"

"Then I'm glad I was gone."

In the morning Mama said to Louis, "I'll bet it was Big
Joe got her to go out with that riff-raff Bronc Hoverty!"

Louis did not argue with her. Recently, to escape from
her persistent heckling, he had spent most of his hours at
the corral or around his makeshift raceway, getting Two-
Step and the chestnut gelding in shape to win big money
at the Fort Norris Indian Fair, which was held during
the middle days of October, when the snows of the early
blizzard had vanished and a few warm days gave the country its last respite before winter.

So there he was one day, ignoring a slight rain, hunkered on his moccasins, with his back against the corral,

braiding a hackamore of whang leather, when Jack Vig
the cattle buyer found him and said, "I was just up on
the ridge looking at your cows, Louie. Are those the ones
Joe engineered the trade on?"

"By gare, those boy of mine has engineered enough
trade for *me*. What has he been talking now?"

"He didn't talk to me, he talked to Foster in at the
Falls. You know, he and Foster's boy, the one that got
killed, they were in the Marines together. Anyhow, they
made the trade for that bull; but, like Foster told him,
they had him entered in the stock shows around, and it
might be a while. Well——"

"You mean you have a bull for me?" asked Louis, with
his eyeballs out.

"Ya, you probably know the deal better than I do, and
Foster's back in South St. Paul, but the girl in at the
office is stewing about freight charges—haulage up here,
that is—and I told her I thought you'd be good for it."

"By gare, yes! Ha! My white-ribbon bull is coming.
Joe! Pete!" The boys were far out of hearing, trying to
remove something from the chestnut's rear hoof without
getting their heads kicked off. "By gare, I can't wait to
hear what that old woman of mine will say now."

Vig laughed and got some papers from a flat folder.
"She been giving you a rough time, Louie? Here, the
girl sent these along to sign. Read it over—I haven't.
Three of those heifers, I guess, and, if you ask me, you're
getting one hell of a good deal."

"Two heifers," said Louis.

Vig's pen was poised. "No, three."

Louis decided there had been a mistake in his favor, for he knew that Joe had taken only two of the heifers to Great Falls. "Okay," he said and signed.

"Then we'll make the pickup when we deliver the bull," said Vig, walking back to his car.

He drove off, leaving Louis to ponder his parting remark—but only for a few seconds, after which Louis laughed, struck the leg of his pants, and said, "So, by gare, all of them try to say Big Joe is a crook!"

He went back to the house with spring in his step, not minding the rain that was coming harder now, but feeling good all over. He refrained from telling Mama, but remarked instead, "Well, by gare, those horse got plenty of run in them. Old Two-Step too. You think your husban' is big failure, eh? You wait—win two-three race at Fort Norris, make plenty money, get those cows back from Staples, we'll be in good shape yet."

"Hah, twenty-five-dollar purse!" jeered Mama. "How far will twenty-five-dollar purse go toward paying off the eight-hundred-and-forty-dollar mortgage on those cows? No, you will never get them back. Big Joe has lost them for us. What cows we have left this winter we will eat, and then we will no longer be in the cattle business."

"Well, I had some hard luck, that is true. But you wait, I have a *big* surprise waiting for you."

He would not tell Mama what his surprise was, but all around the house he went chuckling to himself, tracking wet on the floor from his moccasins, giving Mama an angry curiosity by saying, "You wait, ol' woman, you wait and see!"

The rain turned to snow, and to rain again. The north sides of the coulees were rimmed with snow that marked their long, branching contours as they dwindled against the mountains, where the dark timber was also rimmed by snow. Every morning now Mama had to break the pump plunger free of its ice, and she came to the house telling Louis he should get his winter wood hauled; and this, moving around to keep warm, he agreed to do, but soon the sun came out, and by noon the good warmth made him forget about it.

Sometimes Louis came out, feeling good from breakfast, and there in the Buick was Big Joe, crouched over his Sterno stove, cooking ready-mix pancakes, and Louis' heart went out to him. He started doing Joe little favors —getting him an extra blanket for his bed, saving out a piece of Mama's molasses cake when she was not looking, or a bowl of venison stew from the dry doe that recently had ventured too close to Louis' .38 rifle. As the days went on Louis got very thick with Joe, and they plotted how to get a longer race for the chestnut than the five furlongs that had been the outside distance at Fort Norris the year before.

Said Joe, "I have friends over there at Fort Norris on the tribal council. I'll pull some wires. I'll get you your mile race."

With that assurance, Louis began to make big talk about his horses, belittling every animal on the reservation. Horse to horse, there was no amount of money Louis would not call—but on the cuff, I.O.U., of course, until he sold just one more cow. Mama put up a stubborn fight against selling another cow for money to wager on horse races. "Look at the rain," she cried, waving an arm at the dull, rain-slick gumbo of the yard. "How do you know what that old horse will do in such mud? You remember two years ago that big gray horse of Steve Nord's? He can beat anything in the mud."

"There will be no mud," said Louis. "They will be kicking up dust when fair time comes."

But it rained on, little by little, that day and the next, and there were still heavy clouds on the day following that.

# Chapter XIII

A car bearing a Great Falls license plate had pulled off the county road and was now concealed by pines and frost-brown serviceberry bushes on a little spur leading to a wired-up gate about half a mile down the road from Louis' place. A kid of eighteen, wearing a blue and white sweater with athletic service stripes, sat behind the wheel, smoking a cigarette; an older man, thirty-five perhaps, was outside, standing on the front bumper, with one knee on the hood, looking at Louis' house with binoculars through a rift in the branches.

"I can see it," he said, fooling with the adjustment of the glasses. "It's the car, all right. Hasn't been dented up, either. Body looks to be in first-class shape. It's parked up by the house in some bushes."

"Anybody around?"

"Seems to set awful low. I hope it hasn't got a flat tire. No, if it had a flat it'd be slonched off to one side. It's just the bushes make it look that way."

"Anybody around?" the kid asked again.

"Can't see anybody."

"Luck!"

"Well, I hope so." The man got down and handed the binoculars to the kid, who put them in the glove compartment. From his pocket the man took two keys wired together. "I hope these fit."

He started away, and the kid said, "Good luck."

"Ya. When I come past in that Buick I'll be rolling pretty good. Now there's a chance it'll be low on gas, and if it is I'll yell at you, and you have the can ready. Otherwise I'll keep booming right along until we're over into Chouteau County. I don't want any trouble with the Indian Police or with the local sheriff. You know how they are, always out to throw it into somebody from Great Falls."

He walked down the road, keeping watch in both directions, listening for cars. The morning was very still. He could hear his feet on the road and the rustle of a Chink pheasant racing off through the underbrush. He came into the open then, and, not wanting to expose himself to view from the ranch, abandoned the road and found cover among the box elders that grew in a solid wall long the creek. It was slow going there; the trees were burdened with moisture and ready to drench him each time a branch was disturbed. Wet and cold, he got to the other side of the creek, crept up the steep bank, and rested on one knee. The ranch yard was before him.

There was the gleaming metal top of the Buick, over a long, gentle hump of ground. It was much closer than he had anticipated. Instead of coming around on the cut-bank side of the house, as he had originally intended, he now saw that he could follow a little gully and get almost to the car. Furthermore, if he approached from that direction, the car itself would give him at least partial concealment from anyone who chanced to be in the house.

He anticipated no trouble from the law once he got the car off the Champlain premises. It was not the first time he had performed such a job. Once before he had swiped a car from a Blackfoot up in Glacier Park—a ward of the government, like this Joseph Champlain, who, like him, had secured a car on the easy-payment plan. It was strictly seller beware if an Indian got a piece of merchandise from you on contract, because Indians were legally not responsible, and you had no recourse to law, short of an act of Congress.

He walked up the little gully, hunched far forward, keeping his arms down like an ape. After a while the gully became too shallow, so he rested on one knee and, rising carefully, again located the car. All was quiet. "Well, here goes!" he said to himself, sprang up, and sprinted the final seventy or eighty yards, with the keys ready in his right hand.

He crashed through knee-deep buckbrush, breathed thanks at finding the car door unlocked, and leaped inside.

There was no front seat where he expected it. He tried to save himself, but there was nothing to grab hold of. He fell to the floor on one elbow. He picked himself up and looked around. There was no back seat either. A bedroll

had been folded and pushed away to the rear; an old
wooden rocking chair was at one side. There was no steering gear or shift lever. The instruments of the dash had
mostly been removed. A tiny stove had been installed on
triangular wood blocks to make it sit level on the slanting
floor beneath the dash, and a pipe had been run out
through the ventilator hole. Higher up, beneath the dash,
were shelves made of halves of apple boxes, in which pancake flour, coffee, canned goods, and some old pots and
skillets were stacked.

He decided to get out and check the serial number. Now
he saw that the running boards almost touched the ground.
No tires. No wheels either. He opened the hood. There
was no engine. Nothing. Slowly he closed the hood. He
closed the doors. A woman, broad and dark, had come to
the cabin door to look at him. She did not speak but stood
there watching him as he slunk away across the creek toward where his car was waiting.

Big Joe did not even learn that anyone had been around
his car. He was at Fort Norris, talking to Charley Deersleep, chairman of the tribal fair committee, making
Charley a friend with a gift of twenty-five dollars so he
would see the wisdom of placing the new baseball diamond
inside the racetrack and moving the back fence out to
where the old-time track used to be, thus increasing the
circumference to almost seven furlongs; and as it was
the accepted practice to run the long races twice past the
little makeshift grandstand, Louis would have his mile
race, or maybe just a trifle more. With this accomplished,

Joe raced home on his motorcycle to tell Louis, who then, without Mama's knowledge, sold one more cow to cover his I.O.U. bets and make some more. And to make it perfect, the following morning dawned hot and clear, with blue sky from one horizon to the other.

"See now, ol' woman!" Louis cried. "Now where is that mud-horse of Steve Nord's? He is back there, swallowing dust from my chestnut, by gare!"

Even those folk who lived close to Fort Norris generally abandoned their homes during fair time to pitch their tents or tepees on the flats of Little Beaver Creek, below the parade grounds of the old fort, for the two days the fair was in progress. Those living at greater distance started out with their camp stuff much earlier—already cars from Hill Fifty-Seven in Great Falls had started rolling past, sagging to their last spring leaf under people and equipment—and Louis made his plans as usual to take the horses and wagon and stay at least three nights. He got out the tepee that had been stored in the barn, mended it, and freshened with red paint some of the Indian insignia that Grandpere had put on it years before. Mary packed her things and left with the Beaverbows, for she had accepted their invitation to stay with Nellie and a couple of other girls. The boys were wild with excitement, and Louis had to shout at them all the time to keep them from running the life out of the horses. Grandpere had already donned his ceremonial garb of antelope skin and feathers, to which now were added the stick and scalp, and, thus bedecked, he paraded all day, so that strangers on the county road stared at him as they drove by. Five or six times a day Big Joe would roar up on his motorcycle with some message for Louis, and he would roar away again, for days not sleeping or eating in his car. Even Mama finally caught the spirit and prepared huge quantities of food, which she packed away in cardboard cartons. The fine weather held, and at midmorning the day before the fair they set out, Louis and Mama in the wagon seat, Grandpere, cushioned by quilts and hay, in the box, and the boys coming up behind, riding the race horses. They did not hurry, and got to Fort Norris only in time to erect the tepee before sunset.

From one fire to another went Louis, shaking hands with his old friends, most especially with the French Crees from Canada, whom he had not seen for years; speaking French of the highly nasal Coyote variety, its small vocabulary pieced out by sign language done in the grand manner, so that Mama could see and hear him in one direction or another while she waited supper—but soon her own friends began to congregate, and she served the crowd without him.

Grandpere meanwhile had found a gathering of elderly men, among whom, with great age and dignity, he sat in the place of honor. A tarp was thrown over the rear wheel of Walkingbird's wagon, to reflect the heat of the fire against his back. With his scalp on the stick to gesture with, Grandpere made long talk about the good old days; and he talked about the new days too, for he had been a long time around and he had seen things come and go, and only a fool or a white man thought that things could be fixed up just so to last forever, and someday all this

would go too, cattle, plow, barbwire, roads, railroad—
everything go, and then the buffalo would come back
again. At this juncture there was a skeptical murmur as
if someone wanted to change the subject, but Grandpere
struck the dirt with his stick and went on talking, telling
how on the devilbox he had heard it spoken only the week
before that the Crees across the border in Canada were
again hunting for buffalo; the government had found
so many on its lands that there was no grass left. And now
pretty soon the big bomb would start falling, boom! boom!
Yes, the white man's own devilbox had told him so. Edward
R. Murrow himself had said, "Everybody back to the
caves."

"White man don't live long in cave," said Grandpere.
"No more factory for make penicillin, pretty soon white
men die. No more big town like Havre to buy wheat, buy
beef. No factory for build skunkwagon. No skunkwagon,
no use for roads. No factory build barbwire. Boom! Big
bomb blow 'em all up. Horses come back, buffalo come back,
good country again." He looked around, slowly turning
his head, the fire making the thinnest of glints across his
sunken eyes. "Me, Chief Two Smokes, live long time, see
plenty, see things come, see things go."

He was finished then, and there was silence, unbroken
even by the young men who had gathered around intending to laugh among themselves but instead moved un-
comfortably and pulled their mackinaw jackets more
tightly against the wind that blew down from Canada
across the high prairies of Milk River, with the promise
of winter—the strong cold, *noot' akutawin keskawin*, as

the old men said, feeling in it the primeval urge of their people, the struggle against a bleak land that might well go on after all the gadgets of the new order had been swept away—and just for a moment there was no such comfort in the shine of automobiles parked around as there was in the warmth of the fire.

Early next morning Steve Nord, who had just arrived with his horses, noticed the new length of the racetrack and raised a noisy objection, threatening to withdraw from all events and go home. When it was rumored that Big Joe had connived to have the track lengthened to benefit his father, others joined with Nord in the clamor. The storm raged particularly around Charley Deersleep, who in vain pointed to the ball field and talked knowingly about the distance of the "centerfield fence," although there was no fence but only a rail that the outfielders could jump over when going back after long fly balls. Finally it came to such a point that the tribal council was called to sit in emergency session, with the result that the track was ordered changed back to the half-mile distance.

Now it was Louis' turn to cry for justice, but he cried in vain, for his chestnut was the only horse there that laid any claim to being a distance runner. The distance, thus reduced to five furlongs, proved just to the liking of Pete Brissaud's bay horse, Rex, and the chestnut lumbered home fifth in a field of ten.

Ever since losing to the gray bronc last June, Brissaud had looked for revenge. Now it was his, and, leading Rex, he followed Louis all around the grounds, laughing him-

self sick, for he had proved that nobody for very long got
ahead of him in a horse swap.

"Where is the gray bronc you traded for if you are so
damn sharp?" Louis asked, knowing that the gray had
reverted to his outlaw nature so that Brissaud was afraid
even to put a saddle on him.

"Maybe I'll run him if I take a notion."

"Ha! You didn't even bring that bronc along. I know
why. You can't even catch that bronc."

"I have some tricks up my sleeve."

"You are running the gray tomorrow?"

"If I take a notion."

"I'll tell you what. Bring in your gray bronc, and I
will run against him for five hundred dollaire."

"How far?"

"Half a mile."

"Maybe I will."

"And maybe you won't! Listen, nobody needs to tell me
anything about that bronc; I had him around the place
long tam. Don't talk to me about horse swap. I threw it
into you good." Then Louis looked sad. "Sometam I feel
very bad, treating you, my good friend and neighbor, like
that. You want to swap back, give me three hundred dollaire to boot, okay."

Brissaud laughed until he could not keep his shirttails
in, at such a thing; but, to help Louis, who was having
hard luck at the fair, he would maybe swap back and give
Louis twenty-five dollars. An hour later Brissaud went
away with the chestnut, leaving Louis ownership of the
gray and a hundred and twenty-five dollars. Louis imme-

diately wagered the money on next day's quarter race at
big odds, for it was assumed by everyone that he would run
old Two-Step, a venerable beast which even Big Joe had
been riding around when he was a kid that high.

Mary hunted Louis out and said, "Pa, are you crazy?
Two-Step won't get out of his tracks in a quarter-mile."

Although no one was around, Louis whispered, "Did
I say anything about running old Two-Step? Little Joe
is going to ride the *gray bronc!*"

Mary then wagered all her money—sixty-five dollars.
Big Joe borrowed a hundred and fifty on the motorcycle
and another twenty dollars on the Buick, wagering nearly
all of it against Steve Nord's sorrel, which was the fa-
vorite and would pay the best odds; for in race meets such
as this there is no means of laying bets against the field,
most wagers being made on the relative merits of two
horses.

Louis still felt their wagers were too small, for he must
not only recoup for the race he had lost, he must somehow
come out winner by eight hundred and forty dollars, to
lift the mortgage from the four cows being held by Staples. He borrowed five hundred dollars from Chief Littlehorse, giving a bill of sale for two more cows as security,
and with this money strode the grounds, calling bets with
everybody.

In the meantime Mary, Pete, Little Joe, and the Beaverbow girl had set out with Beaverbow's car and a one-
horse trailer to bring in the gray bronc. At dark they still
had not returned, and Louis sat in the door of the tepee
watching for them, drinking cups of strong green tea. It

became late; the fires went down; the camp was so quiet
that he could hear the jazz band playing in the old cav-
alry quarters beyond the racetrack.

Mama finally put words to her fear, saying, "Oh, I
know something happened to them, that awful gray bronc.
Little Joe shouldn't try to ride that bronc; didn't he almost kill Pete Brissaud inside his corral?"

"Don't worry about those boy. They have maybe a
little trouble corralling him is all."

Grandpere, making small movements in his bed on the
ground, said, "You should have sent *Big* Joe. *He* would
catch the horse."

"Pooh, pooh, Big Joe!" said Mama.

It was past midnight, and frost was giving the grass a
crisp feel beneath Louis' moccasins as he walked around
the camp, when finally he saw Beaverbow's Ford with the
trailer still empty.

"Eh?" he said, coming up and looking.

"Pa, we can't find him," Mary said. "We drove all
over, even down to his cousin's place after it got too dark
to see, and he just isn't there."

Louis cursed Brissaud and got him out of bed, naming
him a thief who lay in wait for his neighbors and friends,
all of which Brissaud, with a voice startled in the tent
darkness, was voluble in denying. The bronc was right
there, but very good at standing still in the bullberry
bushes when he thought somebody was looking for him;
for he had the very devil in him, that bronc, as Louis knew
well enough, having owned him; but just the same, in one
hour Brissaud would be able to find him, though putting

a rope on him might be another matter. Tomorrow, the
first thing, he would go with Louis and get the bronc.

"Tomorrow!" cried Louis. "You will go *now*."

Brissaud pleaded for rest, and Mary said, "Oh, Pa, we
can't do anything tonight. We'll have to wait until morning."

Reassured, Louis got some sleep. At dawn the two
girls, the two boys, and Brissaud set out again, while
Louis put down a few more bets. Noon passed, and it came
time for the first race, a half-mile for saddle colts. To
pass the time Louis laid six dollars to eight on Lafontaine's blue roan against a highly touted colt of Big Rider's, and won. He scarcely got any pleasure out of
the victory because of watching the west road and wondering why the gray bronc did not come. Next came the
potato race; then there was some bronc riding, then a
five-furlong race, and then Clarice Beaudry did her fancy
riding. Now it was midafternoon and close to the feature
race of the day, the quarter-mile free-for-all—for among
fanciers of cow ponies the sprint races are most important.

Stephenpierre got hold of Louis and said, "Don't you
know the race is coming up? Why haven't you saddled
Two-Step?"

Louis, unable to stand on either foot from nervousness,
kept saying, "Goddam, goddam!" while watching the road.
He could see the road for a mile, and there was no sign of
them yet.

Stephenpierre said, "Where's Little Joe? Who's going
to ride Two-Step?"

"Maybe I'll let Gran'pere ride Two-Step," Louis cried

in exasperation. "One of them is about as old as the other."

"Louis, you were crazy to bet all that money on Two-Step."

"Quit talking to me. Haven't I got trouble enough? I didn't bet it on old Two-Step, I bet it to sneak in that gray bronc I traded back from Brissaud."

It then dawned on Stephenpierre why all the kids had set out that morning with Brissaud and the horse trailer. "They're not back?"

"No, they have not caught that goddam horse."

"Louis, if your horse doesn't run you will lose all your money."

"You French fool, don't I know I will lose all my money if my horse doesn't run?"

"But they're saddling for the race now." Louis did not know what to do, and Stephenpierre said, "Quick, you have to stall them off. Saddle old Two-Step. Claim you're having lots of trouble. Maybe you can get them to run the wild-horse race first."

"How can I say I am having trouble with Two-Step? Everybody knows he is so gentle he will go saddle himself." Already Louis was hurrying with Stephenpierre to the corral which served as a paddock. It was true the other horses were saddled, but no one expected him to be long in getting Two-Step ready. Louis killed all the time he could by doing this and that and sending for linament. Finally there was nothing left for him to do but put the saddle on, which he did, nudging Two-Step in the flank, trying to make him buck. But all the horse would do was twitch and move his hips around.

Matoose Old Squaw, councilman in charge of the races, came around and said, "What's the trouble? You are delaying the race."

Louis stepped back, letting the latigo strap swing, and cried, "Can't you see he is bucking himself to a lather?"

Everyone started yelling at Louis, laughing themselves limp at the very idea of old Two-Step bucking himself to a lather. Then suddenly, to confound them all, Two-Step gave a wild snort, burst loose, making men scatter in all directions, and bucked all around the paddock. Stephenpierre, with a movement so casual no one had noticed, had touched the horse's rump with the coal of his cigarette.

Louis took a long time cornering Two-Step, fighting him, trying to get the saddle on. Badly spooked, the horse cooperated by twice getting away and galloping around the enclosure. Finally a Gros Ventre by the name of Skin got everyone's attention and said, "I've seen that horse lots of times, and he was just as gentle as an old squaw. There's something wrong. I think that horse has been given something."

Louis stopped trying to saddle Two-Step and came over, waving his arms, shouting, "M'shu, what is this? Are you saying that I have doped that horse?"

"Look at him. Have any of you ever seen him act like that before?"

"All right," said Louis. "This is a pretty serious thing, to accuse a man of doping a horse. We'll have to have a test on him."

"How can we test him?"

"In the fair at Great Falls every horse that's run has this saliva test."

All the others then jumped into the argument, which became noisy and got nowhere. At last Steve Nord shouted, "Stop, stop! To hell with it. I'll run against old Two-Step, drunk or sober."

Louis was not to be dissuaded from the saliva test. "No, that's not the point. The point is, I am an honest man accused of doping my horse."

"What are we going to do?" Beaupre asked, turning to Matoose Old Squaw. "Are we going to run a race, or are we going to stand around here all day and argue about nothing?"

Matoose was ready to order the race to proceed, but Stephenpierre said in his ear, "If you ask me, it is very unfair to poor Louis Champlain, this thing. First you make the track too small for his chestnut, and then today you let everyone accuse him of doping old Two-Step and don't give him a chance to prove his innocence. You know what's going to happen? All the Crees are going to go home and say that the Gros Ventres are running things to suit themselves, not letting anybody else have a chance."

"What can I do? If that Skin had only kept his mouth shut!"

"Doc Wotala is here from Chinook; I saw his car. Why don't you get him over here to see if the horse has been doped?"

But people were honking their car horns for the race to begin. "I wish I was home," said Matoose. "I didn't want this job in the first place."

Then Louis looked up and saw Beaverbow's Ford with the trailer and the gray bronc!

"Okay," he said. "You don't want to run against Two-Step, have it your own way. I am taking him out of the race, but I have a fee paid for running a horse, and, by gare, I am running my gray bronc."

"That's Brissaud's horse," said Big Rider.

"You want to see the bill of sale signed yesterday?"

Skin was really hostile now. He had fifty dollars against thirty that his sorrel would beat Louis' horse, which, of course, he had assumed to be Two-Step. "Go ahead and run him," he said, "but I collect the bet."

"No, I have a witness, old Matt Horse Chaser, that I said thirty against fifty dollaire on my horse in the race. Eh, you hear that? *My horse.* Did I say Two-Step? No. If you thought it was Two-Step that is your hard luck, because I was all-tam talking about my gray bronc."

"That's right!" cried Little Joe, his chin over the corral pole. "He figured on double-crossing you all the time."

"Joe, go away," said Louis. "Saddle the horse. Limber him up little bit for the race. Goddam, I wish you had got here quicker."

Skin was furious, saying Louis could not get away with it; he would have the Indian Police make old Matt Horse Chaser give him his money back. Others who had laid down money assuming it to be against Two-Step—some of them at three to one—joined in, making a whoop-up that Matoose Old Squaw was unable to cope with. He retreated, indicating in sign language that he was done with the whole sorry business. All the cars were honking now, and

Charley Deersleep came over to see what the trouble was. He listened briefly to both sides of the controversy and said to Skin, "He said 'his horse.' Well, that is his horse. What the hell?"

"He let on like it was Two-Step."

"Are you afraid to bet against that poor little gray bronc?"

With low-hanging head and his tail all matted with cockleburs from hiding in the brush, it was true that the gray bronc did not look like much.

"Okay," Skin said. "To hell with it."

Steve Nord concurred, saying, "Sure, what the hell, let him run the bronc. I will beat him anyhow. I will beat him farther than I would have Two-Step even. I know that bronc. Brissaud had him to the sun dance. He couldn't get him to run in the right direction even."

They had saddled the bronc while he was still in the trailer, and now Little Joe mounted him. They got the bronc out stern first, and he was off with a wild sunfishing leap. Joe stuck to him, bent far over the saddle, holding to mane and saddlehorn. The bronc bucked among the cars parked between paddock and grandstand, and back again.

"Ya-ya!" cried Skin, laughing and holding his stomach. "Look at the race he is running. Hooray, hooray! Some race horse, runs all-time straight up and down."

"I wish I had bet *one hundred* dollars now," said Big Rider.

"Ten to one I would give you against that horse," said Skin.

"Okay," said Louis. "How much will you bet?"

Skin backed down from the ten-to-one figure, but he did wager forty against the fourteen dollars that Louis could still muster.

At last Little Joe got the bronc moving in the right direction. He maneuvered him onto the track. Now that the horse had bucked, he was docile. Joe did not even need to guide him; he jogged around the track to the far side, where the rope starting barrier was erected, and there he stood, crouched a little, his head forward and his ears down. When the barrier went up he was gone a length ahead of the field, taking the rail, never swerving or relinquishing an inch of his advantage, but holding that same length ahead of Big Rider's bay, Skin's sorrel, and that white-blazed roping horse of Steve Nord's; these staged a blanket finish for second, third, and fourth.

Without the aid of alcohol, Louis was a drunken man. He sang and danced and shook hands with his old friends all over again. Triumphant, he and all his family collected money from everywhere. Money filled Louis' pockets so he could not count it all.

With darkness Big Joe roared back on his motorcycle, Mamie Callahan in a thin jacket, blue from cold, holding on behind.

"We won, Joe, we won!" shouted Louis from the tables where the 4-H boys and girls were serving barbecued beef.

"Sure, I know, I was here. Come and look at the ring. Mamie, show Papa the ring."

She did—a huge white flash that dazzled like diamond, though actually it was twenty-five dollars' worth of titanium rutile.

"Wait!" said Louis. "You, my boy——"

"It's going to be a surprise," Joe said, heading for the dance and dragging his giggling burlap blonde with him.

Although this year the rule against drinking was supposed to be strictly enforced, Joe found everyone offering him beer as he danced around telling the big news about himself and Mamie. "When is the happy day going to be?" twenty people asked, and each time Joe said, "Big surprise, you will see." Over the PA system it was announced to all the fair grounds: "Special request of Joe Champlain and Mamie Callahan—'The Night You Set Your Little Shoes by Mine.' " Later it was "Marriage Vows," and then, as beer cans accumulated in heaps in the corners of the hall, more ribald sentiments prevailed and the loudspeakers blared "For Joe Champlain and his bride-to-be—'The Shotgun Wedding Polka.' "

Dancing in the crowded hall, Frank Knife shouted to Joe, "You'd better look out, Joe. I hear tell your bride's father is out on bail."

"Good, then I will go down there and tie knots in his shanty-Irish neck."

Mama found Louis at the 4-H counter, still talking about the horse race, and pulled him aside to say, "Did you hear what was on the loudspeaker? He is going to marry that girl. Where does he think he'll live—in the Buick? I tell you I won't have them there under my nose in the Buick."

"Ol' woman, quit borrowing trouble. Tomorrow he will forget all about it."

"He's bought her a diamond like *that*. Where would he get money to buy such a diamond?"

"Have you forgotten who won the race?"

Mama wanted a glimpse of the diamond she had heard so much about and pushed inside the hall. There she saw Mary dancing with Bronc Hoverty, staying in a corner with him, giggling when he said things in her ear, and the sight made her just sick. She went back outside and moaned to Louis, "Oh, I wish I had not even come."

"Now what is the trouble—winning big race, now you wish you had stayed home? Look, in every pocket money, plenty money, buy back cows."

"Did you see your daughter in there, belly-rubbing with Bronc Hoverty, that no-good?"

"Oh, little dance, young folks have good tam. Anyhow, he's pretty good rider, that Bronc."

"Rodeo rider! You call that good? Me, I have had enough rodeo riders since spring to last me a lifetime."

She lingered, watching the dance hall, for there seemed to be something more than ordinary in the way Bronc and Mary were acting. Then Mrs. Littlehorse saw her and said, "Well, Annie, I hear you are going to have a double wedding in the family."

"What do you mean?"

"Why Joe and Mamie, Mary and Bronc, of course."

"She wouldn't marry Bronc!"

"Oh, I didn't know there was any doubt about it. Billie Jo said that they were all going to Chinook together and get married."

"That Joe!" Mama whispered with a long exhalation of utter loathing. "Joe would do that—his own sister, he would talk her into throwing herself away on that no-account Bronc Hoverty."

"What did you say?" asked Mrs. Littlehorse.

"Nothing. Louis! Where is Louis?"

"Don't you feel well, Annie?"

"I feel all right. Where is Louis? Oh, where did that man go to? He was here just a minute ago."

She stood by the counter where the 4-H kids were cutting beef, its steam making clouds in the cold air, and wondered which way to turn, feeling that Louis rather than herself should try to reason with Mary. One of the boys offered her food, and she shook her head, unable even to say "no," she felt so alone, and she had a big lump in her throat.

Then, as she started away, she saw a Chevrolet of the same color and model as Loren Hankins', and hope leaped inside her. The car had just arrived; she was certain it had not been there when she came over from the tepee. She detected movement and called, "Loren! Yoohoo, Mr. Hankins!" The movement had stopped. For a second she had the unreasonable idea that he was hiding from her. Then two kids popped into view and ran; they had been rifling the glove compartment.

"Loren!" she called hopelessly. Then she heard his steps and saw him. She said, "Loren, quick, before she makes a fool of herself!"

"Oh, Mrs. Champlain, I was just over at your tent, looking for you. What were you—"

"Thank God you have come in time."

"What's the trouble?"

"It's Mary. Joe is trying to talk her into running off and marrying Bronc Hoverty."

Loren looked slightly sick. "Does she want to marry him?"

"Who can tell what a girl will do after her worthless half-brother gives her beer to drink? I tell you, I haven't known she was the same girl since you broke up."

Loren grabbed Mama by the shoulders and turned her so some of the distant light from the 4-H booth struck her face, and said, "She does care about me, doesn't she? It's just because of what happened that day Mother came out to dinner—"

"Of course she does, but she says she couldn't look you in the eye again. She used to hide in the shed every time you drove out; she says she would not fit in with your people down in Helena, that your mother doesn't want you to marry a breed, and that she is right—"

"She wouldn't need to go close to Helena after we were married."

"Well, go up there and stop her before it's too late."

Loren, looking pale and taut around the mouth, marched to the hall. The large anteroom was filled with men, girls, tobacco smoke, and the smell of beer. He tried to get through, but the orchestra had just finished playing a number, and the push of people was against him. "Excuse me, excuse me, please," he kept saying, trying to crowd this way and that, looking above their heads into the hall.

A girl giggled and grabbed hold of his arm, putting her weight on it and looking up at him. "Hello, tall stuff. I'll bet you're wondering about Mary."

It was Billie Jo Littlehorse. "Ya, where is she?"

"Don't you think you're a little late?"

The implication made him go sick and unsteady. He jerked himself loose and cried, "I asked where she was!"

"Inside, I suppose," said Billie Jo, pouting with her red-smeared lips out. "Unless she's already run off with Bronc Hoverty."

Inside the hall, Big Joe had heard that Loren was coming even before Loren reached the outside door. He left his partner and hurried along, looking for Bronc, whom he found dancing with Lola White Calf. He grabbed Bronc, spun him around, and said in his ear, "Hurry up and find Mary, get her the back way out to the car."

"What the hell—"

"You know who is coming? Lydia E. Pinkham." And as further identification Joe coughed, sticking out his tongue and holding his stomach.

"Loren?"

"Yes, Mr. Pipsqueak. Loren."

Bronc had been slightly drunk, but the news sobered him. He said, "Oh, what the hell, Mary told me she didn't care about him any more."

"How do you know what she'll do? She'll feel sorry for him maybe. Come on, get her out of here."

The music stopped, and couples began to leave the floor. Bronc saw Mary on the arm of Boob Dugan. He

ran after her among the couples, and Joe watched his
progress. Then Joe saw Loren's head above the crowd.

"What's going on?" Mamie asked, getting hold of him.

He pushed her off. "Out to the car, quick. Bronc's
car. We're all going to Chinook."

"To get *married?*" she cried in falsetto elation.

"Of course, big double wedding. You wait in the car
with Mary and Bronc, don't say anything to her about
that pipsqueak being here, and I'll come pretty soon the
front way."

Joe burst through the crowd barely in time to run
chest-up against Loren and stop him from entering the
dance hall. "Loren old kid!" Joe cried, getting both arms
around him. "How's my old pal, hey? How about having
a bottle of beer with Joe?"

"Where is she?"

"Who?"

"Mary."

"Mary? Oh, I guess she's over at the tepee, taking care
of Mama. Mama's sick. Mary will be back pretty soon."

"You're a liar."

Joe got free of Loren and stood with his shoulders back
and the muscles big under his red silk shirt. "Hold on,
now. Nobody goes around calling this fellow a liar."

Loren was not interested in quarreling with Joe; he
wanted to get past, for he knew there was a reason why
Joe was trying to block him from the dance hall.

"Oh, no, you don't," said Joe, placing a hand on
Loren's chest and shoving him back.

Loren's response was to set his feet and bring a hay-maker to the point of Joe's chin. Joe's mouth had been open to say something, so the blow had an added potency. Joe staggered and caught himself against the archway. His pomaded hair was knocked loose and fell in strings over his face, and his eyes looked baffled through it. For a second it seemed that he might go down, but he recovered and lurched forward in time to stop Loren from getting inside.

They wrestled, and Loren twisted free. Joe, with his head down, charged, carrying Loren through the crowd. A wall stopped them. There, by superior strength, Joe held Loren, who fought catlike, using every muscle he had, striking Joe with fists, elbows, knees, and the top of his head.

"Goddam you," said Joe, retreating. "Why don't you stand up and fight like a man?"

Joe had a fist ready to flatten his adversary for all time, but Loren swung rights and lefts in a windmill that proved baffling. At last Joe stopped him. He shoved him back with a left-arm sweep and hit him with a tremendous right that was half punch and half shove, fairly lifting Loren off his feet and sending him halfway across the anteroom.

Loren went to one knee. He had lost his glasses and seemed baffled, unable to locate Joe without them; then he charged again, and Joe, weighing his right fist, was ready for him. The fist, however, did not land; the blow was never thrown. Mary had come up behind Joe. With a

scream she leaped on his back. She held him with one arm
around his throat, her other hand clutching his hair, her
knees in the small of his back.

Joe reeled, trying to free himself of her. His head was
bent back, his big nose pointed toward the ceiling. To
make it worse, Hankins was slugging him. He reeled, he
tripped, and sprawled forward, striking the floor with a
thud like a felled beef. Mary was still on him. Her hands
in his hair, one knee on the back of his neck, she repeatedly
lifted his head and pounded it, thump-thump, against the
floor.

"I'll teach you to keep your nose out of my business,"
cried Mary.

"Ow!" moaned Joe. "You're killing me, you're killing
me."

Loren pulled her off, and she stood panting, with her
hair awry and her dress pulled around so it was almost
backside first. She had blood on her wrist, but it was Joe's.
"Loren!" She wept and fell into his arms.

Joe got to his knees, his head hanging down and his
nose running a stream of blood. Finally he made it to
his feet. He was still groggy from that first blow with his
mouth open. He stood with one hand on the wall, the other
trying the swivels of his jaw. Blood ran from his nostrils
around his chin, down his neck, and soaked the front of
his scarlet shirt, turning it brownish. "Pipsqueak," he
said. "Goddam. Hit a man when he's not looking. Then
let a woman do his fighting for him."

Loren had found his glasses, with one lens trampled

out, and had them on like that. He heard what Joe said and was going to start after him again, but Mary got between them.

"Oh, let the big ox go," she said.

Joe said, "You listen to me, you marry him and you won't have anybody to blame except yourself. I wash my hands of the whole thing."

# Chapter XIV

All the way home through the bright morning sunshine Mama was happy as a girl again that Mary and Loren would have their wedding before Christmas after all. Although Loren had assured her that his mother looked forward to another visit in her home, she said no, she would entertain everyone with a wedding breakfast at Big Springs.

"Cost plenty money," Louis said cheerfully.

"And we have plenty money."

Louis did not mention using it to get back the cows, the four mortgaged to Staples and the two for which he had given the bill of sale in borrowing five hundred from Littlehorse. Tomorrow, maybe, would be plenty of time to talk that over with her. After making allowance for the wedding breakfast, there would be plenty left to get back the cows. Right now it was good to find Mama really happy, laying her plans while jogging, clip-clop, bump and creak, in the wagon through the shotgun timber of

the mountains, with everything smelling so good just before the big freeze.

It was late afternoon when they dropped down toward
the ranch, and there, pulling away, was a big red stock
truck with three cows in it.

"Hey, wait!" cried Louis, suspecting they were his
cows. But the truck was far away, and the driver had it
in gear.

"What was it, Louis?" Mama asked.

"I don't know," Louis said, resuming his seat. "I think
that stock truck picked up three of our cows."

When the boys rode alongside, Pete on Two-Step and
Joe on the bronc, Louis sent them to the pasture to check
and make sure.

"There's a bull up there!" Joe called, hitting the yard
at a dead run.

Right behind him, Pete shouted, "Ya, he's a young
bull."

"The old bull's pawing dirt at him. Pa, do you suppose
they'll fight?"

"How about my cows?"

"There's only three left."

"Goddam, they made a mistake and took three *more*
cows. Joe already gave them the three cows for that bull."

Mama said, "When did he trade three cows?"

"The time he went to Great Falls with Bronc Hoverty."

"When he bought the Buick? He took only two cows."

"Of course, but they made a mistake. On the paper they
thought he had given them three cows."

Mama still did not know what he was talking about. He

tried to explain how it was, but at last she stopped him
and said, "He traded no cows. Your cows he used to make
a down payment on that Buick. What you signed was a
paper to turn over three more cows for the young bull."

Louis could not believe it. He vowed to go to Great
Falls pretty soon and see the paper for himself. An hour
later, as Mama got supper, he was seated on the steps
carving a little bear not much bigger than his thumb
when Mary and Loren drove up.

Mary said, "Pa, the kids were telling me they took three
more of your cows."

"Oh, that goddam girl bookkeeper in Great Falls,
pretty soon I'm going down there and get my cows back."

Not making a sound, and standing back of Louis where
he could not see her, Mama said "Joe!" with her lips, and
Mary nodded, understanding.

That evening they talked about the wedding. Mama
took charge of all the plans, telling how she was going to
have the wedding breakfast at the Grand Hotel in Big
Springs, and Mary would have a wedding gown of silk
crepe, so long she would have to stand on a stepladder to
have her picture taken, and of all the flowers she was
going to get from the greenhouse in Havre. At each pew
Mama wanted to have a large spray of white flowers.
"Have you talked to the priest?" Mama asked. Suddenly
she was wringing her hands because Loren was a Presby-
terian. "Oh, dear, they won't *let* you get married in the
church. It will have to be in the rectory, that little stink-
ing old rectory, they won't let a heathen get married inside the church."

"Oh, Ma," said Mary, "they'll let us get married outside the altar rail."

"*I'll* buy the flowers," said Loren.

"No, no, no—"

"The groom is supposed to buy the flowers."

"Not to decorate the church. Some flowers for the bride and her mama and his mama, and maybe for Papa's buttonhole, but not to decorate the church. I may be part Gros Ventre, but I know a thing or two about a wedding just the same. At Fort Belknap when I was a little girl, such big weddings!"

Louis said, rubbing the little bear in his fingers, "Who will be the best man?"

Loren said, "I thought Hy Slager. I had a real good pal, but he's overseas and—"

"Oh, sure, Slager, he's been very good to Mary." Louis had secretly hoped they would make it possible for him to suggest Big Joe and thus bring peace in the family, but no. Poor Joe, he was getting married too. Sometimes Louis felt very sorry for Joe.

Two days later, when Joe was briefly at home to get some clothes out of the Buick, Louis inquired about the trade he had made for the young bull.

"Of course I traded the two cows for the bull," said Joe.

"But now that they brought the bull, they took three more."

"Oh, mistakes, mistakes! Okay, I'll get hold of my friend Foster and have him straighten it out for you."

And with a gold-colored nylon shirt stuffed in his jacket pocket, Joe roared off on the motorcycle.

Mama had Louis take her to Havre, where she visited the florist's and the department stores; then to Big Springs, where she made plans with Mrs. Knight for the wedding breakfast. Again she had to visit Havre, and again Big Springs. Things kept coming up that she hadn't thought of, and the cost grew higher and higher.

"Don't forget," said Louis, "I have to pay five hundred dollaire to Littlehorse."

"He will give us more time."

"Well, I don't know. The Chief is a tough man to bargain with."

"Then why did you borrow from him?"

"Ol' squaw, what are you talking about? If I had not borrowed we would have had no money to bet on the horse race."

Twice while Louis was in Havre or Big Springs the Chief drove over to see about his money. Finally he decided to put his bill of sale into effect and sent Humphrey Hindshot over to drive off the two cows. Louis and Mama learned of it from the boys when they returned home that night.

"Humphrey Hindshot took two cows for Littlehorse," Pete said. "He said he had a bill of sale."

"Sure, sure," said Louis sadly.

Joe said, "There's only one cow left now, Pa. You think the two bulls will fight over her?"

"By gare, no. I don't think that old bull will do much fighting over a cow."

It had become apparent that their money would barely cover the wedding, so there was no hope of getting five hundred dollars for Littlehorse. Mama was even giving up as too expensive some of the things she had set her heart on. It all made Louis a little bit sad, and he tried not to think what he would do if Congréss came around.

Next day Mama was home, going over her list for the twentieth time, when a winch-equipped truck drove in, wheeled around, and backed up to the Buick.

Mama did not go to the door. She sat still with her pencil and paper, watching. There were two men in the truck. While one of them got his tackle hooked to the forepart of the Buick, the other one looked inside.

"For Pete's sake," Mama could hear him say, "look here. He's even got a stove."

But the other man did not look. He said, "Ya, well, toss his stuff out, and let's get it back on the road before somebody raises hell."

The Buick, now only body and frame, and a denuded body and frame at that, lifted like nothing. They swung it up onto the truck and quickly pulled away. Mama, her view of the barren hillside now unobstructed by the Buick, took a great breath.

"Thank goodness," she said, "we are through with that."

When Louis came home he asked about the Buick, but Mama could not even tell him the company name on the truck that had hauled it away.

"I think it was some place in Great Falls," she said.

"Joe will come home and want to know about his car."

"Perhaps he sold it to them."

"Well, he might have, but still I wish you had asked."

But Joe had not sold it. The next afternoon, with Mamie holding on behind, Joe putt-putted up and sat on the motorcycle, looking with dismay at his poor possessions in a heap where his Buick had been. Joe was all dressed up. There was a white carnation in the lapel of his jacket, he wore his gold-colored nylon shirt and new riding pants with big pearl and gold buttons on the pocket flaps. Mamie was also in her best. She had a black velvet wrap on over her frilly pink dress, and she had a corsage of pink rosebuds pinned on.

"Joe, my boy!" said Louis, coming outside to talk about the car. He stopped at sight of the finery. "What goes on?"

"Congratulate me!" cried Joe, getting off the cycle and waving a hand at Mamie. "Let me introduce you to the new Mrs. Champlain."

"Mama, Mama, come quick!" cried Louis. "Our Joe and this beautiful girl are now man and wife."

Mama, at the door, muttered, "Uh! Congratulations!"

"Where's the Buick?" asked Joe.

His father said, "You didn't sell it?"

"No, of course I didn't sell it. What the hell gave you the idea I had sold it?"

"They came for it, and—"

"Who came for it?"

"A truck with a derrick, I don't know, some Great Falls fellows, I guess. I wasn't home. I was over at Brissaud's looking at his sorrel colts, and—"

"Who saw them take it?" Joe looked at Mama and

went toward the house while she stood inside and hooked the screen. "Did you let them take my car?"

"Go away. Is it any of my business what happens to your car, not paid for anyhow? Did you ask me to keep watch and drive them off when they came for the transmission and the engine block?"

"You let them on purpose. You *got* them here to take it."

"No."

"Who was it? Tell me who it was. I'll have the Veteran's Administration after them."

"I don't know, some outfit from Great Falls. I have plenty things to do besides keeping watch of your old car."

"Ha-ya, sure, plenty things for Mary's wedding and that pipsqueak—everything for Mary, big shindig, wedding breakfast, flowers all over church, that is for *her;* but *me,* when I get married, that is a different matter."

Mama muttered, "You did not even tell us you were going to get married."

"Ha!"

"No, and unless I have a look at the license I won't believe it yet!"

Joe had a signed certificate in his hip pocket. He pulled it out with a huge flourish and thrust it toward her. "See there? Married just this morning in Havre. And now I come home with my wife and find out you let them take my car, throw all my stuff out on the ground, everything a man has in the world. Where the hell do you think we're going to live, with my car gone?"

"I don't care where you live."

"Sure, now the truth comes out, you don't care!"

Grandpere, coming up alongside the house as fast as he could hobble, waved the stick with the scalp on it and cried, "Chief, chief! You bring squaw, move into Grandpere's tepee."

"Thanks, Grandpere," said Joe. "Anyhow there's somebody that likes me."

Louis said, "Joe, I like you, we all like you. Now don't lose your temper. You know Mama, ol' squaw, she say some things she doesn't mean. By gare, I tell you what— why don't you go down and fix up the old blacksmith shop, move in there?"

But Joe trod his weight on the starting mechanism and got the motorcycle to exploding. "No," he shouted. "To hell with this place! Joe's got plenty other big fish in the sea."

He went back as far as the turnoff to Callahan's. There he sat, with the motorcycle idling, and looked things over. A growth of grass and weeds, springing to life after the September rains, gave the yard an abandoned look, but there had been fresh travel on the road to the coal mine, and he could see the truck cab above one of the low, extending roofs of the building.

"Are you sure he's out on bail?" Mamie asked.

"Bronc saw him already. He's been at the mine, selling stoker coal like hell to raise money for his fine, if it's not too big."

"He'll probably get a sentence in federal jail too."

"Yup," said Joe, turning the motorcycle to go down.

"Think it's safe?"

"I got nothing against your old man. You know what caused all the trouble between us—it was Glenda."

"I'm sure glad *she*'s gone. I hope she never comes back."

"That was a no-good fellow she ran off with. I'll bet she'll wish back plenty of times for a couple of good guys like me and Callahan when she's out working, earning a living for that no-good she ran away with."

He rode down, going just fast enough to keep the motorcycle in balance, warily staying clear of the buildings. The saloon was closed, and a notice was tacked on it, but the side door to the living quarters stood open, and Joe, leaning far forward, ready to gun the motorcycle, saw Callahan.

Callahan was sitting at the table, eating his midday meal out of cans, jars, and paper cartons.

"Hi!" said Joe, still on the cycle. "Hi, Callahan!"

Callahan rose suddenly and stood with his feet on both sides of his chair, mouth full and eyes staring out at them. "Why, you dirty—"

"Hold on, now, don't lose your temper. We got big news for you." Joe decided it was safe to get off the motorcycle, so he did so, taking Mamie by the hand. He said to Mamie, "You bet we got big news for Papa, haven't we?"

Mamie giggled, turning her head toward Joe and saying, "Uhuh!"

"Show him the rings," said Joe.

She did—the huge titanium rutile and the wedding band, both on her left hand.

"Oh, Jesus!" said Callahan.

It took something out of him. He looked older, despite the fact that he had been off the bottle since his arrest. He retreated to the table and sat down, resting his forearms in the food litter. "You really married?" he asked, staring at them.

"Sure," said Joe.

"Where you going to live?"

"I had a good place," said Joe, "but it was stolen away from me. That damned squaw up there—"

"Say, you're not figuring on moving in here!"

"Well, we thought just to help you out, maybe you would have to spend some time in jail—second offense, you know—we might just camp here a little while."

"Why, you son of a bitch, stand there and talk about living in my place while I'm in the gow, and all the time it was you that turned me in—"

"Hold it, now. There's something to say on both sides. By golly, my back still hurts from the birdshot you tried to kill me with. But let bygones be bygones, I always say. Maybe you don't like me for a son-in-law—okay, maybe I don't like you for a father-in-law either; but what the hell, it's all in the family, now we have to get along together."

Joe stood tall, looking down on Callahan, letting this sink in. Then he said, "Eh!" through his caribou nose, signifying that the subject was disposed of and he never wanted to hear of it again. He sat down at the table and looked at the glass jar Callahan had been eating from.

"What is this? You got some more of these pig's feet?" asked Big Joe.